Praise for *Maiden Flight*

5 Magical Wands "This was a heartwarming story with a twist. I found it touching that Belora felt so strongly about both men, and had to struggle to accept that it was ok to love them both. Wonderfully drawn characters fill a unique and fascinating world of dragons, hot sex and magic. I'm desperately anxious to see where Bianca takes this story and what secrets she'll reveal of Belora's past and the new threat to this world." ~ *Piper Evyns, Enchanted Ramblings*

5 Angels "**Maiden Flight – Dragon Knights Book One** is a gem of a fairytale story! Be forewarned, though – this tale is for adults only, with its sensuous and sexy scenes and multiple partner encounters. There's also a very erotic healing scene with a dragon that is sure to get your blood pounding. …Maiden Flight definitely has a medieval flair to it, and the author's descriptions of her dragons are not to be missed. I'm pleased to award five shimmering angels to Bianca D'Arc's **Maiden Flight – Dragon Knights Book One**, and breathlessly await more books in this series!" ~ *Michelle, Fallen Angel Reviews*

5 Stars "A romance that flies straight to the heart, **Maiden Flight** tempts and teases before delivering a powerful story of super heated love. …As the first book in this series I loved it, Biana D'Arc has penned a book that explores the world of dragons and their partners who must now rid their realm of a menace that could destroy all of them. Buy your copy of this book today and escape to this magical world too." ~ *Sheryl, Ecataromance.com*

Praise for *Border Lair*

5 Stars "The second book from the Dragon Knights series, Border Lair is another amazing installment from Bianca D'Arc. Border Lair has some characters that endear themselves into your imagination, while the others will make you want to wipe them from the face of the earth. The connection between Sir Jared, Darian and Adora is electric; I loved reading about the love they feel for each other while trying desperately to cool myself down from their explosive relationship. The world Bianca D'Arc has created is mystical and highly addictive, with characters that certainly know how to get what they want, while trying to protect the ones they love. If you love reading about dragons and their knights then go out and get your copy of this series because flying high is only one aspect of their flight, the other is the love they create with the woman lucky enough to conquer them." ~ *Sheryl, Ecataromance.com*

4 Stars "Reading Dragon Knights 2: Border Lair was a pleasure. What attracted me to the story was the dragons and fortunately, they held my attention. Dragons Kelzy and Sandor were magnificent creatures with personalities that matched their size … big. If I closed my eyes, I could almost see them now flying through the sky. Their representation in the story was great. …Overall, Dragon Knights 2: Border Lair was an entertaining work of fiction that lacked grammatical errors, contained hot sex and good writing. You really cannot go wrong when reading this story. I plan to get the first installment." ~ *Suni Farrar, Just Erotic Romance Reviews*

LADIES OF THE LAIR

Dragon Knights 1 & 2

By Bianca D'Arc

A SAMHAIN PUBLISHING, LTD. publication

Samhain Publishing, Ltd.
2932 Ross Clark Circle, #384
Dothan, AL 36301
www.samhainpublishing.com

Dragon Nights Books 1 & 2
ISBN: 1-59998-251-X
Copyright © 2006 by Bianca D'Arc

Cover by Scott Carpenter

First Maiden Flight electronic publication: February 2006 ISBN 1-59998-022-3
First Border Lair. electronic publication: May 2006 ISBN 1-59998-063-0

MAIDEN FLIGHT

Dragon Knights Book 1

DEDICATION

To Jess—my patient, thoughtful, whip-cracking editor. I couldn't have done it without you! Thanks for believing in dragons.

CHAPTER ONE

Belora tracked the stag through the forest. Carefully chosen for this hunt, the stag was older, past the prime of his life, and would feed her small family of two for more than a month if she and her mother used it wisely. On silent feet, she followed him down to the water, a small trickle of a stream that fed into the huge lake beyond.

Taking careful aim with her bow, Belora offered up a silent prayer of hope and thanks to the Mother of All, and to the spirit of the stag that would give its life so that she and her mother could live. She loosed the arrow, watching it sail home to her target, embedding itself deep in the stag's heart. Her aim was true.

As expected, the stag took off, pumping away the last of its life in a desperate attempt to escape. She followed, saddened by the poor creature's flight, but knowing it must be so. The old stag ran into a clearing, flailing wildly. He was nearing his end, she knew, and again she prayed to the Mother of All that it would be swift.

The stag faltered in its running stride, a shadow seeming to pass over from above. A moment later, the stag was gone, clasped tightly in a magnificent dragon's talons, winging away toward the far end of the small clearing.

Belora took off as fast as her tired feet would carry her, after the dragon who had stolen her prize.

Coming out of the swooping dive, the dragon neatly pinned the stag's quivering body between the talons of his right foreleg. He'd made a clean kill, stabbing the beast through the heart with his sharp talon even before lifting it into the air. It struggled for a few moments more, then lay dead in his grasp. The dragon rejoiced in the skillful kill.

He came to a neat landing nearby and dropped the dead stag to the ground with satisfaction. That's when he noticed the little stick protruding from the other side of the beast. It was an arrow.

"Oh no, you don't!"

The irate, high pitched human voice made the dragon look up quizzically at the small female now facing him down with hands perched in tight fists on her hips. A longbow was slung over her shoulder, the string resting between generous breasts that heaved in irritation.

"I shot that stag well before you swooped down and picked him up. He's my kill. What's more, that stag will feed me and my mother for a month or more. For you, he's just a snack! You leave him be."

She fairly glowed with indignant anger and it was truly a sight to behold. Luminous green eyes sparkled in her pretty, flushed face. She seemed to have no fear of him, fearsome dragon that he was, with blood on his talons and fire in his eyes. She had courage all right, and it impressed the hell out of him.

He could feel her anger, and a rudimentary channel opened between her mind and his. She was one of the rare humans then, who could communicate with his kind. This intrigued him, and one thought kept running through his mind—Gareth had to see this.

What's your name, pretty one? The dragon spoke directly into her mind, surprising her a bit, but her mother had told her stories about the dragon she'd known as a child. Belora knew dragons communicated with humans mind to mind. It was part of their ancient magic.

"I'm Belora." She renewed her forceful stance. She could not let this dragon sense any fear. She needed that stag. "Will you yield my kill to me?"

Why are you not afraid of my kind? Do you know dragons?

"Not me. My mother knew a dragon once though. She told me about your kind." Belora knew she had to convince him soon. The longer this dragged on, the more likely he was to haul her before some tribunal for poaching. "So what about the stag?"

From where I stand, it was my talon that made the kill. Not your puny arrow. But you have a good argument. I'll give you that.

The dragon moved closer to her as she fumed in response, but she didn't realize she was being set up until it was much too late. While she ranted and argued with him, the dragon moved in closer still, until he had the stag wrapped in the talons on one huge foreleg and she was much too close to the other. Just as she realized her mistake, he swooped in and made his move.

He reached out quicker than thought and snapped the padded digits of his left foreleg around her waist, trapping her arms inside the cage his wickedly sharp talons made around her. She screamed in frustration and more than a bit of fear. The dragon only chuckled.

Don't worry little one. The dragon beat his huge wings two or three times and then they were airborne. She couldn't help the little yelp of fright that escaped as her feet left the ground. He could easily just open his claw and drop her to the ground far below. That would solve his problem quite easily, she thought with growing horror.

But dragons were supposed to be noble creatures! In all the tales she'd heard about dragons, she'd never heard of one going to such lengths to toy with a human before. They were mankind's friends, not enemies, and they weren't supposed to go around snatching up maidens only to hurtle them to their deaths.

As they gained altitude and he did not release her to die a nasty and painful death, she began to calm. She was held in one foreleg, the slain deer in the other. She looked around and realized she had never seen such a beautiful sight. The view from above was breathtaking. She could see the huge mountain lake as they approached it, and if she craned her neck to look behind, she could see the forest canopy, green and fertile, hiding the secrets of the creatures that lived within.

She and her mother lived there, under the thick cover of trees, and had for many years. It was their haven, their home. Nothing as magical as this had ever happened to Belora, living isolated in the forest, and she decided to enjoy this moment out of time, flying high above the world. She would likely never have the chance again, for it was rare that a dragon transport a human that was not his knight partner. She knew that from the stories and legends the old ones told of knights and dragons. Even her mother, who had been friends with a dragon in her youth, had never flown with one. It was a rare and magical experience.

Do you like the view, little one?

"It's beautiful!" Belora had to shout to be heard over the racing wind.

The dragon chuckled smokily, thoughtfully directing the stream of smoke out behind him and away from her. She realized from the gesture that he was well used to being around humans and carrying them as he flew, but she guessed he didn't carry too many in his claws. The legends all said knights rode on the backs of their dragon partners.

"Where are you taking me?" She pulled her eyes from the gorgeous vista long enough to question her predicament. If he was taking her to a tribunal, she was in big trouble. She'd rather know now if she would be facing arrest when they landed.

Fear not, little one. I said you had a good case for the stag. We will let the knight decide.

They cruised over the edge of the large mountain lake. The water sparkled below as the dragon dropped a bit lower. A moist breeze off the water teased her senses.

"What knight?"

Rather than calming her fears, the news that there was a knight in the area only made things worse. She'd been poaching, plain and simple. Mere peasants weren't allowed to kill the deer to feed their families, but the dragons were welcome to them as a snack at any time.

That knight, the dragon thought back at her. It took her a moment to understand his meaning, but when she looked down and just ahead of them, she saw a sleek male body cutting through the waters of the lake. He swam like a fish or like one of the great sea creatures she had heard stories about. She found herself distracted by the sun gleaming off the powerful muscles of his arms as he sliced through the water, heading for shore. Something about the man's hard body pulled at her most feminine core though she had never felt the like before.

I am Kelvan and that's Gareth, my knight.

Her eyes followed the man cutting through the waters below. She'd never seen a dragon in person before, much less a knight. Surprisingly, the hard-muscled man intrigued her even more than the amazing blue-green dragon who spoke so effortlessly in her mind.

The thought gave her pause. She'd met any number of men from the nearby village and never had such a reaction to the mere sight of one, but there was something about this man. Without even seeing his face clearly, she felt something deep down inside her stir to life. It was as if something in him called out to her—to the deep parts of her femininity that had never been awakened before. She wanted to know this man. She wanted to see him smile, and she wanted to know what those shining muscles would feel like under her hands.

The thought shocked her. Shocked, and excited her, if she were being honest. The thought of his strong arms wrapped around her made her insides quiver. The thought of his lips trailing over her untried body caused moisture to blossom between her thighs. She felt desire for this unknown man, the likes of which she had never experienced, but oh, how she wanted to experience it now!

The scandalous thought roused her from her contemplation of the handsome man. He was just a knight, she tried to tell herself. She didn't even know him. He would probably be old and unattractive when she finally saw his face clearly. No matter what she tried to tell herself, though, she kept looking back at the man cutting through the water so effortlessly, as if drawn. She tried to shake off the almost magnetic pull the man had on her, but it was surprisingly hard.

"You're a fighting dragon, then?"

The dragon didn't grace her obvious statement with an answer.

"There are no dragon enclaves this far east. Where do you hail from?"

Not that it is any of your business, but the king has asked us to set up a new Lair just to the south of here. You will be seeing more of us patrolling the skies in days to come.

"But why?" His startling news was enough to make her forget the knight for the moment. "The border with Skithdron has been peaceful for many years." She knew it had not always been so. The wild skiths—snake-like creatures larger than five full-grown men who spit deadly burning venom—

were often found along the border region, harrying herds and killing unsuspecting farmers who crossed their paths.

The native skiths gave the neighboring kingdom its name and heraldic symbol, much as the dragons were the symbol of her land, but that's where all similarity ended. Dragons were reasoning creatures of high intelligence where skiths were pack hunters intent only on killing and destruction. It was rumored they could be herded against the enemy, and in legends of older times, it was believed this border region had been decimated by herds of skiths sent as a first wave by the neighboring army that had almost taken the region completely. The only thing that saved the land had been the native dragons, fighting the hated skiths back with flame. It was the only thing a full-grown skith was afraid of.

The dragon directed a stream of rumbling smoke away from her as he scoffed. Her mother had warned her that when dragons became angry they sometimes had a hard time controlling their fire.

Skithdron has a new king. One not worthy of the title. War is coming. It is only a question of when. Again there was a belch of smoke that he thoughtfully directed out behind them as he flew.

"I didn't know." She tried to quell the frightened quaver in her voice as she shouted to be heard over the rushing wind.

She knew things had to be serious indeed if the king had sent a contingent of knights and fighting dragons to make their home on the border. Her chest tightened as she realized they could be in serious danger. They might have to flee yet again, losing the snug little home in the forest that had sheltered them safely for so long.

"Thank heaven the king sent you here. We're all but unprotected here on the border."

Not anymore. The dragon seemed to chuckle and preen as he circled lower, searching for a landing site.

Gareth, I've got a live one here. The dragon communicated telepathically with his partner, who still cut through the waters below.

You found your deer then? I'm almost through with my swim. We can get back underway as soon as you finish your snack.

Not quite. The dragon swooped lower as he prepared to land on the far shore. *There was a poacher there before me and we quarreled over the kill. I've brought her to you to decide who keeps the stag.*

Her?

Indeed, the dragon replied dryly. *She has no fear of my kind and the ability to communicate with us too. I thought you ought to see her before we departed.*

Intriguing. The knight neared shore as the dragon landed lightly, setting both the deer and his wriggling human burden down on the ground gentle as could be.

Hmm. Beautiful too. And feisty.

Beautiful?

In the way of humans. Quite beautiful, I believe. And quite upset with me. She did not come willingly.

He released her, sat back, and watched the little human fume at him. She raged and paced, shrieking about being taken by force, but the dragon paid her words no mind. Gareth would sort her out soon enough. In the meantime, she was quite amusing to watch with her antics.

Gareth got his first look at the woman—girl, really—as he stepped from the water. The cool wetness of the water as it sluiced down his limbs barely registered in his mind as he strode toward the girl. She stomped around, ineffectively arguing in front of the impassive dragon. Gareth was struck by her lithe form, her soft hair waving in the warm summer wind, and the passion in her stance. She showed absolutely no fear of Kelvan, his dragon partner, though he outsized her many times over. No, this little woman was fearless and rather focused in her anger.

She was too thin as well. It was more than obvious that she needed that stag to feed herself and her family. If they were all as thin as she was, they needed much more than just the one stag. Perhaps he and Kelvan could do something to help her the next time they came through this way, he thought absently, not even realizing he was already looking forward to the next time he could see the girl.

He knew almost immediately that he wanted to see her again. Something about her drew him. There was a light in her, a fire that called to him. He didn't understand it, but it was beyond question. She pulled him in like a moth to a flame and he went willingly. The fire in her glittering green gaze mesmerized and the vulnerability in her bowed lips made him want to fall to his knees and give her everything he had, everything he was. The desire to please her, to protect her and cherish her blindsided him. He didn't even know her! Yet everything about her called to him. He watched as she berated the dragon—or tried to. Kelvan seemed just as in awe of her as he was.

She worked up a good head of steam as he neared, though she seemed completely unaware of his approach. Kelvan shifted his head, finally alerting her to his presence. She turned to face him, gasped, and suddenly stopped talking.

Maybe it was because he was naked, he realized belatedly, enjoying the way her eyes seemed glued to his groin. Of course, such attention caused his staff to grow rapidly, as did the enchanting stain of embarrassment on her cheeks. Slowly, he reached for his clothing, which lay in a pile only feet from where she stood, still watching him.

"Keep looking at me like that, mistress, and you will reap the consequences."

The girl gasped as her eyes shot up to his. Finally. Her mouth closed with a snap as she seemed to gather her wits.

"Your pardon, my lord, but I'm not used to meeting unclothed knights of the realm."

The sarcasm fairly dripped from her words and he grew even more intrigued. He shrugged into his shirt, leaving it unlaced for the moment and faced her, now clothed more decently in breeches and shirt.

"My partner here tells me you claim this very large stag as your kill."

He thought his statement masterfully done, complimenting her hunting skill while making no mention of the fact that they all knew she had been poaching. The fact that she was in the wrong according to the law bothered him much less than the thinness of her lithe little body. He would rather she take the deer and feed herself and her family. Kelvan could always hunt another or wait until they arrived back at the Lair to feed fully. He knew from long association with dragon kind that it would be no hardship for the huge creature who was his dearest friend in the world and closest companion.

"I shot him well before this great lug lumbered in from above."

Lumbered! I'm insulted. I never lumber.

"Mistress—" Gareth shook his head theatrically. "You have insulted a dragon. That is never wise."

The petite beauty looked up over her shoulder at the dragon and rolled her eyes.

"All right then, how about swooped in majestically?" She paused to see the dragon's reaction and then went for the kill. "And stole my deer."

Kelvan snorted, careful to keep his flame far from the humans, though he choked the woman momentarily with his sooty wheeze. While she coughed, Gareth smiled up at his partner.

This is a strange one indeed. And quite as beautiful as you said.

She lights your fire, then?

Gareth had to fake a cough to hide his start of laughter. *Indeed.*

Good. You need a hard fuck. You've been much too tense lately. I'll go hunt another deer while you settle things with the girl.

Kelvan winged away, blowing the slight woman straight into his knight's arms, belching dragon laughter as he headed back toward the forest. The shell-shocked girl looked up at the knight, clinging to him to hold her steady in the fierce wind created by the dragon's massive wings.

"Where's he going?"

Gareth smiled down at her, holding her tightly in his arms. "To hunt another deer. You can have the stag, with our compliments."

Her whole face lit up and it was a sight to behold. Gareth realized this young woman possessed more than mere beauty. She had a light that radiated from within the likes of which he had seldom seen before. A rare jewel, indeed, and he knew he must have her, if only for this moment.

"Really?" Her wide eyes held hope for the first time and happiness that made her glow.

"Yes, really." He tightened his arms around her, his gaze roving over her lips hungrily. He felt her breath start as her body responded to his. It was a good sign, as was the fact that she was in no way trying to be free of his hold. Rather, she seemed more than comfortable in his embrace, clinging to him in a way that was most gratifying. "Kelvan and I will fly you back to your home and deliver the deer there for you. Later."

"Later?" Her voice was soft as her eyes spoke of the pleasure he was bringing her with the soft, circular motions of his hands on her back.

"Much later."

His head dipped and his lips claimed hers in a sweet kiss that soon turned passionate. Though willing, the hesitancy with which she followed his passion told him a great deal. She was quite obviously untried but a willing partner in the ecstasy he demanded and returned to her. He pulled back after a long satisfying time, but didn't release her.

"You are very beautiful, Mistress Belora."

She blushed so prettily he had to bend down and kiss her again.

"And very young."

"Not so young." There was a teasing challenge in her tone. "I have eighteen winters."

Gareth clicked his tongue and shook his head. "Just a babe you are."

"How old are you then? You can't be that much older than me. I won't believe it. You're in your prime."

"I take that as a compliment, mistress, that you think me prime. I have twenty-six winters though, so you see, I'm an old man compared to you."

"Not too old." She chuckled as he squeezed her playfully.

"Never too old to appreciate a beauty such as yours. A man would have to be dead not to want you."

She gasped as his hands stroked intimately down her back and cupped the curve of her ass. He pulled her against his hard frame, letting her know how much he wanted her. The next move he would leave up to her. She was so young and obviously untried. He would have to give her some choice, but he prayed to the Mother she would choose to make love with him. He needed her on a soul deep level he had never experienced with any woman before. He thought he'd go mad if she turned him away now.

"And do *you* want me, sir knight?" The coquettish smile in her eyes gave him hope.

He actually growled as he undulated his hips against hers. "I want you more than any woman I've ever known."

"Pretty words, sir. I bet you've said the same to all the maids you've bedded." She laughed as he stroked his hands up her sides to frame her face.

"I've never said anything of the kind before. For that matter, I've never felt this way before. My word as a knight of the realm. You are special, Belora. I know we've only just met, but I feel as if I've known you all my life. As if I've been waiting for you." He felt his heart lodge somewhere in his throat as he gazed down into her mesmerizing green eyes. "Tell me you feel the same."

Her expression sobered and her breath caught. A dazzling light came from her beautiful eyes that humbled him.

"I thought I was being fanciful." Her whispered words made something fragile inside him tremble. "You truly feel it too?"

He kissed her lips sweetly. "I do."

His mouth ground down on hers with savage intent as she clutched at his arms. His hands roamed her lithe body, stroking her curves and supporting her when she sagged against him.

"Will you lie with me, beautiful Belora?" His words were impassioned whispers against the soft, warm column of her neck. "Will you give me the gift of your body?"

She pulled back and it nearly killed him to let her draw even slightly away.

"I've never been with a man, Gareth." His heart stopped beating as he waited for her hesitant words. "But my mother's a healer. I know what to expect and I want to be with you. Will you teach me what I need to know to please you?"

He gathered her back into his arms and hugged her close. A slight and strange wetness formed behind his eyes as he realized the import of this moment. This small woman's trust meant more to him than anything in the world except perhaps for his bond with Kelvan. It was on the same level as that momentous occasion and that alone told him this was a special moment—a special woman. He'd be damned if he hadn't just found his mate.

It was a heady thought. A frightening thought. A thought for later consideration. Much later. For now, he had to concentrate on the beautiful woman in his arms.

"You need do nothing but be yourself to please me, sweet Belora."

Words failed him at that point and he turned his attentions to showing her how beautiful she was. He lifted her rough tunic slowly over her head, memorizing every one of her maidenly blushes. He'd never had a maiden before, but he had bedded many experienced women and knew well how to please them. He would make certain this first time for Belora was as good as he could possibly make it. He wanted her to remember this loving with joy.

When she was bare, he laid her down on the soft pile of their discarded clothing and spread her flowing hair around her lovely face. She was shy, but willing, he could easily read from the soft expression on her face.

He stroked her breast with one large hand. He was a big man but he could be gentle when he needed to be and this was one of those times. At least for now, he would give her gentleness. If it turned out she could handle more, he would give it to her later by all means. With pleasure.

She shivered as he stroked down to the point of her breast, pinching her pert nipple with just enough force to make her squeal in pleasure. He leaned lower and replaced his hands with his lips. Sucking her deep into his warmth, he watched as her eyes followed his movements with more than a little shock and rising desire.

"Gareth!" she keened as he bit down gently on her nipple, releasing her with a pop to pay the same homage to her other breast.

His hands were busy learning the curves of her waist, her hips, her thighs and what lay between. One hand parted the neat curls above her mound and found their way into her folds while she squirmed. He lifted his head and watched her carefully as he drew her nipple between his teeth with a little edge of roughness. She was with him all the way and it sent a thrill of dominance through him. She liked what he was doing to her. No, she *loved* what he was doing to her. He could tell by her sexy eyes and shivering body.

"You'll never regret giving yourself to me, Belora. I swear it on my honor."

"The only way I'll regret this is if you stop now, Gareth."

He laughed heartily at her honest, soul-baring answer. This was a woman who wasn't afraid to take life by the horns. He was half in love with her already and they'd only just met.

"I'd never leave you wanting, sweet Belora. I need you every bit as much as you probably need me by now."

"No one could need you more than I. It's not possible. What have you done to me, Gareth? What kind of magic is this?"

She gasped as he moved his hand, coating his fingers in her slick excitement. Holding her gaze, he slid one large finger into her core and watched carefully as he stretched tissues that had never known the touch of a man. The thought excited him beyond reason, but he held tightly to his control. This woman was special. He would make sure she enjoyed every moment they had together.

"It's the purest form of magic, sweet. The magic of man and woman."

He leaned in close and kissed her deep, catching her cries of excitement in his mouth as he added a second finger inside her tight channel. He knew it might hurt her, but she was so deep in her pleasure, she was beyond pain now. This first time it would be a blessing to her to break through her barrier fast before she had time to worry and tense up. She was in the perfect place now, if he could just keep her there until he was buried deep inside her.

He slid over her, placing himself between her spread thighs, holding her eyes and overwhelming her senses with deep, passionate kisses that kept her off balance. His fingers began pumping in and out of her channel, preparing her, drawing forth her liquid.

He brought his wet fingers to his cock and coated himself with her essence, hoping to make his passage easier on her this first time. Before she had time to think, he pressed forward, the cap of his raging erection sinking in with little trouble. He straightened over her, bracing his arms on either side of her face as he moved steadily forward.

"Do it now, Gareth. Come into me now!"

"Your wish," he surged forward, breaking through the barrier, "is my command." She jerked beneath him momentarily and he held still, watching the tightness around her sweet mouth ease as she got used to his presence in her body. "Better now?"

She tilted her head as if considering exactly how she felt. He loved that thoughtfulness about her. He loved her adventurous spirit. And he feared given half a chance, he would love her. Period.

"It feels odd, but very pleasurable. Isn't there more?"

Gareth grinned down at her questioning eyes. "Much more. We've only just begun."

"Oh, good."

With a chuckle, Gareth began to move in her, watching her eyes light up as she discovered what came next. She was delightful to him. Fresh, eager and open to new experiences, she was a treasure. He'd never felt so lighthearted while making love, never knew it could feel this right, this pure, this perfect.

She clamped her legs around him and he could feel her excitement rising fast. She was so responsive to him, it made it all that much better. He moved his hand between them and teased her clit until she tensed and cried out, experiencing her first orgasm while he remained hard within her. He watched her through it all, entranced by the look in her luminous eyes, the sheer pleasure on her pretty face.

He rode her throughout, helping her milk it for all it was worth. When she came back to earth, he was there, looking down into her beautiful eyes.

"Ready for more?" His smile teased her and she blushed so prettily he had to lean down and kiss her luscious lips. Rolling, he reversed their positions, keeping himself tight within her, watching the surprise enter her expression. "Do you ride?"

"We can no longer afford to keep a horse."

"Who needs a horse when you can ride me?" His teasing tone brought a spark of excitement to her eyes and she straightened, letting her beautiful breasts swing as she positioned herself atop him.

"Am I doing it right?" She began a slow up and down motion on him that made him groan in appreciation.

"Any righter and I'd be a dead man." His head flopped back to the ground as she increased her pace. "You're a natural, sweet. Keep on as you're going and we'll soon touch the stars together."

"Oh, Gareth!"

She was close; he could see it in the tensing of her sweet mouth. He moved his hands up to cup her bouncing breasts, enjoying the look and feel of them in his hands as she rode him. He pinched her nipples and teased them with his thumbs, flicking them as she moved faster and faster in search of her goal.

"Come for me now, sweet. Let go and come now!"

She convulsed over him, straining as he pumped hard within her and spilled a torrent of his seed within her tight depths.

"Oh!" She convulsed again as he watched, close to awe at the pleasure this small, untried woman had given him. He had never come so hard or so long in his life and still he emptied into her as if she had been made for him.

He stroked her hair, her back, her soft skin, even as his cock relaxed within her. Not seeing any reason to move further, he dragged a dry towel over her back and settled in for a short rest. He would have her again before this day was through, but for now she was wiped out.

CHAPTER TWO

Belora woke on her back beneath Gareth, his cock hard once more within her. He stroked lightly, in and out, and she realized she was very wet and very excited. This man had shown her the most amazing things and it seemed there was still more to learn. The attraction she had felt on first seeing him in the water now resolved into an amazing affection for the handsome, thoughtful man. He was so gentle with her, so caring in his way, yet so exciting. He'd shown her things about herself she had only been able to guess at before and given her a new confidence in her femininity she had never had before.

"About time you woke up." His soft grin eased the hard words.

She stretched up, stroking his stubbly cheek with her soft hand. She loved the masculine feel of him.

"Someone tired me out."

"Hmm. We'll have to see what we can do about that."

He rocked gently, in no hurry now to sate the hunger growing inside her. She climaxed twice before he let loose with his own completion, nearly drowning her in his seed. She knew a baby could come of what they'd just done, but didn't care. Or rather, she kind of liked the idea of having this knight's baby, even if she never saw him again.

Here was a man worthy of fathering children. He was brave, strong, gallant and a considerate lover. She well knew her initiation into sex could have been much more painful than it had been. In fact, aside from that one moment when he tore through her barrier, it had been nothing but pleasure.

No, if she got pregnant from this day's work, it was the will of the Mother. Such pleasure could not be wrong and if she had this man's child, the baby would be healthy, smart, and as strong as its father. It would be a blessing.

"Come, Belora." He tugged her to her feet though the lethargy of good, hot loving weighed her down. She wanted to sleep again, but it seemed he wouldn't let her.

"Where are we going?"

"For a quick dip in the lake."

"What?" Her tiredness left her in a rush. "That water's cold!"

"Invigorating," he countered, drawing her closer to where the clear waves lapped against the pebbly shore. "We need to clean you off or you'll be uncomfortable."

Her heart melted at his soft words. She knew in that moment that he was caring for her again. He was the expert at sex and knew what was best for her. So far he had proven that he always put her pleasure and comfort before his own and that was a good quality in a man, she decided.

"All right, but let's make this quick. I don't relish freezing my butt off."

He let her precede him so he could leer at the butt in question.

"No, that would be a definite shame. I'll make sure that your beautiful butt doesn't go anywhere."

He grabbed her ass in his hands and pushed her toward the clear water of the lake. They splashed in, laughing and smiling as he pulled her close into his arms. He took them only waist deep into the water before tugging her to a halt. Holding her eyes with his, he swept his big hands down into the water, cupping them between her legs, and ran his calloused fingers through her folds. As he cleaned her, each sweep growing bolder, a fire kindled and leapt in her womb.

He plunged two fingers up into her sore channel, but backed off when she winced just the tiniest bit.

"I'm sorry," she said softly as he drew back.

"No, I should have realized you'd be sore after all we've done today."

"But I want more."

He shook his head with a soft smile. "You can't have it. Not that way at least."

"What other way is there?"

Now the fire returned to in his eyes. "There are many other ways, my sweet innocent."

"Not so innocent anymore, thanks to you, sir knight." She knew she was blushing from the heat rushing up her neck, but couldn't help it. Besides, he seemed to enjoy it as he traced the flush on her cheeks with one strong hand. His other hand lingered below the water, tracing her folds and soothing her aches with gentle touches.

"I doubt there's anything in this world that could take your innocence completely from you. It's part of your soul, shining out through your lovely eyes." He bent down and kissed her eyelids so softly it brought a tear to her eye.

She started to shiver but it wasn't from the cold.

"Let's get you out of the water. You're right. It is kind of chilly."

Instead of letting her walk out, he hoisted her up in his arms and carried her to shore. After drying her with his towel, he laid her down on the soft pile of their clothing and settled himself on his haunches between her bare legs.

"What are you doing?" She was just a bit nervous, lying there exposed to his gaze. Her eyes followed his every move, her mouth going dry and her stomach clenching in anticipation that was mixed with just a hint of fear. This was all so new to her, but this man, this moment, felt so right. The smile in his eyes reassured her, the passion in his gaze heated her blood.

"Just enjoying the view. You're gorgeous, Belora." He leaned forward and placed a smacking kiss on the soft swell of her tummy as she laughed. "And while I'm here, I might as well show you one of those other ways of giving pleasure. What do you say?"

He raised his eyes to hers and smiled in that devilish way of his that made her insides clench.

"All right. I think."

"Oh, don't worry. You're going to love this."

He moved downward, shocking her as his hands spread her pussy lips apart and his tongue delved inside. She nearly bucked off the ground; the pleasure was so intense. He laved her most intimate places with his hot tongue, stroking down her slit and back up, pausing to seek inside the sore little hole that had never known such passion before that day. All pain was forgotten as shivers of delight danced up and down her spine. She'd never felt so wanton, so desirable as she did with this knight. He soothed her with long licks, exciting her with the odd foray down to the tight pucker of her anus and back up to circle and tease her clit. Her legs trembled and her muscles went weak, anticipation building as he stroked her higher and higher.

"Gareth?" She didn't know how she could stand the sensations running through her body. It was frightening and profound at the same time.

"Shh, sweet. Just enjoy. This is for you." His whispered words brushed in soft puffs of heated air against her clit, making her temperature rise higher. It wouldn't be long now.

She looked down and saw Gareth's sparkling eyes looking up at her from between her legs. Something about the sight of him, pleasuring her so thoroughly and seeming to enjoy it, sent her soaring higher. When he bit down gently, but unexpectedly on her clit, she screamed and convulsed in yet another orgasm. He rode her through it, keeping his warm mouth on her fiery cunt.

"Gareth! Oh, Gareth." Her whispered pleas escaped unnoticed from her lips as he curled her into his arms, much, much later. She could feel his hard cock against her, but he made no move to relieve his own tension.

When reason returned, she sat up and pushed him down onto the bed of clothing. The surprise in his eyes made her bold.

"Surely if you can make me come with your mouth, I can do the same?"

Gareth placed his hands on her arms. "You don't have to do this, Belora. This last time was for you. I don't expect anything."

"Nonsense. I want to learn you the way you've learned me." She moved closer, settling her face closer and closer to his thick erection. "I would take you in my body again, but I'm too sore. Let me do this for you, Gareth."

He let go of her arms and lay back with a silly grin on his face. "If you insist."

"Tell me what to do."

"Just touch me, Belora. Wrap your fingers around the base and suck the tip of my cock into your mouth. Use your tongue." She followed his instructions and was gratified to hear his harsh groan and feel the fingers tightening in her hair. He obviously liked what she was doing so she sucked harder. "Yes, just like that. Oh, Belora!"

She began to move up and down on him, in time with the tugging motions of his hand in her hair. He wasn't controlling her, but coaching her, she realized, and she took full advantage of his lesson to bring him to the brink of ecstasy. At the same time, she was learning intimate things about him. His musky scent, his salty taste, the rhythmic way he liked to be licked. She felt wicked and divine at the same time, learning how to pleasure a man such as this. She sucked lightly, then harder, following his cues as she learned the new landscape before her. Never had she imagined, even in her wildest dreams, taking a man in her mouth this way. It was something out of her realm of experience, but something she knew she wanted to experience again and again. With this man, and this man alone.

"Let go now if you don't want me to come in your mouth," he warned. "I'm that close."

But she wanted his cum. She wanted it all. She wanted to taste him, to swallow him down, and take his essence into herself. She sucked harder and he gasped, coming hard as she gulped it down, licking and tasting, moaning her own enjoyment. She hadn't expected to enjoy making him come as much as she had, but it gave her a sense of her own feminine power and allowed her to express the softer feelings she inexplicably had for this hard knight who had stolen her heart with only his smile.

They lay down again for a while, basking in the lethargy that she was learning came after incredible sex. They enjoyed watching the late afternoon sun glinting off the lake and the dragon flying low over the forest in the distance.

She turned in his arms to look up at his hard chiseled face. "You know, I've never seen a dragon in these parts before, much less a knight."

"You'll see more of us soon. We've founded a Lair just to the north of here by the king's command, and will be patrolling the border from now on."

"That sounds like trouble. Your dragon friend said we might see war from Skithdron."

He nodded once. "It's true. There's unrest to the east. More skith attacks than usual for one thing, and political maneuvering between the kings and politicians."

"My mother said she'd heard rumors, but we were hoping it was just talk."

"Unfortunately not."

She lay back against him, staring at the sky and thinking hard while he idly drew soft circles on her bare skin with his fingertips.

"Will I ever see you again?" Her tone was curious, not possessive, but the words caused a tightening in his heart.

"I hope I'll see you often. In fact, I want you to come back with me to the new Lair, Belora. I want more than just this. Will you come with me?"

"I want to, more than you can know, but there's more to consider than just my desires."

"What could be more important than this?" His hands skimmed her back, bringing her close to his heart.

"My mother relies on me, Gareth." Her voice was small. "I can't just leave her."

Gareth set her back slightly so he could look into her eyes. "You are a noble creature, my Belora. Kelvan and I will take you to your home and speak with your mother. As Kel is fond of saying, the Mother of All will find a way." He stroked her cheek. "You're truly not afraid of Kelvan, are you?"

She gave him a puzzled smile. "Why would I be afraid of a dragon? They're noble creatures, especially those who are in service to the lands and fight to protect us."

"And you can hear him when he speaks to you?" Gareth held his breath. So much depended on her answer.

"Well, yes, of course. Can't everyone?"

He shook his head and laughed lightly. "Not everyone, Belora. Only a few are blessed with the ability."

She tilted her head, thinking. "That's strange. I thought everyone could. My mother can, I know that for certain. She was friends with a dragon when she was little."

He kissed her lightly. "Then the Mother of All has definitely put you in our path for a reason. If we are meant to be together—and I feel close to certain we are—it will all work out. All I ask is that you at least come back with us to visit the Lair. I want you to see it and learn a little of our ways." He stroked her hair back from her face, his heart shining in his eyes. "If you think you could live there, well, then I'll have another question to ask you, but we'll take first things first. Let us go see your mother and then we'll go to the Lair for a visit. Do you approve?"

"All right. A short visit."

Adora watched in awe as a mighty dragon landed in the small clearing in front of her cabin in the woods. She'd not seen a dragon since she was a little girl, and this one was a beauty. Blue and green with the iridescent sparkle of his kind, this dragon reminded her of her childhood friend. Even more amazing, this dragon bore a young knight on his back along with her daughter! She wiped her hands on her apron and rushed out to greet them.

"Belora, my dear, you've brought guests." Adora smiled as her girl raced from the dragon's side to hug her.

"This is Gareth and Kelvan." Belora's excitement was evident as she took her mother's hands in hers, pulling her forward to meet them. "Gareth, Kelvan, this is my mother, Adora."

Adora surprised them all by bowing low to Kelvan in the old way first, before she even acknowledged his rider. The dragon preened openly at the show of respect and stood to his full height, returning the courtesy with a formal sweep of his wings.

"You honor my humble home with your presence, Sir Kelvan. Be welcome here."

The honor is mine, Madam. Your daughter claimed you once knew my kind and I am pleased to see the old ways preserved in your memory. You do both our peoples proud. Kelvan included them all in his silent speech.

Adora blushed prettily as she straightened. "You are a handsome dragon, Sir Kelvan, and a pretty talker."

The dragon rumbled in a way resembling laughter and all the humans smiled as he laid the dead stag at the lady's feet.

An offering for your table, Madam. Courtesy of your daughter.

"And Kelvan too, Mama. That's how we met. I shot the stag, but he didn't see me and snagged it from above for a snack. I disputed his claim to the stag and he brought me to Gareth to see who was in the right."

"Ah yes, you bring me not only a dragon, but a knight as well." Adora clapped her hands together in joy though her tone was mischievous. "You are Sir Gareth?"

The young man strode forward to stand before her. "I am."

"Welcome to our home, sir. It has been many years since I last saw a dragon and I must admit complete ignorance of the knights who work with them. The dragon I knew as a child had no partner at the time."

Gareth smiled kindly down at her. "We are not much different from normal men, Lady, except that we can hear the dragons as you do and partner with them to protect the innocent."

"It is a noble calling."

Gareth inclined his head to acknowledge her words.

"But worrisome. If you are here, trouble must not be far behind."

You are perceptive, Madam. The dragon's powerful voice sounded through all their minds. Trouble brews on the border and the king has dispatched us to create a new Lair not far from here. You must be cautious in your travels and dealings with strangers. The skiths are growing restless.

Adora gasped but did not otherwise show the fear his stark words brought to her soul. Her keen mind worked around the dire news as she made her guests welcome and turned the subject to more pleasant matters.

She asked them about the new Lair they were building and prepared refreshments while Kelvan, in an uncharacteristically thoughtful move for a dragon, dragged the stag away into the forest to prepare it for the women. A few swipes with his razor sharp claws and it was ready.

When he came back, they were sitting around the fire pit in front of the small cottage, talking amiably. Being certain he had everyone's attention, Kelvan covered one nostril with an overly large digit and exhaled a burst of flame over the spitted stag. When the flame subsided, the animal was fully cooked, just right for human consumption.

Dinner is served.

They laughed at the dragon's wry humor.

After dinner, Gareth and Belora took a walk down to the stream to gather water and steal a few moments alone together. It was obvious to Adora that her beautiful daughter was deeply in love, as was the tall young man at her side. His heart was in his eyes as he looked down at her girl, and she knew it was a long, lasting kind of love that filled his heart. Though she had never known a knight before, she knew dragons and the men they chose to fight with had the highest qualities of nobility and honor. She had little to worry about as far as her daughter's match was concerned, but still her heart was a little heavy watching them.

He loves true and deep, Lady. It's the nature of knights to decide what they want quickly and pursue it. Many recognize their life mates within moments of meeting. The Mother guides them in all things. Fear not for your girl. The dragon came up to sit across from her, his wings folded loosely against his sides as he sat on his haunches.

"I fear not for her, though I thank you for your words of comfort. If anything, I fear for my own future, selfish as it seems." Adora shook herself and changed the subject before the dragon had a chance to interject. "But it's not important. I knew a dragon when I was a child. I used to bring her melons from our garden and she would always slice a little piece for me as a treat. You remind me of her, Sir Kelvan. You have similar coloring in your wings and around your eyes. Her name was Kelzy." She sighed, lost in memory. "She had a scar running near her left ear."

And another on her right foreleg.

"Yes! How did you know?"

Kelvan bowed his head to the side. *She is my mother.* His voice was solemn. *And you are Adora. She speaks of you often.*

"She lives still?" A smile bloomed on her pretty face.

Kelvan chuckled softly in his dragonish way. *Our kind does not age as you do. When you knew her, she had suffered the loss of her knight and needed some time to recover. We bond quite closely to our partners, you know. She's one of the elders in charge of building our new Lair and teaches the younger ranks how to fight and work with the knights. She chose my knight for me, in fact, even before I could claim him.*

"She chose well." Adora's eyes followed the progress of the young couple across the small clearing. They were strolling slowly, oblivious to all except each other.

He is a good man through and through. You have naught to fear for your daughter or yourself.

"It is selfish of me, I know, but I fear being alone. I've already lost children and it nearly killed me. Still, I want my girl to be happy, and her happiness lies with the young knight. It's obvious to see."

Then come with us to the new Lair. I am certain my mother would welcome you.

"I refuse to be a burden. This is Belora's time. I don't want to interfere."

You would not be a burden, Lady Adora. We always need help in the Lair, and there are so few humans able to deal well with my kind. We already know you and your daughter can. We would welcome you both.

Adora considered his words carefully, mulling over the possibilities in her mind. "I can cook and clean, I suppose. I also know of healing herbs. It's how we've made do out here in the forest."

Healing skills are always needed among the fighters. You would be more than welcome, Lady. What can it hurt to come for a visit? I know my mother will want to see you. If you do not come back with us, at least for a visit, I can nearly guarantee she will make the trip out here herself to make certain you are all right. She is not a young dragon any longer. Won't you spare her such an arduous journey? I can have you there and back again the next day, if you will consent to come for a visit.

Adora was torn, but she did so want to see the dragon who had been her childhood friend once more. "Perhaps a short visit. Just to see Lady Kelzy. I have thought of her often and missed her greatly. But I must return to care for my patients. I am all the help the local village has, and I can't just abandon them."

Yet you do not live in the village.

"By choice. Not because they would not have us. When I came here, I was hurt deeply by the loss of my children. Twin girls as bright as the sun." She paused while she collected herself. Her baby girls were gone and it left a hole in her heart that was wide and deep. How she missed them still, years later. Nothing would ever make up for losing her beloved twin daughters. The only consolation she had was that Belora was still with her, still safe. She sighed deeply before continuing. "I couldn't bear to be with other people and my work often brings me into the forest to gather herbs. I enjoy the solitude and don't have much. This place was empty and available. It needed a good cleaning and still needs some repair, but it's home. It welcomed me, helped me heal, and sheltered Belora as she grew. This place has been good to me."

Kelvan bowed his head in respect. *I can feel the love in your words for this place. Our new Lair begins to feel that way to me as well, though I've only been there a short time. Perhaps because my mother was able to set it up to her specifications it has always felt like home. I have come to learn that home is wherever those you love are, so for me, home will always be with Gareth and his mate.*

"You think Belora is his mate?"

I do. He moves slowly to claim her though, because she does not know our ways. I think that once she sees how we live and learns more about us, she'll fit in well. The Mother of All would not be so cruel as to bring them together only to break their hearts. They both watched the two young people walking back from the stream, hand in hand. It was obvious how much in love the two were, though they had only met that day. *You must come for a visit, Lady. It will help if you can see how your daughter will live and know that she is not gone from you forever. I'll fly her back to see you as often as possible if you choose to stay here. I understand the importance of family.*

"You are a kind and noble being, Sir Kelvan." Adora reached up and placed her small palm on his knee joint. "I'll go with you to visit your new home and see Lady Kelzy once more. But only for a short time. With war coming, my duty is to the people of the village who depend on me."

If you were male, you would surely be a knight, Lady. Your heart is compassionate and strong.

"I think that's the most beautiful thing anyone has ever said to me." She smiled softly and turned back to watch the younger couple, kissing in the dappled moonlight, distantly in the forest. She thought they looked right together—her baby girl with a handsome and strong knight who so obviously cared for her. It was like a dream come true. For Belora.

Adora sighed wistfully, resigned to knowing that this time was for her daughter, but still it saddened her that she would never know such a love again. Her time was over.

CHAPTER THREE

The dragon tried not to gloat as his mind sought out that of his partner. *Adora has agreed to come with us for a short visit to the Lair. She wants to see my mother, and I told her Kelzy was far too old and decrepit to fly all this way out to see her.*

Gareth burst into laughter and sent his thoughts back to the dragon as all knights were trained to do. *Kelzy will singe your hide for even suggesting that she's too old to fly this short a distance. Your mother is one of our finest fighters, Kel, and by dragon reckoning, she's still quite young.*

You know that and I know that, but Adora doesn't. You should be thanking me for getting her to agree so easily to come along. These females belong at the Lair, Gareth. You know that as well as I do. We need them.

You're right, Kel. Gareth sighed. *I've only just met her, but I know in my heart, Belora is mine. And her mother seems a treasure. We don't have enough healers at our new Lair if it comes to war. There are so few women who can deal well with dragons and knights alike. We need every one.*

These two are special. My mother saw the light in Adora as a child, so clearly that she talks of her to this day and her girl is just the same. If she consents to be your mate, you will be truly blessed.

Don't you think you're getting ahead of yourself a bit? First we have to see if she can live at the Lair.

But you want her.

Hell yes! I want her. But don't forget, she must choose me, Kel. Without her trust and her love, it will never work.

The Mother of All would not put her in our path only to take her away. She is not so cruel.

I hope you're right, my friend. I hope you're right.

Kelvan alighted on the ledge carved out from the stone face of the cliff for just that purpose. It was wide enough for several dragons to take off and land on at any one time and there was one already there, waiting for them.

"Kelzy!" Adora whispered in a choked voice as she caught sight of the waiting blue-green dragon.

Belora squeezed her mother's hand and they shared a smile as Kelvan came to a complete stop. Gareth jumped down first, helping the women down. Adora made her way directly to the dragon and made a deep bow before her.

"Lady Kelzy, it is so good to see you again."

Adora? Is it really you? The huge dragon stepped closer, all formality forgotten as she lowered her head to the human's height. *Adora, my child,* the dragon's voice was so gentle in her mind, *give us a hug, dear.*

The woman threw herself at the dragon, her arms wrapping tightly around her huge neck, weeping openly. The dragon did something then that dragons seldom did. She wrapped her great wings around the woman, encasing her in their magical warmth as Adora clung to her long lost childhood friend.

Kelzy knew she was overly emotional for a dragon and unseemingly fond of her human friends, but this little woman hugging her so tightly was the closest thing she had to a daughter. Kelzy had missed her terribly during those years they'd been separated. Finding her again so unexpectedly was a miracle.

"Mama Kelzy, I've missed you so," Adora whispered.

Kelzy crooned in her mind, soothing the woman's fears and basking in the joy of having the child of her heart near once more. Kelzy knew the others were watching them, but didn't care. She had always been her own dragon and didn't care for those that would comment on her uncharacteristic display. Adora was special and always had been. Losing track of the small human girl had been one of the saddest things that had ever happened to Kelzy and finding her again was a gift from the Mother.

When Adora finally gathered her emotions and stepped back, Kelzy let her go with joy in her heart. Her great eyes turned to her grown son and his partner. She did a double take when she spotted a younger human woman with the same light around her as Adora. This was Adora's child and, if she wasn't much mistaken, her light was already affecting the broad shouldered knight at her side. Kelzy felt an extreme satisfaction. Her boy would have Adora's child as his partner's mate. It all suddenly made sense.

You have a beautiful girl, Kelzy told her. *She will make a fine addition to our community.*

Adora reached back and brought her daughter closer. "My daughter, Belora."

Belora made her bow prettily and said all the right words, impressing the dragon and no doubt making her mother proud.

And where is your man?

"I'm a widow. Have been for many years. We live, simply, in the forest."

That will not do. You must stay here, with us. I have need of you, Adora. There is much work to be done and so few to do it.

"I—"

Don't answer now. Come see how we live here and learn a bit of our ways and needs. Then, if you still feel like living all alone in your forest, I will take you back myself.

Adora smiled up at the dragon, love shining in her eyes, but started as she looked just past the dragon's tall shoulder. Kelzy turned her great head to see what had startled her long lost daughter and puffed a small cloud of smoke in wry amusement.

Don't let his looks frighten you, dear. This is Jared, my partner. Be nice, Jared, this girl is as a daughter to me. Kelzy was speaking to the minds of both humans, linking them just slightly.

Adora was startled by the feeling of the knight's curiosity that reached through the small link formed by the dragon. She had never experienced such a thing before and it was surprising.

"I'm honored to meet you, Madam."

The knight's rumbling voice caught Adora off guard, warming her insides in a way they hadn't been warmed in too many years. The man was striking. Older than she, he had a jagged scar running down one cheek, all too close to his eye though the silvery blue depths of his irises remained unhurt and stunningly alert. His hair was dark with light streaks of silver near his temples that only made him appear more dangerous somehow. She got the impression that this man seldom smiled but was competent and deadly in his chosen profession.

A tall man, he was muscular in a lithe sort of way, but solid and all too handsome for his own good. The only relief was that he didn't seem to be aware of his rugged appeal, or if he was, he disdained such things in favor of more sober pursuits. He seemed very serious and almost grim, but Adora saw a sadness in his eyes that called to the sorrow in her own soul. Instinctively, her heart went out to him, though he gave no indication of wanting or needing any sort of sympathy or even camaraderie.

"The honor is mine, Sir Jared." Adora realized belatedly that she was staring rather rudely and made her bow quickly, averting her gaze to the ground while she knew her cheeks flamed.

Honestly, Jared, make an effort. You're frightening the poor child. Kelzy's teasing voice was just a bit exasperated in both of their minds and Adora had to stifle a giggle.

Jared was humbled by the woman's beauty. Her green eyes were luminous as she raised them once more to his. Though Kelzy insisted on referring to her as a girl, there was no doubt in his mind that this was a woman. She had the rounded curves he enjoyed and a sparkle in her eyes when she looked at him that set his teeth on edge.

He was a widower and the loss of his wife so many years before had been hard on him. Since then, he had found pleasure where he could, but had no desire to marry again or become involved in anything remotely long-term.

But here was a woman who was already close to his partner—the only female he allowed in his life. Undoubtedly Kelzy would want this woman near. Their relationship pre-dated his own with the dragon and was obviously as close, or perhaps even closer, than the relationship between he and Kelzy, bonded as they were. This woman would most likely be underfoot and he couldn't ignore her.

His heart didn't want to ignore her, and that's what unsettled him most. It had been a very long time indeed since a woman had such an impact on him. The odd echo of her feelings he could touch through the link with Kelzy when the dragon spoke to them both was the most unsettling phenomenon he had ever felt. He wondered if all mated knights had this sort of non-verbal feedback through the links with their dragons. He hadn't been partnered with a dragon when he was married, so he had never experienced it for himself. In fact, it had been his wife's death that brought Kelzy to him. His pain had drawn the dragon from her own pain of losing her first knight partner and they bonded as they helped each other through the emotional upheaval of losing someone they loved.

"Kelzy has of course told me about you as a child. I know she missed you greatly." He remembered his manners with a little nudge from the flat of Kelzy's sharp front talon against his calf.

"No more than I missed her."

The woman glowed. There was no other word for it. Her goodness and light shone in her eyes and around her curved womanly body in a way that made him want to move closer.

Adora, you will stay in our suite. It is quite obvious my son's knight and your girl wish to be alone together. Kelzy's satisfied tone had both Adora and Jared looking back at Gareth and Belora who were currently locked at the lips. *We have plenty of room and I suspect we'll talk long into the night. I want to know everything that's happened to you since last we saw each other. And I want to know all about your girl too, since no doubt she will soon be part of my son's human family.*

The woman's soft eyes went from her little girl up to meet his. He knew she waited for him to second the invitation since it was his suite too and he could do no less than step forward, even though his internal alarms warned him from getting involved. This soft woman could well break what little was left of his heart.

"You should stay with us. There is plenty of room, as Kelzy says."

He thought he detected relief and a spark of interest in her luminous eyes, but dared not read too much into it. He was a confirmed bachelor now.

He didn't need love in his life. It made him soft. It made him hurt. Kelzy was the only female he needed. At least she wasn't likely to die and leave him alone and hurting.

Without further ado, they left the younger couple and headed for Kelzy's suite. Jared escorted her though it was obvious to Adora that he was careful to maintain a certain distance. The man alarmed her a bit, but she sensed a deep sensitivity in him and her sixth sense about people was seldom wrong. This man had been hurt badly in his life and the gruff exterior was probably all for show. Besides, she reasoned, Mama Kelzy was an excellent judge of character and the dragon chose the knight, not the other way around.

Adora learned the dragons had warm sand pits that were fired by the earth from below and their human partners built rooms for themselves around them. Each single dragon or mated dragon pair had their own wallow which was divided from the rest of the Lair by a ring of rooms that made up their suite. The knights and their mate would live in the suite with their dragons, some having guest rooms attached as well as utility and storage rooms.

The arrangement appeared quite cozy and served both the knights and their dragon partners well, but Adora noticed quickly that there were far fewer women in the Lair than men. The dragons seemed to be about fifty percent female and fifty percent male and all partnered with male knights, but there were few mated dragons and only those mated pairs seemed to have mated knights.

Adora intended to ask about it, but all the wondrous things she was learning and seeing for the first time quickly distracted her. As they passed a huge steaming chamber, Jared told her the pools within were heated, as the wallows were, from the earth beneath, and the water had a fragrant mineral quality that she had never before encountered.

Since it was already past time for the evening meal, Jared volunteered to go to the kitchens and bring something back for Adora while she freshened up from the long flight. Kelzy sat down for a good roll in her heated sand wallow and both females were content for the moment.

An hour later, he found Adora, now changed out of her traveling clothes and wearing a simple nightgown, cuddled up under Kelzy's wing. She slept soundly in the dragon's warm wallow with her.

It was unheard of. Shocking. Yet somehow it softened his heart to see this strong woman tucked up like a child against the side of the kindest dragon Jared had ever known.

Don't wake her. Kelzy said softly in his mind. *She's had a hard time of it.*

You really weren't kidding when you said she was like a daughter to you, were you? Jared spoke mind to mind with Kelzy to avoid making noise that might wake the small woman sleeping so peacefully next to the huge dragon.

She could be no closer to my heart if she were a dragonet. This girl has the purest heart of any human I've ever known. Don't you see the light from her soul? It's in everything she touches, in all that she does. The Mother of All had blessed her as a child and I'm gratified to see that her heart has never wavered. It's as pure today as it was when she was little.

Her daughter has that glow too, he agreed absently as he watched the small woman sleep.

Then you do see it! I knew you, of all the knights here, would. Kelzy reached out with one smooth talon and touched his booted foot gently. She was very demonstrative for a dragon and often shocked the others with her displays of emotion. Jared shuddered to think what the others would say if they saw her sharing her wallow with a human. There had already been talk about her allowing the human to hug her.

She's special, Jared. You must help me convince her to come live here with us. We need her. The Lair needs her and her daughter or the Mother would not have put them in my son's path.

I will, of course, help in whatever way I can, Kelzy, but you should know I'm not looking for a wife.

Did I say anything about you marrying her? Honestly, Jared. What makes you think I'd even think you were good enough for her? I won't let my girl consort with just any knight. So you'd better warn off your lusty friends.

Methinks you protest a bit too much, Kelz. Jared had to stifle a chuckle as he walked away from the odd pair snuggled in the warm sand.

Belora watched with interest as Kelvan strode into the large chamber, heading straight for the pit of warm sand at its center. With obvious relish, he kicked up a little cloud of sand as he settled in for a good roll and made dragonish purrs of contentment as the warm, dry sand rubbed against his scales, polishing them to a brilliant shine.

The set up of the knight's quarters intrigued Belora. Everything was built around Kelvan's slightly oval wallow. A small room for eating and preparing small, private meals sat off to one side with sealed ewers of what looked like beer keeping cold in the trickle of water down the side of the stone wall. She went over to investigate and realized that by moving a small trap, the flow of water could be increased or decreased to nothing at all. A large stone basin lay beneath with a drain that led off somewhere below, presumably down further into the mountain from which this Lair was carved.

"Magic," she breathed, moving the trap to watch the flow of icy clear water.

"And a good dose of science as well." Gareth chuckled as he leaned back against the doorframe, watching her. "His Majesty sent a mage to help us redirect the energies of the earth so we could heat our baths and the dragons' wallows, but he also sent a skilled architect who could direct the flow of water for washing and drinking. The two worked hand in hand to design this place for both humans and dragons to live comfortably."

"It's a marvel."

"You haven't seen all of it yet." Gareth held out his hand to her. She took it and moved through the rooms with him. "Let me give you the tour of our quarters at least. You already saw Kelvan's wallow. The dragons' wallows are the centerpiece of each set of rooms though they vary in size according to location in the mountain, how many dragons need to live there and other factors. Since I am still unmated, Kelvan's wallow is sized for one dragon only."

And a great hardship it is. I barely have room to spin around. A great flick of his tail sent a shower of sand over the chuckling humans.

"I keep brooms on hand to sweep the sand back in the wallow each day, else I'd soon feel like I was living on a beach." He took one of the brooms leaning up against the circular wall and began sweeping the warm sand back into the pit.

Better a beach than a hermitage.

"What does he mean?" Belora looked from Kelvan's smoky snort of disgust to Gareth's shaking head.

"My partner thinks I spend too much time alone." He pulled her close into his arms. "But I won't be alone tonight, will I?"

Belora giggled. She actually giggled. She was shocked such a flirty, feminine sound came out of her body, but there it was. Something about this knight brought out the floozy in her, but it felt good. Freeing.

"No, you won't be alone tonight, Gareth." Blushing, she reached for his hand. "Why don't you show me your room? And your bed."

"All in good time." He patted her hand. "But I bet you're still too sore to test the bed yet. Not to worry, I have a solution." He pulled aside a screen that hid the entrance to a small bathing chamber. It had a stone tub sunk partially into the floor and another of those trap devices that Gareth pulled to allow water to trickle into the tub in a steady rhythm.

"This water is from the mineral springs. By the time it makes its way here from there it's little more than lukewarm but we have Kel to help us warm it again, if we ask him nicely. A hot soak in the mineral water and a little dragon magic will put you right again in no time."

"Dragon magic?" She turned to watch the large dragon. He craned his neck out of the sand and up on the warm stone floor so that his great head rested only a few scant feet away from the bathing tub. His jewel like eyes settled on her unflinchingly. It was slightly unnerving.

Didn't your mother tell you that a dragon's breath and touch has healing properties? I will gladly expend my energies to soothe your torn flesh if it means I can share in your pleasure again like this afternoon. I have never felt the like.

"You... you felt that?" Belora blushed to the roots of her hair, looking from dragon to knight and back again for some explanation.

We bond closely with our knights. We're always present in each other's minds. We each feel what the other feels. It's our greatest strength and perhaps also our main weakness, but it is the way of things. When you joined with Gareth, I felt the echo of his pleasure and your own. His wide mouth opened in a toothy grin. It was marvelous.

Embarrassed beyond belief, Belora didn't know what to think.

"Don't worry, sweet." Gareth took her in his arms as the tub filled behind him. There was a small stool just to the side at the foot of the tub and he led her to it. "It's the way of things for knights and their dragon partners. There's nothing to be ashamed of."

"I... I just didn't realize."

"I know." Gareth soothed her with his hands, undoing buttons as he stroked her shoulders and arms. "And I would have told you sooner, but we've been a bit busy today."

She chuckled. "To say the least."

"Now, how about that hot bath?" He reached out to close the water trap. "Kel, will you do the honors?"

Gladly. Breathing deeply, the dragon aimed a wonderfully warm exhalation of hot air at the full tub, heating the chamber and the water as easy as that. He returned his head to its reclining position at the foot of the tub, watching the humans lazily.

"Is he going to watch? I can't... um... take off my clothes in front of him." She blushed again, unreasonable bashfulness taking over her mind.

Why not? You are a beautiful woman, but even if you weren't, I'm a dragon. Not human.

"But..."

Your modesty is misplaced. I'll feel everything Gareth feels, even know what you're feeling through my link with you both. I couldn't be any more present if I were human and could fuck you myself. She gasped, but he forged ahead. *Won't you let me enjoy what little pleasure I can gain from this? Until Gareth mates, I cannot claim my own dragoness. It's strictly forbidden, and for good reason.*

"Is that true?"

Gareth nodded. "Just as he feels my passion, I'll feel his. Dragon mating is, from what I've been told, overpowering to humans. Unless I have a mate to be with during his mating flights, it would drive me mad. Even among mates, sometimes the humans get into a frenzy that can be dangerous."

"Oh, my." She turned compassionate eyes to the dragon lolling in the huge archway. "So you've never…"

He stirred himself to shake his head sadly. *Until Gareth mates, I cannot.*

Belora walked slowly over to the dragon, feeling both sets of male eyes trained on her as she moved unexpectedly. She knelt down by Kel's massive head and leaned forward to kiss the ridge just between his eyes.

"You are a good and noble creature, Sir Kelvan. I'm sorry to have doubted you."

With a nod, she stood and removed all her clothing, standing before the dragon as if for inspection as he sighed out a warm puff of air that tickled her. She laughed and turned toward Gareth, who had shed his own clothing. He reached for her, and together they tumbled into the warm bath, locked at the lips as if they hadn't kissed in years rather than mere minutes.

The water lulled her and when a long, hot tongue dipped into the water and circled her ankle, she squealed. Apparently the dragon wanted to participate. She lifted her leg as he tugged upward, then allowed him to do the same to her other leg, draping both over the lips of the massive tub on either side. She was spread before him, Gareth to her side, watching now as the dragon's tongue returned to the hot, clear water.

"What's he doing?" The nervous edge was back in her voice.

"Healing you," Gareth whispered against her breast, just bobbing above the water. He licked her nipple and bit down as Kelvan's tongue slipped up her passage.

It was warm. No, it was downright hot, and large. But everywhere the long, leathery tongue touched, she felt healing fire. This was dragon energy, exciting even as it healed. She felt herself responding to the two male touches on her body—to Gareth, sucking her nipples and stroking her ass with his hands, and to Kelvan, his big dragonish tongue bringing healing to her sore tissues.

You taste divine. No wonder Gareth enjoyed going down on you so much this afternoon. If I were human I'd live between your thighs.

The dragon's tongue retreated with a last, hot flick over her clit and she cried out at the stimulation. She had almost come from having a dragon heal her. Could things get any weirder?

Apparently they could. When Gareth lifted her from the tub long moments later after washing every square inch of her body—some twice and three times—he spread her out on the warm stone floor near Kelvan's massive head.

"Just one more thing to be certain you'll feel no pain from what we do together." Gareth looked up at Kelvan and spread her thighs far apart, holding them there and spreading her wide with his hands. "Kel?"

My pleasure.

The dragon rumbled and brought forth a belch of smoke unlike anything she'd experienced from him before. It was vapor more than smoke and everywhere the cloud of sweet cinnamon smelling fire enveloped her, she felt a tingling not unlike magic. She realized quickly that this was the phenomenon known as the dragon's breath. It was indeed magical, and very, very special. Dragons expended a great deal of energy to put forth such a healing vapor and they did not do it lightly.

She felt euphoric as the mist faded, her skin tingling with the touch of magic and her body raring to go. It felt as if the long afternoon of loving had taken no toll whatsoever on her untried body, and she knew it was all because of Kelvan and his willingness to expend his precious magic on her wellbeing.

She scrambled up on her knees and went over to him, uncaring of her nudity now. What difference a few minutes can make, she realized in one small part of her mind that worried over such things.

"May I touch you?" she asked formally.

Kelvan lifted his head and stared at her as if considering her request. Slowly, he nodded his great head and she moved forward to place her hands on the ridges just below his enormous eyes. Holding his jeweled gaze, she focused her own small power and sent what healing magic she could back to him. His eyes widened as Gareth stood abruptly to watch.

You are a healer? A true healer?

Belora shrugged and sat back. "I have only a small gift when compared with my mother, but as you know, healers cannot usually heal themselves. Thank you for expending your energy for me, Sir Kelvan. I hope I've returned at least a bit of what you gave me."

More than I gave, if truth be known. You have more of a gift than you realize. Your energy has the flavor of dragons.

She yawned and shrugged, setting her pretty breasts to bouncing and she noted both males watched their movement attentively.

"It's time for bed."

Gareth scooped her up in his arms and carried her into the sleeping chamber. All the arched doorways in the large suite of rooms were wide so Kelvan could lay his head down right in the middle of them. He followed them right into the chamber and lay his head down opposite the pile of sumptuous furs and stuffed pillows that waited. Belora had never been in such a luxurious bed. She stretched and smiled as she felt Gareth come up beside her, his hands roving over her tingling body.

"I hope you're not too tired to make love."

"I don't think I'll ever be too tired to make love with you, Gareth. You make me feel so alive."

CHAPTER FOUR

Gareth looked from the dragon in his doorway to the gorgeous woman lying in his bed and realized he had never been more content. Right here he had everything he would ever need in life. His dragon partner had been the main focus of his life for so long, he had not quite realized how a mate would complete the circle. Yet Belora's presence in his room, in his bed, in his heart, made him see things in a whole new light.

She was the woman for him. Of that he had no doubt. Now he only need convince her of it and gentle her to their ways. Life in a dragon's Lair was odd to most humans, but necessary to the nature of both the dragons and their human partners. He prayed to the Mother of All that Belora would be able to accept their ways. No doubt they were hardest on the woman involved, but the benefits were great. The old adage held true in this case—the greatest prize often demanded the greatest sacrifice.

Gently he came down next to Belora, touching her softly, knowing she welcomed his touch, his love. It was a heady feeling. Slowly he lowered his head to her body, licking the mineral saltiness of the bathwater from her dewy skin, lapping at her much the way Kelvan had done. She was that sweet.

"What you do to me, Gareth. I never knew…"

He sucked her nipple into his mouth and she gasped, unable to complete her thoughts. He kept at it until she was shivering, moving on the bed sensuously. A puff of warm air from the doorway had her lifting her head to meet the jeweled gaze of the dragon, watching them.

To warm you, Mistress. You looked cold.

She giggled. "I wasn't cold, Kelvan, and well you know it."

Gareth lifted above her, blocking her view of the dragon.

"You don't mind that he's here? Truly?"

She tilted her head as if considering. "It still seems a little strange, but I think I'm all right with it. I mean, it's not like he's human after all."

"How would you feel if he were?" Gareth's eyes darkened.

"You mean having another man watch us?" She shivered against him and the look in her eyes was not one of fear as she mulled over the startling thought. Her reaction gave him hope. "I don't know. That seems stranger still. I was a virgin until this morning, Gareth. Give me some time to adjust."

"I know I'm rushing you, sweet. Just kick me if I go too fast, okay?" He leaned down and kissed her. "But having you here in my bed makes me think of all sorts of strange notions." He nibbled on her neck, working his way down her body as she squirmed in pleasure. "And for the record, being watched doesn't bother me. Quite the opposite, in fact. To have other men able to see what belongs to me—what they'll never have—it's a tantalizing thought."

She wiggled again as he neared her sex, spreading her legs with his big hands and settling himself between them. He stared down at her for a long while, slowly threading his fingers through the neat hair at the juncture of her thighs before spreading the outer lips of her pussy and touching within.

He knew that together, he and Kelvan had healed the worst of her hurts but still he did his best to be extra gentle. He would die rather than injure this special woman, the other half of his heart. He leaned forward and took her in his mouth, swirling his tongue through her folds and right up into her channel as she cried out.

She came almost at once as the dragon puffed warm air over them and rumbled low in his throat, reminding her of his presence in the archway, watching. Gareth rode her through the orgasm, stroking her ever higher with his tongue and questing fingers. He brought her wetness down to the tiny hole of her anus and probed gently within, setting off another series of shockwaves.

"You like that?" he breathed against her skin.

She could only moan as he continued teasing her. When he judged she was ready, he sat back, flipping her over and massaging the rounded cheeks of her ass.

"Get on your hands and knees, pet."

She looked back at him, uncertain, but his slap to her ass made her squeal and move. The spank had not really hurt; he had meant it only to tease. The widening of her eyes and her panting breaths told him all he needed to know about her reaction to it. She moved to her hands and knees uncertainly but he soothed her, parting the cheeks of her ass with gentle fingers so he could inspect her in detail.

When he could hold back no longer, he moved up and brought his cock to the entrance of her dripping pussy. She was beyond excited. She was primed. Pushing in, he went slow as she moaned.

"It feels so much bigger this way." Her gasping words reached his ears and brought a satisfied smile to his face.

"Too big?" He teased by stopping about halfway in.

"No!" She moved back against him, trying to take him deeper. "It feels so good! Don't stop."

He chuckled and moved forward, seating himself fully. He just stayed there for a moment, savoring the sensation but then his needs grew fierce once again and he started to move. She was moaning beneath him as he used his hands to steady her, playing with the little hole of her anus and teasing her response.

She jerked and cried out as his finger dipped into her ass, just to the first knuckle. He kept it there, noting her reactions as his pace increased. He was close now and she was downright explosive beneath him.

When he was ready to explode, he pushed his finger in deeper, at the same time reaching around to tease her clit with his other hand. She came like fireworks, clenching around him and milking his cock until he shuddered and cried out, jetting his seed deep within her.

They collapsed together onto the pile of bedding and he folded her gently into his arms. Drifting off to sleep, he realized he had never reached higher plateau of pleasure in his life and possibly never would again with any other woman. Belora was it for him. His mate.

He smiled as sleep claimed him, knowing she was in his arms where she belonged.

Gareth woke in the night when Belora moved restlessly in her sleep. He wasn't used to sleeping with a woman, but waking with Belora in his arms was an entirely satisfying experience. He soothed her and she settled back against him. He looked around the room and found Kelvan's head still resting in the doorway, watching them.

Gareth, there's something strange about her healing energy.

Strange? Strange in a bad way?

No! It feels... it feels almost like... no, I must be wrong.

Spit it out, Kel.

No, I shouldn't say anything unless I'm sure. Let me think on this a bit more, but by all means, don't let her go back to that hut in the forest. If I'm right, she is more precious than you know.

Go to sleep, Kel. We can puzzle out your cryptic words tomorrow. Gareth threw a pillow at the dragon and cuddled closer to his woman. Everything would work out now that they were together. He could feel it.

The next morning after a small meal in the communal area where both Belora and her mother were introduced to most of those who lived in the Lair, Gareth and Kelzy went off to train. Belora and her mother made friends with a few of the women, but it was Silla, a woman about her mother's age that took them under her wing. When both Belora and her mother volunteered to help with the daily chores it was Silla who showed them where to go and what to do to help. Belora helped with the washing while her mother went off with the Lair's healer to discuss what might be needed in the stillroom.

It was almost dark when Kelvan alighted on the ledge outside the suite where Belora waited for them. She beamed when Gareth walked in, looking a bit ragged, beside his magnificent dragon.

"Did you have a good day?" He wrapped her in his arms and kissed her with a grin.

"Wonderful, actually. The others are so friendly, and the dragons! They are just amazing. I think I could live here forever and never become bored."

Belora's smiling face enchanted him as she pulled away from him to fold the last of the linens. He'd told her to relax and enjoy her time here while he trained, but she insisted on pitching in with the wash when she saw the other women working. He admired her spirit and her giving heart, but he also wanted to pamper her. After seeing her house in the forest, he knew she hadn't led an easy life.

He wanted to make her life easy. He wanted to spoil her and shower her with love, attention, and all the material things she had never had before, but he knew her innate goodness wouldn't let her rest idle while others worked, and now he was glad of it. Working alongside the other women today had been a good thing, he realized, because it showed her up close how good her life could be if she chose to stay with him in the Border Lair. He grabbed her by the waist and twirled her around, unable to contain the joy he felt at her unguarded words.

"Gareth! Put me down!"

He did, but then he knelt at her feet himself, smiling up at her. "You have no idea the joy that fills me to hear you speak of my home in such a way."

"You must know how special this place is."

"I do. But even more special, is you, Belora, my beloved."

"Why do you kneel?" She tried to tug his arms up, but he would not budge.

"It's tradition for a knight to humble himself before the woman he chooses when he asks the most important question he will ever ask of her."

She gasped. "What question is that?"

He tugged both her of her soft hands into his and stared up into her eyes. "I love you, Belora. Will you be my wife?"

She gaped at him. She seemed hardly able speak, but the smile that spread across her soft lips was answer in itself. "Yes, Gareth. I love you too!"

He drew her into his arms and kissed her hard, hugging her tight and lifting her off the ground with his eagerness. He moved her to the bedroom and lay her down on the soft furs, kissing every inch of her body as he undressed her. He made short work of his own clothing and soon they were skin to skin. *The way it should always be,* he thought.

He rose up above her and took her legs in his hands, caressing them boldly before placing one on each side of his body. He knew what he wanted and couldn't wait. He tested her readiness with one hand before smiling in deep satisfaction. She was wet and more than ready.

"Take me, beloved. Squeeze me with your beautiful body and bring me pleasure like I've never known."

He entered her slowly, careful lest he hurt her, but once seated he groaned in bliss. His eyes squeezed shut for a moment as he savored the feeling of her warm body around him. When he opened his eyes and looked down into hers, he saw the tears there and stilled in panic.

"Did I hurt you?" He moved to lever himself off of her, but she surprised him by wrapping her legs around his waist and holding on tight.

"You could never hurt me, Gareth." Her whispered voice was full of wonder and her watery eyes shone with happiness. He began to relax and settled back onto her though he was curious about her reaction. "I'm just a little overwhelmed, I guess, by the beauty of this—of you. I love you so much."

The glow of her words pierced his heart. "As I love you, Belora. Never doubt that."

"I want to stay with you forever."

He began to move inside her, unable to hold back any longer.

"I want you too, Belora. For always and ever." He moved more urgently then, his mind blocking out the reality that she still didn't know all that would be expected of her as his mate, but he would deal with that later. It was enough for now to know that she wanted him and would accept him as her mate. The rest would come later.

He pounded home, again and again, bringing her to repeated peaks. She climaxed almost continuously under him while he steadily increased his pace, altering his position slightly to reach deeper or differently each time she came down from a yet higher peak. He played her body, manipulating her senses to bring her the most pleasure he knew how to give. When she finally sobbed at the highest climax yet, he knew he could hold out no longer.

With a harsh groan, he increased yet again, bringing her to the final, mind-blowing climax in which he joined her. He came for what seemed like hours, deep within the woman he loved. Potent and powerful, his climax wrung him out from deep within his soul while Belora shattered and shook with her own orgasm around him.

It went on for a long, long time and when it was over, he was completely drained. He had only enough energy to roll off her, pull the covers up over them both and tuck her into his arms securely before falling into the deepest, most peaceful sleep he'd known in years.

All was right with the world. Belora loved him and wanted to be with him. Life could hardly get better than this.

So you have claimed your mate. You know what this means, don't you? Kelvan's voice sounded through Gareth's mind the next day, lower than usual and more excited. Kelvan looked over at his partner with a curious tilt to his head. *Now that you have found your mate, I am free to take mine.*

"You already have a female in mind?"

I do. The dragon's rumble sounded suspiciously gruff.

"This sounds serious. Have you waited long to claim your lady love, Kelvan? Truly, I had no idea I was holding you up." Gareth was only half teasing.

You know it's not safe for a fighting dragon to mate before his human partner. I knew you would find your mate sooner rather than later and I think I have exhibited extraordinary patience with you. Of course, as it turned out, I even had to find your mate for you to speed things along.

"That you did, my friend, and I'll thank you every day for it as long as I live." Gareth watched his little mate a few yards distant, moving gracefully in her way. She literally took his breath away. To think, she was his and his alone—at least until Kelvan took his mate. Then they would probably expand their circle of love to include Kelvan's mate and her partner. "So who is your lady?"

And more importantly who is her partner, right? Kelvan supplied with some humor. *Don't worry, Gareth. We dragons take all into consideration when we choose our partners and mates. The Mother of All has no little influence in it either. Seldom has there been an incompatible partnering among our kind. You know this to be true.*

"Yes, but I still worry about exactly who I'm expected to share my mate with." Gareth's skin itched to think of the possibilities. He had never confronted the reality of mating among dragon kind before and had never really considered the problems it could cause for their human partners. He began to sweat as he thought of what would come when Kelvan finally took his mate. It could be glorious. Or it could be disastrous.

You will be pleased then, I think, to learn that my mate is Rohtina.

A huge grin spread across Gareth's face. "And Lars is her partner. Kel, this couldn't have worked out better!"

The dragon dipped his great head. *The Mother of All knows what She is about after all.*

"That She does."

A speculative gleam entered his eye. He and Lars were close. He knew and trusted the man and they worked well together. When their dragons mated, they would become part of a fighting unit, partners that would share everything—including the pleasure their dragons found in each other with the sole human female among the tightly knit group. If Gareth had to pick a man to bring pleasure to his beloved mate, he could not have picked better himself. Lars was a good man and he would love Belora as much as he did. He would also help Gareth give her the greatest sexual pleasure a human woman could know. The dragons would see to it.

Jared, will you talk some sense into her? She insists she's only here for a visit, but she must stay. Make her realize how much we need her. Kelzy's voice was tinged with frustration when Jared walked back into their apartments to find the two females squared off in full argument mode. He had forgotten just how much females could squabble over inconsequential things.

"We cannot just commandeer the woman, Kelzy. She has her own life and must make her own decisions."

"Thank you, Sir Jared." Adora turned the full power of her gaze on him and he looked away uncomfortably. The woman seemed to see right through him with her pale, healer's gaze and it was jarring to say the least. "As I've told Mama Kelzy, I have responsibilities to the villagers. I'm their only source of medical help and they depend on me. I can't just abandon them."

"Why do you call her that?"

"What?" Adora seemed confused for a moment as she tilted her head up at him, her beautiful green eyes frowning.

"You call a dragon 'mama.' Didn't you realize? It's a bit odd, to say the least, but then Kelzy's always been a little overly demonstrative with humans, or so her fellow dragons would criticize."

They're just busybodies. Who I consort with as friends and family is none of their business, dragon, human or otherwise.

"I didn't realize I still called you that, Lady Kelzy. I'm sorry." Adora's blushing cheeks spoke of her embarrassment.

Now see what you've done, Jared? Sweetheart, you don't have to use titles with me. You are the daughter of my heart. It warms my soul to know you still think of me as your surrogate mother.

Kelzy stepped forward and Adora reached her hand out to stroke the dragon's tough, jewel toned hide. The two females so obviously cared for one another.

"When I was very little, I got lost in the woods and stumbled into Kelzy's cave. I could barely speak, but I knew the word 'mama.' Kelzy returned me to my family, who were searching frantically through the woods. I know they were frightened to see her, but when they saw me on her back, smiling away and calling her mama, they knew I was safe. She deposited me back with my mother and father and after that they let me go see her whenever I wanted. She raised me as much as my parents did, watching out for me when I ventured into the woods."

None of them could hear me or speak with me, but Adora had the strongest gift I have ever encountered. They may have raised you, but they were not your blood kin.

"What?"

I never told you this because I didn't think it my place back then, but it was obvious to me that your mother and father were not your birth parents. They adopted you. If they had

-55-

been your blood kin, at least one of them would have been able to communicate with me. It's an inherited trait, passed down through the bloodlines, usually on the father's side. The man you called father had no such ability nor did any of your siblings.

"Then who are my parents?" Adora's voice trembled just a bit and her wide eyes looked shaken and a little lost.

I couldn't say and for that I'm sorry. I often thought to go on a quest to see where you came from. After all, females with the dragon gift are rare and we need every one we can find. Especially with war coming.

"Then war is definitely on the way?" Adora's eyes darkened with worry.

"Yes." It was Jared who answered, his voice firm. "There's no escaping it now. The Skithdronian king has been working toward all out war for a long time and he's just about ready now, we think, to launch it."

Which is why you must stay here with us, Adora. You will have no protection in the forest. The skiths will ravage man and beast alike when they are loosed.

"Which is why I *must* go back. I'm the only healer within twenty leagues. I can't just abandon those people."

"We're flying patrols now. When the skiths come, we'll engage them whenever and wherever we find them." Jared kept his voice calm and deadly. He surprised even himself with the sentiments he was feeling. "We're here to protect the people and lands. What good can one unprotected healer do out there? Wouldn't your talents be better used here?"

"You may very well be right, Sir Jared, but I have to go back. They depend on me. I'm not so conceited as to think that my destiny lay in such a grand place. I'm a simple healer, not one to be worthy of working with your knights."

Sheep dung! That is the most ridiculous thing I've ever heard you say, Adora. And here I thought you were smart for a human.

Adora smiled softly. "I love you too, Mama Kelzy, but the fact remains, I must return to my cottage."

Cottage? My son tells me it was no more than a hut! How can I leave you in such a place?

Adora stroked the dragon's shiny scales soothingly. "Because you must. It's what I have to do."

"But you'll at least stay for your daughter's wedding, won't you?" Jared surprised himself by asking.

She nodded. "I'll stay for the mating feast, but I must go home the next day."

Kelzy snorted smoke, clearly upset. We will take you then, but don't expect me to be happy about it.

"Kel will seek his mate soon." Gareth knew he had to tread lightly. Belora had not been raised in the Lair and did not know the way of things among dragon matings.

"He's already chosen a mate?" Belora spoke softly, wrapped in his arms in the dark of the night.

"He hasn't made his formal declaration yet, but he will soon. That means we'll be adding to our family as well."

She turned to peer up at him in the darkness. "How so?"

"When dragons mate, their human partners cannot help but share in the event. It's because of the close bond we share with our dragon partners. Kelvan intends to mate with Rohtina. Her partner is named Lars. He and I have been friends for a very long time. When Kel claims his mate, we will become family of a sort. Lars and I will train with our dragon partners and will go into battle together from then on. We will patrol together and work together—even live together in the same set of apartments."

"Does this Lars have a wife?"

Gareth shook his head. "No. There are so few women born with ability to hear the dragons, many of the knights never find a woman to share their lives. It was a miracle when Kelvan found you. He would have given you the stag, but he made an issue out of it so he would be able to bring you to me. He suspected the Mother of All put you in our path so that I could find you and make you mine, and I quite agree."

"Praise the Mother, then. She certainly knows what She's doing." She reached up and kissed him deeply, caressing his cheek with her soft fingers.

"As soon as we move the rest of your things from your cabin into our new apartments, there will be a mating ceremony held for us. It's basically an excuse to eat, drink and be merry as our fellows wish us well. There will even be dancing."

"Oh, Gareth! I don't know how to dance."

"Not to worry. I didn't expect you would know our style of dance anyway, so I talked to your mother and she's setting up some practice for us."

"What's different about your kind of dancing?"

He shifted uncomfortably. "Since there are so few women among us, our dances are designed around sets of three—two men and one woman. We don't dance often, but a mating ceremony is one of the times when tradition requires it, and it really is a lot of fun. Don't worry. You'll enjoy it. I promise."

CHAPTER FIVE

Lars was a big man, the same tall height as Gareth, but even more muscular. Where Gareth had the sleek muscles of a racehorse, Lars had a stockier sort of strength. His hair was the color of pale wheat and his eyes a sparkling turquoise blue that crinkled at the corners when he smiled. His smile, when it appeared, was open, generous and surprisingly kind, though it seemed he was a quiet man by nature.

Belora took one look at him and had to fight the odd feeling in the depths of her womb. Was it right to be so attracted to a man after pledging your life to another? She wasn't sure, but she found it impossible not to notice the tingle in her skin when he took her hand in the moves of the dances they were teaching her. She caught his eyes twinkling at her at times with an odd sort of speculation and a definite masculine appreciation that fairly took her breath away.

She thought she intercepted a look or two between the men that made her loins burn. When she caught Gareth's eye he was wholly approving of her, encouraging her to learn the more intricate steps of the progressively harder dances they showed her. By the time they moved on to the "mating dance" that would culminate the feast in their honor, her blood was sizzling with desire and the two men were more than familiar with the feel of her body under their guiding hands. It was an amazing feeling.

"Let's take a short break before we begin the next one."

Gareth moved over to a small side table where a jug of wine and several earthen cups stood. He poured for each of them and served with good grace as Lars helped Belora to sit on the pretty, warm bricks that edged Kelvan's wallow. They had shown her about five different dances, each one progressively harder. They involved a bit more touching than she was used to, but touching two such handsome men was no hardship, she thought with an inward grin.

"Will I be expected to dance with other people?" she asked over the rim of her wine cup as Gareth sat down beside her.

"No. Just us. Lars is our third since he and Rohtina will be joining our family."

"I think Kelvan and Tina will enjoy the larger quarters. I went by there today and it's nicely placed." Lars sat beside them and gazed over the warm sands of the smaller sized wallow. When his dragon partner and Kelvan mated, they would require a much larger space to share.

"I'm going to start moving my stuff over tomorrow. How about you?" Gareth moved closer to her, pulling her back against his chest as his free arm tucked around her waist. She was surprised by the intimate move, but neither man seemed to think anything of it, so after a few moments, she relaxed back against him.

"I figured I'd do the same. Tina has some stuff she's collected over the years that she wants me to shift for her. Little sparkly stones and bits she's found in her journeys."

"Women of every species like their gems." Gareth and Lars chuckled but Belora gasped as Gareth's large hand moved up to cup her breast. She couldn't believe he would fondle her in front of his friend, regardless of whether or not they were becoming some sort of family. She stiffened and would have pulled away, but Lars took her hand in his surprisingly gentle grasp and held her eyes.

"Don't be embarrassed. It is our way to be free amongst our family. I've accepted that I will never find a woman as Gareth has found you. Let me share in what you have together, at least in this way for now."

"I'm not used to this. Your ways are very strange to me." She settled back against Gareth with a little trembling in her limbs, but didn't object further as his hand moved down inside the V of her blouse to cup her bare breast and flick the nipple so it stood out against the soft fabric. She knew Lars could see it clearly as his eyes dipped to focus on her nipples, blossoming under Gareth's skillful touch.

"I know, love, but this will be your home now. I hope you'll try to adjust to our ways." Gareth dipped to kiss her neck as he spoke softly next to her ear. "I won't rush you, but I need you to be open to new experiences. Can you do that for me? For us all?"

His hand squeezed her nipple hard and she felt little tremors of excitement course through her womb. She found she liked the hot flash of Lars' turquoise eyes as he licked his firm lips, his eyes glued to Gareth's manipulations under her shirt. It was definitely a new experience, but she found she wasn't afraid. She trusted Gareth with her very life. It was little stretch to trust him with her pleasure. He would never hurt her or make her do anything she didn't want to do. She knew that in her soul and it allowed her to let go and let him lead their pleasure.

She nodded as he moved his hand out of her blouse and turned her in his arms to face her. His eyes held hers and sought her answer.

"I trust you and I'll try."

A broad smile spread across his lips before they claimed hers in a deep, happy kiss. He lingered over her lips before turning her once more in his arms. Lars had moved closer while they kissed and now he was only inches from her aroused body. Gareth pushed her gently toward his friend, encouraging her with his voice.

"Kiss Lars, sweet. Let him know there are no hard feelings. Welcome him to our family and let him know just a tiny bit of what we share."

She looked back at him questioningly, but his eyes were encouraging and his hands open, willing to let her decide whether she would go through with his suggestion or not. It was the freedom to choose that made her move forward. A kiss was a small thing, after all, and it was not like it was any kind of hardship to share a kiss with such a handsome and kind man. She turned back and smiled at Lars as she moved into his strong arms.

He clasped her against his chest and moved his head down, his turquoise eyes dazzling her as he drew closer, oh, so slowly. When his firm lips met hers, her eyes shut in self-defense as his scent, his feel, and his amazingly gentle touch flooded her senses with warmth. His lips caressed hers for a long moment before his tongue sought entrance, taking the kiss deeper. She was surprised, but more than willing, swept up in the passion of the man and the moment.

Lars kissed like a dream. Gentle as only a very strong man can be, he tempered his strength with a deep passion that she could feel as his muscular arms trembled the tiniest bit. He made a small, inarticulate sound of pleasure as she wrapped her arms around him. It spurred her on and she answered the sweeping intimacies of his tongue in her mouth with her own daring forays into his warmth. She felt hot all over and realized vaguely that Gareth had moved up behind them, enclosing her between the two men. His hands teased her nipples and stoked her fire.

When at long last the kiss broke, all three were panting. Belora shot shocked eyes up to Lars and was greeted with a stunned smile.

"You are beautiful, milady, and much too good for a scoundrel like Gareth. I wish I had met you first."

She laughed and the tension of the moment was broken. She realized that while Gareth had been palming her breasts, Lars' hands were up under her skirts, skimming her legs. They now rested on her thighs, his fingers dangerously close to the juncture that fairly wept with arousal.

"In the mating dance, you will be expected to kiss us both and we will both handle your body in ever more intimate ways—lifting you up in our arms, twirling you around, touching you all over. You must give over control to us completely." Gareth's breath pulsed against her ear and made her shiver. "Can you handle it?" He spoke it like a dare.

"I can handle it, but will everyone be watching?"

Lars nodded. "The mated pairs will be dancing with us, but the single knights will certainly enjoy the show, dreaming of the day they find their own mate and are able to claim her before the entire enclave. It's a rite of passage and something we do to solidify our families and share our pleasure with our fellows. It's important."

The earnestness of his words touched her heart. It made an odd sort of sense and it made her want to perform this strange dance with these two strong men, for the good of the Lair.

"All right. I guess it won't be so bad if we're not the only ones doing it."

Gareth chuckled as he rose and lifted her up by the arms. Lars stood in front of her and they moved back to the cleared area where they'd been practicing before.

"We'll all be dressed differently of course, so we'll just pantomime some of the parts we can only do while in the ceremonial clothing."

Gareth moved in front of his mate-to-be and positioned her for the start of the dance. He was much closer to her than he had been for any of the other dances she'd learned that day and Lars stood so close to her back, she could feel his warmth. She did the moves as they taught them to her but quickly realized just a few minutes into this strange dance that he was not kidding when he said she would have to give over control to them both.

After a few initial moves, she was simply swept off her feet by first Gareth, then Lars, passed between them as her feet barely touched the ground. The two brawny men did most of the work as they swung her around in their strong arms, her body held tight to their own while little tingles of electricity raced through her frame. Gareth made her burn with his barest touch, but the look in Lars' turquoise eyes as he held her close nearly made her insides melt. The set of his jaw proclaimed how very hungry he was for her and she could feel his shocking erection against her abdomen as he held her close.

"That's enough for now, I think." Gareth's voice was calm as he stood behind them. Lars' mesmerizing eyes were fused to her own. Gradually, he released her and she slid down his hard body to rest once more on unsteady feet. Her entire body trembled and she could feel that he was hard as granite against her. A muscle ticked in his jaw but otherwise he indicated none of his discomfort.

Gareth snuck his arm around her waist from behind and pulled her unresisting body back against him as she swayed on her feet. She was glad of his support though her dazed eyes were still locked on Lars.

"We'll see you later, Lars. Thanks for your assistance." Gareth's words were formal but his tone was warm. She realized he knew exactly what afflicted his friend as he fit her bottom against his own raging hard-on.

After a long moment Lars nodded, bowed slightly to her, and left the chamber.

"Will he be all right?"

Gareth chuckled behind her, pulling her soft body closer against his. "Nothing a few strokes of his hand won't cure. Would you like to help him?"

She was shocked, but also titillated by the teasing remark. "Would you want me to?"

Gareth turned her in his arms. "Oh, yes. I'd enjoy watching that."

She stiffened in his arms. "You'd enjoy seeing me pleasure other men?"

"Not just any other man. Only Lars. He will be our family soon, Belora. It's only right that you should be able to share pleasure with him. It's normal and healthy for our kind."

"I don't understand your ways at all." She shook her head but relaxed once more against his hard body.

"It's all right. We have time yet." He hugged her close, tucking her head under his chin. "Does the idea repulse you though? Could you make him welcome in our family, do you think?"

She snuggled into him. "He's so quiet, yet I sense in him a great well of feeling kept tightly under wraps. He's so alone." Her voice was quiet with thought and sympathy.

"Lars has been alone for a long time. His parents and siblings were killed right in front of him during the Northern Wars when he was only a small boy. His partner, Rohtina, found him among those left for dead a few days later. He was badly injured, but managed to cling to her back until she could get him back to the Lair. For years he spoke to no one but Rohtina, his dragon partner." Gareth sighed as he tucked her hair behind her ear and held her close. "He's only a year or so younger than me and we became friends early on when we were still just boys really. Others thought him strange and it was hard for him to find welcome from some of the other knights, but we've been close friends for many years. I love him as a brother though I've never said the words to him I know he feels the same, though he rarely speaks at all."

"Now I begin to understand what lies beneath." Her mind spun and her heart opened with sympathy and a nurturing kind of love for Lars. It encompassed Gareth too, for the protective way he spoke of his heart-scarred friend.

"Because Rohtina will be Kelvan's mate, our friendship will now become a true partnership. We will be family, a fighting unit when on duty and a partnership in whatever we do. All five of us will live together in one large suite and any children we have will also be his to nurture and raise. When the dragonets come, likewise we will all help in whatever way Kel and Tina need us to. The five of us will be family in the truest sense."

"Am I expected to… uh… to have sex with him?" She didn't really know if she was nervous about the answer or excited. Either way, her breath was coming faster and something inside her womb clenched in anticipation.

"Neither of us will ever force you to do anything you don't want to do."

"But is that how the other mated pairs work?"

"Most, yes. There are so few women among us that it's normal for one woman to be wife to both knights if their dragons are mated. Kel says the Mother of All knows what She's doing when She pairs off the dragons and their knights. But not all matings work the same way. There are no real rules about it. Each woman pretty much decides for herself what she's comfortable with and how the relationship will work. It'll be up to you if you accept Lars in your bed or even how far you will go with him. You could limit yourself to just kissing him, which is a common enough courtesy. Or you could move further into sharing oral pleasure and the like. Or you could take him as you take me, or take us both at the same time."

His words and the deep tone of his voice made her squirm. She pressed her legs together and felt the wetness already on her thighs from this hot conversation. She realized it wasn't fear that made her feel this way. No, she rather liked the idea of what Gareth was proposing. She felt the same instant attraction to Lars as she had felt the moment she had seen Gareth. Something about both men called out to her heart and her very soul. It was not logical, but it was, nonetheless. Something about them felt right and good. She would be a fool not to explore where this might lead.

"Do you really want this? Wouldn't you be jealous if I took him as my lover?"

Gareth stared down at her with serious eyes. "If you took any other man as a lover I would kill him outright." She gasped at the deadly intent in his eyes. "But Lars is my brother. Our dragon partners are going to be mates. It's inevitable that the three of us will be caught up in the fever as our dragon partners mate, and they'll do so often now that they're finally free to join. I couldn't let Lars face that alone. I must admit the idea of watching you with him, of filling you at the same time as he does, excites me. There's no other man I would share you with. Only him. I know that if I should fall in battle, he'll be there to take care of you and vice versa. We're a team now. The Mother of All has ordained it. We'll both love you until the day we die, if you let us."

Belora thought about Gareth's shocking words as they ate and later as he led her to the communal hot baths. She had heard about them, of course, but had not visited the hot springs yet herself.

The chamber was large and the main pool absolutely huge. It could have qualified as a small lake, she thought idly, but the bubbling, effervescent surface and slightly metallic smell of the water made it much different from any other lake she had ever seen.

There were a few men there before them and they all looked up as Gareth and Belora entered. Several shouted greetings to Gareth or lifted their hands to wave while eyeing Belora with great interest. She began to wonder just how this bathing business was supposed to be accomplished without great embarrassment. She tugged on Gareth's hand and he stopped to look down at her.

"I hope you don't expect me to get naked in front of all of them." Her whispered words carried to him alone though she knew all the men present watched them closely.

"There's no shame in nakedness, Belora. Besides, remember what I said before? I think I'll enjoy knowing that my friends and comrades can look but never touch my mate. Many of them may never find mates of their own. Seeing the happiness of others is the only real glimpse of joy left to them besides the momentary pleasure they can find with a whore or some other random woman who doesn't mind the great huge dragon lurking about outside in her garden, scaring the neighbors."

Belora giggled at the picture he painted with his words and his lips softened into a loving smile. He stroked back her hair and caressed her cheek.

"Besides, we won't be in the main pool. There are smaller pools designed for a bit more privacy. We'll use one of those, okay?"

"Will they be able to see us?"

"Maybe. If they were in the right spot."

She chuckled. "How much do you want to bet they'll all want to move suddenly to the one area from which they can see me naked?"

"You've got a point there." He chuckled as she did. "But then, you'll be seeing them naked too, so it kind of evens out."

"Hmm." She looked around his broad body to get another exaggerated look at the muscular men sitting or wading in the fairly shallow water near the edge. "I hadn't thought of that. That blonde man has a spectacular ass. Do you think he'll mind me ogling him?"

"He might not, but I certainly will." Gareth growled with a grin as he chased her toward the far end of the cavern where the more private pools lay.

A bit breathless from both the exertion and the heat of the cavern, she came to a sudden halt before one of the pools. Lars was there. Already naked and in the water.

"And when were you going to tell me about this?" She arched her brow and looked from Lars to Gareth with teasing accusation in her eyes. She gasped aloud when Lars stood from the water, his nude body gleaming wetly in the low light of the cavern. He was solid muscle and had a long, thick cock that was rock hard and aimed right at her.

"I'll leave if you wish it."

He made to step out of the pool but halted when Belora took one almost unconscious step toward him, her eyes entranced with his waving cock. She realized this was a further part of Gareth's plan to make her aware of the things that would be expected of her as his wife and get her used to Lars as well. As far as plans went, she had to agree it was a good one. A woman would have to be dead not to be attracted to the masculine perfection and puppy-like eagerness of them both. They wanted so much to please her and for her to accept them. It was touching really. And very flattering.

"Don't leave, Lars. If I'm really going to marry into this world, I need to know if I can handle it, right?" She turned around and punched Gareth in the arm. "Don't think I don't recognize your plotting hand in this little scene, but in this case, you're probably right. I'm willing to try and see where this goes. He can stay and watch, but if I want to call a halt at any time, you have to promise to stop."

"Of course!" Gareth pulled her close and hugged her. "Your wishes will always come first. Always!"

She nodded against his chest and stroked his arms. "I thought you'd say that, but I had to be sure. This is kind of scary for me."

He soothed her and hugged her tightly. "You're so brave, my sweet." He bent to whisper in her ear. "I love you so much. Do you realize how very special you are to me? I will never love again. Only you, Belora. For the rest of our lives."

He kissed her then, pouring all his love into his kiss and she clung to him. Before she knew it, she felt the wafting warm air of the cave against her bare skin. Gareth had tugged her robe away until she was standing naked in his strong arms. Her eyes shot to Lars as Gareth pulled back, easing from their kiss.

Lars watched her every move, his eyes dark turquoise in the dim light, his gaze intense as he saw her nude body for the first time. Gareth spun her in his arms and pulled her back against his front, wrapping one muscular forearm around her waist as the other hand moved up to cup her breast, displaying her for his friend.

Entranced by the look on Lars' angular face, Belora felt a slick wetness seeping down the insides of her thighs. She had never been so excited by the mere look of a man before. Lars eased back into the water, seating himself on an underwater ledge at the far side of the small pool, one hand disappearing under the transparent surface to curve around his hard cock, stroking slowly as he watched Belora in Gareth's arms.

She licked her lips, thinking of forbidden things. But perhaps they weren't so forbidden after all. If she were going to go through with this, she could have both of these handsome, heart-strong men all to herself for the rest of their lives. Something in her heart felt warm and secure at the thought yet her mind worried over how such a relationship would work.

"Don't think so hard, sweet." Gareth's warm breath puffed against her ear as he spoke and his hands caressed her, the one at her waist slipping down to tease the neat curls at the juncture of her thighs. "Just feel."

He slipped his fingers into her folds and her knees went weak. One hand squeezed her nipple, the other her clit, and her eyes closed in yearning ecstasy. Slowly, he moved his fingers over her clit, pressing and rotating in little swirls over the sensitive flesh, making her squirm. His other hand dropped down and then he was spreading her pussy wide, allowing Lars to see everything he was doing, showcasing her responsive clit for the other man.

"See how he looks at you? If you let him, he would suck your clit while I sucked your nipples."

The words inflamed her and she groaned, shivering in his arms. Her eyes opened to see Lars stroking himself under the water more firmly now, his eyes feasting on the sight of her feminine core as Gareth used two fingers to probe deep inside her. She was slick with excitement and his passage was made easier by the fact that she was near peak from nothing more than his stroking and Lars' hot gaze.

He pumped his fingers into her tight core a few more times before she came hard on his hand, stifling her cry against his shoulder as he supported her spasming body. He held her, crooning to her as he pulled his fingers from her body, bringing them to his lips and licking them.

"Mmm. Delicious." He turned her slightly in his arms and brought the still wet fingers to her mouth. "Taste," he whispered. "Suck them clean." She opened her lips as his fingers pushed inside. She tasted herself on his flesh and the look in his eyes nearly drove her wild.

"Do you have any idea what you do to me?"

He removed his fingers and kissed her deeply. A moment later, her world spun as he hoisted her up in his arms and stepped into the pool. He lowered her into the warm water, supporting her as she learned the feel of the warm mineral springs. She smiled at him, still a bit nervous of the other man sharing the wide pool, watching them from the other end. There were a few feet between where Gareth held her and Lars sat watching. It would be so easy to bridge that space physically, but mentally she just wasn't quite ready.

"The water's so warm and bubbly." She marveled at the feel of tiny bubbles bursting against her skin, leaving her feeling clean and relaxed.

"It's fed from the earth below with just a bit of magic to keep it warm and flowing."

"It's wonderful."

"Not nearly as wonderful as you, Belora."

She smiled as he levered himself away and sat on the ledge of the pool, his raging hard-on out of the water. She licked her lips again, wanting nothing more than to taste him as she had once before. Her eyes must have spoken of her desire because he chuckled and pulled her between his spread knees, his legs wrapping around her and crossing at the ankles behind her back.

"Oh, yes, I can see we both want the same thing. Taste me, Belora. Take me in your sweet mouth."

He guided her head gently toward his cock and she liked the way her breasts felt caressed by the millions of tiny bubbles in the water. She tingled all over as his hands tangled in her hair, urging her to do what she wanted. With a sigh of satisfaction, she placed her lips around his hard cock, sliding down and using her tongue the way he had coached her to do. Satisfaction filled her when he groaned in pleasure.

She knew Lars could see every movement. The thought didn't disturb her as much as she thought it would. In fact, it tickled her sense of adventure and made her want to give him a show worth remembering. The idea that he was so close, so much a part of this even though he was only an observer, made her hot.

No doubt about it. She was wanton.

She smiled around Gareth's cock as she realized it was he who had awakened these raging desires within her. Gareth was her first lover, but if he had his way, she would take Lars before long as well. At first the thought had shocked and scared her, but now that she was getting to know the strong, silent knight, the idea was more and more appealing. She wondered what his cock would taste like and how he would respond to her sucking. Maybe, she thought with a blush and a feeling of incredulity, it was time to find out.

Gareth stopped her with a slight tug on her hair. A surprising disappointment swept through her, but she trusted him to lead their love play. He knew things about lovemaking that she had never experienced and she would follow his lead.

"As much as I love the feel of your talented tongue on my cock and balls, if we don't stop now, I'll come much sooner than I'd like."

He dropped into the pool and brought his lips to hers, working her around in the wide pool until they were just a few feet from Lars. Gareth's strong arms lifted her out of the water and set her on the edge of the pool. She was surprised by the sudden move and grabbed onto his shoulders for balance, but his smile set her at ease and reignited the fires in her belly. Sweet Mother, how she loved this man!

"Are you ready for me, sweet?" Holding her eyes, he parted her pussy lips with one hand and entered her channel with the fingers of the other. He smiled devilishly as her slick wetness coated his fingers. "You want my cock, Belora? Tell me if you do."

"Yes," she whimpered.

"Yes? What do you want, love? Tell me." His eyes challenged her, while his fingers continued to tease.

"I want your cock, Gareth. In me. I want your cock in me now." Her whispered words seemed to galvanize him.

He stepped up onto the ledge that put him at the perfect height to slide home into her pussy with one solid thrust. She cried out lightly as he slid home, only then realizing that Lars was standing right beside them now, watching all in intimate detail as his hand squeezed his rampant cock.

Her eyes locked with Lars' turquoise gaze for a long moment and she realized that his presence seemed somehow right. Only one thing could make it better, she thought with a shock. That he could find satisfaction at the same time they did.

"Let me," she whispered, bringing both knights' eyes to her face. Gareth followed the trail of her eyes with his and nodded at Lars, a broad smile spreading across his strong lips.

Lars wasted no time, moving up to stand the edge of the pool, his hard length level with her mouth. She knew he was giving her the choice of how she would pleasure him and the fear inside her made her want to start slow. She brought one hand up to circle his pulsing cock as Gareth resumed stroking in and out of her pussy. His hands and mouth teased her nipples while Lars watched, the only contact between them her hand on his cock. She realized he was letting her call the shots, letting her decide how far this would go. The thought made her feel safe and cherished. This strong man was allowing her to choose what she would give him with no complaint. The idea humbled and warmed her, showing her without words how noble a man he really was.

Leaning slightly, she licked his length and looked up into his smoldering turquoise gaze. Holding his eyes, she took him deep in her mouth and used her tongue to learn his shape, his taste, and his feel. He was spectacular.

She sucked him deep as Gareth thrust into her core, bringing her closer and closer to orgasm. She knew when she flew to the stars this time, she would take both of these special, beloved men with her. Gareth bit her nipple and pinched the other hard as he drove into her faster and faster. She felt her climax starting from deep within and she pulled hard on Lars' hot cock, coaxing his climax with the suction of her mouth. He came as she did, followed only seconds later by Gareth's spurting deep inside her womb.

The three of them lounged in the pool for long moments, enjoying the restorative power of the bubbly water. They sat on the ledge, each submerged slightly, Gareth's arm thrown casually around Belora's shoulder as his hand dipped down to toy with her nipple. Lars sat on her other side, not touching, but watching her with a renewed heat and pure male appreciation.

"Thank you." Lars' soft voice came to her from out of the dimness of the cavern, making her look over to meet his intense gaze.

She smiled softly at him and leaned up to kiss his lips sweetly. He took the kiss deeper, and she slipped into his arms for a long, languid moment.

"I don't know yet if I can go much further with this, Lars." She pulled away from him to sit on her own between the two men. She had to tell them what was going on in her mind. She didn't want them getting the wrong idea that suddenly she was okay with the crazy lifestyle in the Lair. "I'll be brutally honest with you. Now that things have cooled a bit, I'm a little shocked by what I just did, but it felt good. I don't regret it, but I have to think about this a bit more."

Gareth's hand stroked her wet hair. "Take the time you need, my love. I'm sorry if you feel pressured. We don't mean to rush you."

"I don't feel pressured, but it's a lot to take in all at once. Just give me some more time, okay? I didn't want you assuming I was fine with everything when in my mind I still have some reservations."

Lars smiled kindly at her. "Honesty in all things is important between mates. Or potential mates."

Feeling somewhat better, she dipped into the pool, bathing her hair in the effervescent water. After a few more relaxing minutes, they all gathered their robes and left the pool. Gareth and Belora headed for his suite and Lars walked away toward where his dragon waited.

CHAPTER SIX

When Gareth and Kelvan took off for patrol early the next morning, Belora went to visit her mother in Kelzy's suite.

I heard you went to the springs last eve. Kelzy's voice sounded in the minds of both mother and daughter though Adora knew the dragon addressed her daughter. The blush staining Belora's fair cheeks amused her, but she also felt a pang of regret for her little girl who was now a woman grown.

"Um... yes. It was very educational."

Kelzy snorted smoke in dragonish laughter. *I bet.*

"Mama Kelzy, are you teasing my girl?" Adora gathered her daughter close for a long hug. "I've missed you, honey girl. What have you been doing with yourself?"

"Trying to decide if I'm going to stay."

Belora looked so torn. Adora kept her arm around her shoulders and guided her to sit with her at the edge of Kelzy's wallow. She shot a concerned glance to the dragon.

I thought your mating feast was set for this evening?

"It is, but I'm just not sure I can go through with it." Her eyes looked pained and confused.

"Why not?"

"Oh, Mama, it's so different here. The things they expect of me... I just don't know if it's right or if I can do it."

"What things?" Adora's voice held all the anger of an enraged mother hen. She had spent most of her life protecting this girl. She'd done the best she could to raise her strong and comfortable in herself. She couldn't fathom what the knights would ask of her that would put such fear and self-doubt in her eyes, but she didn't like it. Indignation filled her, the inner fire that she usually kept well banked, rising to take on anyone who would hurt her baby.

Belora blushed a fiery red. "Um... sexual things. There are so few women here, you see. And when Kelvan mates, they expect me to... oh, this is hard to talk about, even with you, Mama."

Kelzy shook her great head and sighed warm air around them. Adora pinned her with a steely gaze.

"Just what is making my brave baby girl so confused? And what has your son to do with it?"

Kelzy shifted in her wallow. *It's always hardest on those not raised in a Lair. Adora, you have to realize the bond between dragon and knight is soul deep. What he feels, we feel and vice versa. When Jared takes a woman, I feel it and if I'm ever lucky enough to be able to mate again, it will undoubtedly drive Jared into an uncontrollable lust. That's why fighting dragons—those of us with knights—are forbidden to mate unless either our knight or our mate's knight has a wife. When the lust rides us all, the knights will turn to their wife to share the mating fever safely.*

"Wife? Only one wife for two knights?!"

Kelzy nodded her great head. *There are so few women who can live among dragons. Our knights have learned to share. But their love and protection for their wife runs deeper than any regular tie. They live dangerous lives. If one knight falls, he knows his partner will be there to take care of their wife and young. It's the way of fighting knights and dragons. It has been this way for centuries.*

"Well, that's some dirty little secret you have there." Adora was shocked, but turned over the problem in her mind. "So just who else is my baby expected to marry tonight?"

"His name is Lars." Belora's voice was reserved, her face flushed and eyes confused. "He's wonderful, Mama. Really. He's quiet and so thoughtful and he has the gentlest heart."

"You sound half in love with him already!" Adora was scandalized, and more than a little intrigued. Still, it didn't sit quite right, her inexperienced baby girl being expected to welcome two brawny knights into her life and her bed.

Belora seemed to think about it. "You know, maybe I am. Gareth brought him around and helped us get to know each other. I like him a lot, but I don't know if I can let them both…" She trailed off in embarrassment once more.

"They are expected to have her at the same time?" Adora turned accusing eyes to the dragon.

When the mating heat is upon them all, it will be inevitable. Most of the human women involved in such arrangements seem to enjoy it immensely. Think of the benefits, child. Two men at your beck and call at all times. Two men who will love you and put your happiness and safety above all. Two men to help around the Lair and father your babies.

"This isn't some kind of perverse partner-swapping arrangement, is it?" Adora wanted to know.

By the Mother, where do you get such notions? Of course it isn't! Once mated, knights remain true to their mates for the rest of their lives. This isn't some whim. The Mother guides the knights in their selection of a mate, just as She guides us dragons. Is it any wonder your daughter already has feelings for the knight of my son's future mate? The Mother of All knows what She is doing after all.

"I love Gareth, Mama. I loved him almost from the first moment I saw him and I want to spend the rest of my life with him. But I feel things for Lars too. It's hard to describe. He's so different from Gareth, so special. I want to bring him out of his shell and tease him until he laughs. He doesn't laugh nearly enough. I like his kisses and I love the way he treats me as if I'm made of spun glass."

Adora didn't know what to think but the look in her daughter's eyes was oddly reassuring. "I think I need to meet this Lars."

He'll be here in a few minutes. I just sent for Rohtina, his partner, to bring him here. She wants to meet you too, by the way. How could a sensible man like Gareth overlook introducing the two females who will be expected to share a suite? I thought he was smarter than that. Honestly!

Kelzy huffed while the two human women listened to the sounds of an approaching dragon. Apparently, Rohtina was prompt and somewhat eager to meet them if her fast tread was any indication. When she came through the huge archway, Adora caught her breath.

She was a gorgeous young dragon in a golden red hue that shone like the morning sun. Her eyes were amber jewels, bright with intelligence and eagerly taking in all there was to see. Intelligence sparkled there and a perky humor, if she didn't miss her guess.

Adora and her daughter stood to greet Rohtina with a formal bow, which was graciously returned. Straightening, Adora noted the tall blonde man at the dragon's side. No wonder her daughter was half in love with him already. He was even more beautiful than his dragon partner! These two together shone like the sun between her iridescent golden red scales and his silvery blonde perfection, they were nearly blinding.

Adora strode forward. "Lady Rohtina, I've just learned that your knight expects to be mate to my daughter."

This is true, Madam. The dragon projected her thoughts to all in the room. Her voice was melodic and gentle, quite different from Kelzy's more martial tone.

"You'll understand that I raised my daughter with quite a different expectation than having two husbands?"

That is my understanding, but you must also understand that things are different among knights and dragons.

Don't you dare lecture my girl, Tina, Kelzy interjected with a hint of amusement. *Though she doesn't understand Lair life, she knows more about our kind than most of the knights.*

Rohtina bowed her head in respect to the older dragon. *If you say so.*

At this point, Belora broke out laughing. Lars chuckled too, followed by the rest of them. Belora moved forward to face the pretty female dragon.

"I like you, Lady Rohtina. You've got spunk."

I like the way you make my knight feel. I don't think he's ever been this happy or hopeful.

Lars' fair skin flushed at his dragon partner's candid words, but Belora moved forward to take his hand in hers. She brought him to her mother and made introductions, including him in the group of females. Adora saw immediately that this young man had hidden depths. From the way his shoulders immediately relaxed, Belora's touch obviously comforted him. She also liked the gentle way he cradled her daughter's small hand in his own.

"What are your intentions toward my daughter?" Adora asked boldly.

"Mother!"

"No, Belora, she has every right to ask such a question." Lars raised Belora's small hand, stroking her palm soothingly. "My intention is to love her and protect her all of our lives. I will be true to her, cherish her, and put her happiness above my own."

"But you've only just met." Adora didn't understand how her sensible baby girl could fall in love with two men in nearly as many days, much less how those two men could claim to love her just as deeply, just as fast.

"Gareth knew her the moment he saw her. It's the way of knights to know their mate almost on sight. I like to think I would have recognized her too, had I been the first to meet her. As it stands, since Rohtina told me of her intention to mate with Kelvan, I've been introduced and found time to get to know Belora. But my heart knew her already. When I first looked into her eyes, I knew I'd found what I'd been seeking."

"Why didn't you say anything before now?" Belora's whisper carried in the quiet room.

Lars shrugged, his turquoise eyes locking on her as if she were the only one in the room. "It wasn't yet time. Now it is. You're ready to hear it and I'm ready to say it. I love you, Belora. If you let me, I'll love you truly for the rest of our lives." He sank down to one knee, humbling himself before her. "Will you be my wife?"

Tears streamed down her face as Belora reached down and kissed Lars on the lips, dragging him upward so she could put her arms around his thick, muscular frame. He wrapped her up in his arms and kissed her deeply, holding her close as the others watched, knowing they had been forgotten.

Just for the record, you understand, what's your answer? Kelzy's amused voice broke them apart.

"Oh, I think she said yes, Mama Kelzy." Adora leaned comfortably back against Kelzy's sparkling foreleg, watching her daughter with amusement.

Lars and his partner seemed to be surprised by Adora's familiarity with the older dragon.

Well, I think that's settled, isn't it?

"I'm still not totally sure I'm comfortable with this two husband arrangement."

Child, do you trust me?

"Well, of course I trust you. You raised me, didn't you?" Again the two newcomers were surprised by the conversation, but didn't interject.

Then trust me on this. It's the way of Lair life and no hardship on the woman, I can assure you. Your girl will come to no harm with her two mates and will, in all likelihood, be very happy.

"You promise?" Adora held out her little human hand to the huge dragon.

I promise. Kelzy put one huge talon carefully into the small woman's hand and they shook once as if in some childhood ritual. It was totally charming and utterly strange behavior for a fighting dragon—especially one of Kelzy's stature.

"Okay then."

Now off with you three. Adora and I have plans to discuss for tonight and plots to hatch. Kelzy swept one of her great wings toward the entrance shooing her guests out.

Belora hugged her mother once and headed out with Lars and his dragon partner.

"Your mother is definitely and interesting woman," he mused as he settled his arm around her waist.

"Lady Kelzy practically raised her from the time she was just a toddler 'til she was about ten years old."

Kelzy? Raise a human child? The others talk about her strange ways but I didn't realize there was some truth to the tales.

"Lady Kelzy was the best thing that ever happened to my mother." Belora defended her mother and the older dragon fiercely. "She has a kind heart and a pure soul. If the other dragons have a problem with that then they're just bigoted idiots."

Rohtina stopped short on the wide ledge they were traversing to turn her large head toward Belora. She blinked her golden topaz eyes down at her for a moment, considering her.

You're brave for a human female. I think we'll get along just fine.

Rohtina moved to the edge of the cliff and launched herself magnificently into the sky while Lars and Belora watched.

"Either she hates me or we're starting to find some common ground."

Lars reached down and placed a kiss on her hair. "Oh, she likes you all right. You just passed her test."

"That was a test?" She spun in Lars' arms to look up at him as he nodded.

"She holds Kelzy in high esteem. You probably don't realize it, but Kelzy and her partner Jared are the leaders of this Lair. They oversaw its construction and Kelzy leads the dragons here. She holds a lot of power and is one of the most respected dragons in the land. She serves the royal family directly. Others may gossip about her sometimes undragonish ways, but my Tina admires her greatly. She wants to be just like her, and of course Kelvan is a lot like his mama, and she loves Kelvan."

"I had no idea."

"Tina's hard to read until you get to know her."

"Sort of like her partner, you mean?" Belora teased him with her smile.

He nodded with a self-depreciating grin. "I'd have to admit you're probably right on that one."

It warmed her heart to see his smile. She reached up and palmed his cheek, urging him down so she could place a light kiss on his lips. One kiss turned to two, then two turned to more until they were all but necking right in the open, for anyone to see.

Gareth came upon them long moments later, his chuckle finally penetrating the fog of desire that swirled around them.

"I see you two have come to terms."

Belora eased down and a little apart from Lars. Both were breathing hard.

"I asked her to be my wife and she agreed," Lars reported, never removing his hot turquoise gaze from her.

Gareth slapped his friend on the back in congratulations, but Lars was so solidly built it barely made an impression. Gareth grinned happily when Belora finally tore her gaze from Lars to realize they'd drawn a small crowd of onlookers.

Single knights were watching them, some with appreciation, some with longing in their eyes. It was disconcerting at first until she realized all looked on them with true happiness that their fellows had found a woman to share their lives. She realized in that moment that she, in a small way, represented hope for them all. Hope that they would find women willing to be their wives and share their lives.

No doubt it was hard for most human women to accept dragons in their midst, but the idea of having two husbands was also a bit daunting. Daunting and exciting at the same time.

The mating feast was a grand affair. Every soul in the Lair had gathered in the communal area, up on the bluff above the entrance to the Lair. Up on the flat, there was enough room for all the dragons and the humans as well. A huge fire had been lit at the center of the gathering along with several smaller ones for cooking and for those who wished more intimate circles, but the guests of honor were gathered at the center, where the dancing was.

Belora and her new mates had already danced all of the dances they'd taught her during her brief lesson, some three and four times. The party in full swing, the other mated trios joined them while the unmated knights watched and clapped their hands in time with the music. Belora felt the pull of the men's eyes on her, but her full attention focused on her two mates and on the two mighty dragons who watched, their necks twining together as their own passions rose steadily through the evening.

There had been excellent food served to them as the celebration began, joined by fine wines and beers, and even sweets for dessert. Then the tables had been cleared away to make room for the raucous dancing. But first, the ceremony.

As the elders of the Lair, Kelzy and Jared waited in the center of the clearing, the huge dragon a witness and support behind her knight, the General of the winged forces of this Lair. It was before Jared they would promise themselves to each other and with his words of blessing, they would officially be wed.

The ceremonial words were short, but no less beautiful for their brevity. Belora's mother wept openly as she watched her little girl pledge her life to the two strong knights that stood tall and strong at her sides. Gareth and Lars took turns promising their love and protection for all time to the woman they both loved and then it was the dragons' turn.

Kelvan and his beautiful Rohtina stood behind the humans, surrounding them and protecting them as they shared in the joining ceremony. They pledged their lives to each other in the presence of Kelzy and Jared, receiving slightly altered words of blessing from the dragon in return for their promises to share their fire and their flight with only each other for as long as their knights and their mate should live.

Belora realized belatedly that dragon joining had to depend greatly on the humans involved—at least among fighting dragons who were paired with human knights. Since dragons lived far longer than their human partners, they could mate only while the humans had their own partners, unless they wanted to break the laws that bound human and dragon together and drive their bonded partner insane with need at the same time. It was just not done. Belora shed a tear when she realized just how greatly the dragons sacrificed to protect their human partners and what such a partnership really meant.

"Whom the Mother has joined, in Her wisdom, let none put asunder." Jared's voice boomed out so that all could hear, echoed by Kelzy's triumphant trumpeting call. The other dragons joined in, howling their happiness to the heavens as the ceremony concluded and Belora felt the thunder of their call rumble through her body. It was an amazing feeling.

Moments later, the dancing began in earnest and her new mates swept her up into their strong arms and twirled her around and around, making her dizzy with happiness. She danced with them and noticed the other trios joining them in the space set aside for dancing. There were more family groups in the Lair than she had realized. Every woman she had met was on the dance floor with two knights each and she realized that there were no single women in the Lair, only a wealth of single men who had little hope of finding a mate who could fit in with their odd lifestyle.

They had been dancing for hours, though it was such fun it seemed like only a few minutes to Belora. Her two men had grown increasingly bold as the night wore on, handling her body with possession and a masterful strength that excited her blood more than she had thought possible. Lars was coming out of his shell more and more too, it seemed, equal with Gareth on every count both in his provocative actions and in her heart.

Before the feast, they had gifted her with a special outfit, crafted of the finest, softest leather. It was a strange garment, consisting of a short, floaty skirt and a halter top covered by a wrap that preserved her modesty on top. She had been afraid she might be cold, but the fires and increased tempo of the dancing kept her warm as the night wore on.

When the mating dance began, she did the few steps required of her, then gave herself almost completely over to the control of her two men. Smiling up into their faces as they lifted and twirled her around, passing her from one to the other of them, she was warmed by the love and fire flashing back from their eyes to hers. How she loved them both!

At one point, they let her back on her feet for a moment. Gareth twirled her about, stealing the wrap from about her upper body, leaving her clad only in the brief halter and skirt. She gasped as the night wind caressed her body, but only a moment later she was twirled into Lars' strong arms. He held her close; his own shirt gone now and her skin brushed his with longing. When she next saw Gareth, his shirt was gone as well.

The dance progressed, their flesh making contact in tantalizing, mesmerizing, and gratifying brushes that only heightened her excitement and desire for her men. She wanted them. Oh, how she wanted them! Separately, together, however she could get them.

"Now we come to it, my love." Gareth spoke in a low, harsh voice as he held her off her feet, her breasts soft against his hard, bare chest. "The dance is nearly over and the true wedding rite begins."

Lars pressed up behind her, sandwiching her warm body between them. Her eyes widened and all around them she noted that the other married trios were in the same position. The dance ended, but all held quiet while the dragons around began their trumpeting calls. Two by two, the dragons were twining their necks around each other, moving off toward the ledge from which they could easily launch skyward. Two by two, they took to the sky, their knight partners and their mate disappearing from the dance floor to seek the shadowed bowers that were a natural part of the bluff.

Last to seek the sky were the newly mated Kelvan and Rohtina. When they beat their great wings in time and launched skyward, all the unmated dragons bellowed and breathed fire up to the stars in a magnificent send-off. As Kel and Tina took to the air, Belora was lifted in her mates' arms and led to the beautiful bower in the shelter of magnificent fir trees that had been reserved for them alone this night of nights.

The married women of the Lair had prepared this special love nest with all the comforts of their home below, decorating it specially for this one perfect night. Soft pillows covered a bed of piled furs. Lars lifted her high and placed her gently on the center of the fur bed, coming down almost immediately to one side while Gareth claimed the other. Both men had fire in their eyes as their dragons twined around each other in an intricate dance in the sky.

Belora knew that both knights were intimately bound to their dragons and that as the dragons' lust grew, so would theirs. The other women had warned her that this first time could be somewhat overwhelming since both dragons were very young and had never mated before. The dragons might not realize how their passions would inflame their partners or themselves and they could easily work themselves and their knights into a frenzy before morning.

The women said this uniformly with a twinkle in their eye and a look almost of longing while reassuring Belora that she would enjoy every single moment of it. But the caution remained. They warned her not to deny the knights this one, most important night of their union. This night, she must remain passive and allow the men their ease. All the women assured her that taking a passive role, at least this once, would be more rewarding than she could imagine and she trusted their judgment. After all, these women had lived through it. They knew what they were talking about. She would have to trust their judgment in this and in other things as she learned from them the everyday ways of life in the Lair.

Gareth turned her in his arms and kissed her deeply. She moaned and writhed as Lars' hands began a slow torture of the flesh of her hips and lower. One of his hands slipped between the cheeks of her ass, teasing the puckered hole there while the other played in her pussy, slipping and sliding in her eager readiness.

"Tell me you want this," Gareth breathed when he let her up for air, his eyes blazing with fire into her own. "Tell me you want us both."

"I do!" Her voice was a squeak of pleasure as Lars dipped his fingers deep inside her pussy, pulsing and scissoring through her sensitive tissues. "I want you both."

Gareth sat back, glancing over at Lars as some kind of unspoken communication seemed to pass between the two. Lars pulled back as well and she could see the fire reflected in his turquoise eyes, now burning with golden flickers as he watched her.

"We talked about this," Gareth caressed her face as if he could not help but touch her in some way. "Lars gets your pussy first, I'll come behind. He wants to be inside you so badly, Belora. As do I."

"Behind?" She squealed just a bit as Lars' incredibly strong hands grasped her roughly and turned her toward him. He didn't hurt her. He couldn't hurt her. He was so gentle, even with all his vast strength. But she thrilled at the small hint of roughness, the only clue he gave her that he was near the edge of his control. She liked the idea more than she could say.

"Yes, Belora." Gareth stroked her ass cheeks as Lars pulled her on top of him, adjusting her legs so she straddled his massive body. His thick erection nestled just at the apex of her thighs, waiting impatiently to go where it longed to bury itself inside her. Gareth's hands, meanwhile, stroked between her cheeks, slathering a warm, slippery substance that smelled faintly of cinnamon, making his path easier as he probed into her. She gasped. It felt surprisingly good.

"I'm going to take your ass this time," he went on to say, all the while playing inside her, bringing her passions to a new level, "while Lars has your pussy. It's something I've wanted for a long time. I've dreamed of this moment, my love. Of making you come around us both so hard, you forget your own name. Forget anything existed beyond the pleasure we could give you."

She must have seemed frightened for Lars tightened his strong arms around her, bringing her eyes to his. He kissed her softly, his fire receding for the tiniest moment while he seemed to assure himself that she was truly okay.

"If you don't want this, just say the word." Lars kissed her softly, coaxing her to tell him the truth of her feelings. "We'll never hurt you, my love. We want only your pleasure."

She kissed him back with more pressure, hoping to bring that fire back to his eyes. Squirming, she was able to take just the tip of his bulging cock inside her pussy as she did her best to inflame him. She lifted her head after a long, long moment to view her handiwork, smiling down at him.

"I trust you both. More than that, I love you. I know you won't hurt me." She pecked at the corner of his lips, biting lightly, glad to see the fire leap once more, even brighter in his eyes. "If you two want this and think it will increase my pleasure, I believe you." She leaned just a little father back—as far as Lars' tight arms would let her go and turned her head to wink up at Gareth who appeared to be listening closely. "Do your worst, boys."

She giggled as Lars clamped down with his arms, bringing her body tight against his as he kissed her long and deep. Gareth went back to preparing her back entrance and she was able to take just a bit more of Lars' hot hardness within her aching sheath.

How she wanted them!

She heard a far off roar and knew the dragons were nearing their own peaks of ecstasy. Lars grunted and slid all the way inside her. She was surprised at the sudden move, but thrilled by the feel of him, so wide and thick inside her. He felt different from Gareth, but just as sexy and exciting. How she loved them both!

"You fit around him like a glove, Belora." Gareth's words were harsh behind her. "Now take me too. Relax, open and take me, my love."

He pushed gently at first, but with firm pressure against the small opening he had made wider with his gliding touch. It was hard at first for her to accept this, but she knew she must. The other wives had warned her in not so many words about this sort of thing, each admitting that great pleasure could be had from letting the men have their way. Keeping that in mind, along with her ever-expanding love for both of these warriors, she relaxed and submitted to their pleasure in whatever way they would take it.

Gareth eased inside, a harsh groan coming from his lips as he seated himself fully within Belora's tight, virgin ass.

"Yes, that's it. Sweet Mother, Belora!"

Both men began to move as the fire from their dragons intensified. Bonded on a soul-deep level with the great beasts that even now tangled in the air high above, mating in a frenzy that could kill them if they didn't finish in time to break apart and spread their wings to fly high once more. The free fall of dragon mating was something he had never experienced before though the older knights talked about it once in a while. Feeling the echoes of Kelvan's pleasure through their link and the incredible pleasure he was finding within Belora's willing body was incredible.

No words could do this sensation justice. For a moment, he felt completely joined. As he was joined to Kel, so was Kel joined to Tina and Tina to Lars. Through the thin links that joined them, he could almost feel echoes of what Lars was feeling, and he knew exactly when to press down and when to retreat to bring them all the most pleasure.

His eyes sought Lars' and an understanding passed between them. They were already as close as brothers, but this experience bonded them anew. He could feel the other man through the thin barrier of Belora's body that separated them and he knew Lars' heart and the love that mirrored his own for the small woman giving them so much of her trust, heart and love. In that moment he knew this partnership was right. They were a family now and would be together until they died.

The dragons came in a rush of pleasure that seemed to go on and on and it fired the passions in both Gareth and Lars. He felt all four of them explode in his mind even as he felt Belora reaching out to join them. Her mind opened and then suddenly, she was part of the tenuous link they all shared, part of the family of dragons and knights.

Gareth was astounded as the pleasure they all felt doubled back and mirrored itself through each one of them. It was like nothing he'd ever heard described. It was completely unique. It was devastating.

He came with a harsh groan as Lars continued to pump his release into their wife's wondrous body. She shuddered around both of them, coaxing them yet higher even as their dragons began beating their wings out in the starry sky, seeking higher ground to begin their love play anew.

And still there was Belora, in the back of his mind, sharing the most extraordinary link. She seemed unaware of it, but he knew. Looking into Lars' eyes, he knew too that the other man felt it as well. Astounding. Somehow, Belora was part of them all—part of the union of knight and dragon in a way he was not sure should be possible.

But exploration of that odd thought would have to wait. The dragons were gaining height again as were their passions. The echoes were undeniable as both cocks hardened and lengthened inside their woman once more. This would be a long, supremely pleasurable night. Thinking would come later.

Much later.

CHAPTER SEVEN

I don't want to leave you here, baby. Kelzy paced heavily as she eyed the hut in the forest with disdain.

Jared had taken one look at the sagging roof and took off into the forest. He had come back a few minutes later with some stout branches and silently set to work making repairs while Kelzy argued with her adopted daughter about staying in the forlorn forest cottage all alone.

"I've lived here for years, Mama Kelzy. It's perfectly safe, I assure you."

That was before that Skithdronian nutcase started riling up the skiths and threatening invasion. What can you do against a hunting pack of skiths on your doorstep, Adora? They'll cut you to ribbons! They're vicious creatures!

"Some people say that about dragons, you know." Adora's soft voice was cajoling but it didn't work on Kelzy in this mood.

Don't try to make a comparison between my kind and those spineless, stinking, soulless skiths. They are purely evil, you know. Not thinking creatures at all, which is why that so-called king can herd them about so easily into doing his dirty work. A dragon would never be so easily led. The only thing a skith cares for is blood, carnage, and its next meal.

"And of course, how many heads they can take." Jared came around the back of the small house toward them, shirtless.

Adora took a step back, her eyes glued to the hard male chest displayed so brazenly before her. It had been years since she had confronted her own feminine desires. Frankly she had thought she was well past such desires, but seeing Jared's hard body, sweaty from working to fix her sagging roof and so unconsciously sexy, she felt something long dormant deep inside her womb stir to life. In her work as a healer, she had of course seen her share of naked males, and she had been married for several years, but Jared was something different altogether.

This was a knight who trained hard and looked it. He had muscles on top of his muscles and a washboard stomach that made her long to stroke him. Adora became breathless as she watched him move casually toward her, his stride supremely male and confident. The supple ripple of his riding leathers surrounded a cock she was sure was of more than generous proportions. He was a vital male animal, totally unaware of his allure to a woman long denied the pleasures of the flesh.

Do you like what you see? Kelzy's voice purred through her mind and she knew the dragon was speaking only to her, well aware of her striking reaction to the gorgeous specimen of man in his prime displayed before her.

"Hush! Please don't embarrass me." Adora flushed hotly, leaning close to Kelzy's flank and speaking in a low whisper she knew the dragon alone would hear.

It's no crime to enjoy the look of a handsome male, Adora, and my knight is more handsome than most. Look your fill, baby, and remember that if you lived with me he would be your protector. He would keep you safe if you lived with us in the Lair. He would be your family, just as you are mine.

"I can't go back with you." Adora stood from Kelzy's side, her spoken words saying far more than the knight would know. "My responsibility is here and here I must stay. At least for now."

I don't like it at all, Adora.

"I'll have to agree with Kelzy. Your home is livable, but in disrepair." Jared wiped his hands on his strong, muscled thighs before stretching to put his shirt back on. Adora tried not to watch, but the sensuous ripple of each hard muscle caught her attention. "I've fixed what I can of the roof, but this place won't hold you safe against one skith, let alone a hunting pack. If they come, your best bet will be to run, perhaps climb a tree out of their range. They don't climb particularly well, but you have to be wary of their venomous spray."

"I've seen what they can do. A farmer from the village ran into a feral one last season and was badly burned."

And yet you still want to stay here? Knowing they may come in force? Kelzy's voice rose in alarm.

"I must." Adora placed a warm palm on the dragon's knee stroking comfortingly.

The knight strode to the small pack Kelzy had worn to carry some supplies and things she wanted Adora to have from the Lair. He pulled out a deep brown bundle and handed it to her.

"Take this then. It's a specially treated hide. It's what we make the battle leathers from and it will repel skith venom somewhat. Make clothing for yourself from it. Leggings would be better than a skirt. They'll protect your legs more. Make slippers or boots and a shirt if you can. Try to cover as much of your skin as you can while still being able to move quickly if need be." He pressed the heavy bundle of leather into her astonished hands. This was a very costly gift and one she knew was not lightly given. "I tried to get some ready made garments, but we had nothing in your size and there was no time to have them made. I asked them to pick the softest hide we had in the storeroom so it would be easier for you to sew and kinder to your skin. There's lacing and needles inside the bundle too, in case you didn't have what you'd need on hand."

Tears formed behind her eyes and she choked up for a moment, unable to speak. She reached up to kiss his cheek softly, clearly surprising him. With one hand, she held the precious leather and with the other, she pulled him close for a quick hug.

"Thank you, Sir Jared." She whispered into his ear as she pulled back, and then turned to her home quickly so she could tuck away the fabric and gain a moment to regain her composure.

When she came back out, she was more in control.

He already protects you. Kelzy's voice was soft in her mind.

"Sir Jared, your gift is beyond generous. I will set to work on the garments you suggest this very eve." She tried to make up for her loss of composure with sincere thanks to the man whose thoughtfulness had taken her totally by surprise.

"That's good." He nodded approvingly and held out a cloth wrapped bundle to her. "Kelzy asked me to pack these as well."

She took the large bundle, surprised that it weighed very little. Unwrapping the cloth, the sparkle of dragon scale was bright in her eye.

"What's this?" She looked from the shimmering blue-green scales to the dragon.

Just a few scales I have shed over the years. We grow new ones, you know, when our scales have been damaged or worn. Our knights save the shed scales to use in shielding or armor, sometimes in weapons. If you incorporate a few of my scales into your clothing in strategic places, they may shield you more effectively.

"Mama Kelzy, I can't accept these. There are fighting knights who need these precious scales, your own included." She looked to Jared who watched with grim interest. She knew he supported Kelzy's decision to give them to her and it touched her deeply. This was a precious, personal gift. Too rare and too valuable to waste on her though.

Let us do this small thing, Adora. If I cannot be with you, at least a part of me will be. Let me think of you, shielded at least a little by my shed scales and my love. Wear them for me, Adora, so I can fly away with at least some feeling of peace in my heart. I won't be able to leave you otherwise.

Adora went to the dragon, touched by her palpable emotion. Putting her arms around Kelzy's thick neck, she hugged her, closing her eyes as Kelzy's sparkling wings enclosed her in a warm embrace. They held each other for long, long moments.

"I love you, Mama Kelzy."

I love you too, child. We'll come visit when we can.

Adora realized that Kelzy would bring Jared whenever she found time away from her duties at the Lair to come visit her. The idea appealed to her more than she thought it should, but she let go that thought as Kelzy pulled away.

"Watch the creatures of the forest," Jared counseled as he prepared to leave, climbing aboard Kelzy's back with a lithe grace that belied his huge size. "The animals will know when skiths are about and the birds will go quiet and fly away. The game animals flee and even the rodents scurry away. Listen to them and look to the trees whenever you're outside. Know which ones you can climb high—at least twenty feet off the ground. More if you can manage it. Trees with thick leaves may provide some barrier to venom spray if there are enough leaves between you and the skiths. Plan ahead, Adora. It could save you."

She took his words to heart, nodding solemnly. "I'll do as you suggest, Sir Jared. Thank you once more for the leather and for fixing my roof."

"I wish I could do more, but I'm not much of a carpenter."

"You managed in a few minutes more than I could do in a year so compared to me you're an expert and I thank you." Her hesitant smile earned her a return grin from him. It lit his solemn face and made her feel good for having caused it.

Kelzy turned with him settled on her back, preparing to take off.

Be careful, child. Your daughter and her mate will come to see you and we'll stop by when we can, but do as Jared says and prepare. War is coming and the skiths will pour over the border first. Beware of them. Kelzy moved farther out into the small clearing from which she would have a clear path to the sky. *I couldn't bear to lose you again now that I've finally found you. Take care, child, and if you change your mind, come back to the Lair with Kelvan or pack your things and I'll take you back the next time I visit, okay? Promise me now.*

"I promise." Adora waved to Jared who held up his hand in goodbye. Kelzy flapped her great, sparkling wings and a moment later was airborne.

"I love you, Mama Kelzy."

The clearing was empty and the beautiful blue-green dragon winged off into the sun. Adora was alone.

Newly mated as they were, Kelvan and Rohtina, along with their knights, were given a few days freedom from drilling and patrolling. They made the most of it, flying off to the forest and beyond to frolic and play, mate and explore. Belora went with them, of course, sometimes riding with Gareth on Kelvan's broad back and sometimes with Lars on the sparkling golden Rohtina.

Both men made Belora feel warm and secure no matter what flying antics their dragon partners engaged in, swooping and diving at each other like children. One memorable day, they spent at the lake where Gareth and

Belora had first met, the three of them fucking hard and fast while the dragons mated in the skies above the lake, plummeting to earth to take an unlikely swim in the cool waters as they floated in the aftermath.

They also spent time moving into their new quarters. Lars brought Rohtina's things—shed scales, lots of pretty rocks and gems she had found in her travels and asked him to collect, a few exotic plants, and the oils and potions that helped keep dragon scales supple and shiny. Gareth had similar items from Kelvan's stash and together the two knights organized the small room set aside for the dragons' belongings.

Belora helped settle the men's clothing, taking the opportunity to clean and tidy everything they owned. She repaired the few things that needed it and made note of their sizes so she could begin work on new things for them. She wasn't a terribly gifted seamstress, but it was an occupation she enjoyed and she knew they wouldn't be embarrassed to wear the plain things she could make for them. She also took charge of the small kitchen area, combining the meager stores from each of the knights' previous dwellings and procuring a few things she felt they would need now that she was in residence.

Her mother had taught her how to brew potions and make ointments, lotions, and tinctures. Although she was not a truly gifted healer, she knew the basics and even a bit more than most herbalists. She took the opportunities that presented themselves as they traveled around during those few days to gather some herbs that she knew she could use and set up an area in the kitchen where she could work. She made fragrant bathing salts, gentle herbal soaps, and lotions for her skin as well as ointments that could be used to heal most cuts and abrasions, potions and tinctures to keep on hand to cure coughs and colds and other useful items.

She set it all up and knew she would have time when the men were back to drilling and patrolling to do the real work of making remedies for both her own household and to share with the rest of the Lair. She knew that Silla, the older woman who had been so kind to her mother, was the closest they had to a true healer in this new Lair. She would undoubtedly welcome Belora's help and the few potions and cures she could add to the Lair's supplies.

The dragons liked to play in their new, much larger wallow too. Belora and the knights spent a great deal of time sweeping sand back into the large oval pit at the center of their suite, but they didn't mind. The dragons were so happy together, their joy infectious.

Of course, that wasn't the only thing that passed from the dragons to the knights and their new wife. Several times, Kelvan and Rohtina had flown off to frolic and caught their human partners almost unaware when the mating heat would surge. At such times, Lars and Gareth would come looking for her with such wild lust in their eyes, she knew the dragons were unconsciously feeding their lusts to their partners.

At such times, Belora would feel an echo of the incredible fever the dragon lust inspired and open her arms wide to her two lovers, welcoming them between her thighs and into her soul. They would take her together at such times, both needing to be inside her at the same moment in order to fulfill the dragon lust riding them so hard.

Gareth was speaking with General Jared Armand, Kelzy's partner, when a sudden urge from Kelvan caught him unawares. His dick started to harden and he cursed, looking desperately for a way out. He had to get to Belora, and fast. But first he had to extricate himself from this discussion with his commanding officer.

Jared saw his fidgeting and chuckled. "Dragons giving you trouble?"

"You could say that." Gareth breathed a sigh of relief that his commander was so understanding.

"Get out of here, Gareth. Find your mate." He slapped him on the back and turned away, moving on to another knight who wanted his attention.

Gareth took off at a run for his quarters, praying to the Mother of All that Belora would be there. The knights cheered him as he passed, knowing or guessing what emergency took him so unceremoniously away from the common areas.

When he finally reached his quarters, the pain in his loins was almost unbearable. Kelvan and Rohtina were already joined, rolling and plunging in the way of dragons, high up in the sky, reaching for the sun. Gareth was nearly insane from the pressure.

He loped through the door and began tearing at his clothes even before he reached the bedchamber.

"Thank the Mother!"

Belora was there, already on the bed, with Lars' big cock in her tight pussy, her bare ass facing him… inviting him. Lars saw his friend in the door and moved his big hands to spread her cheeks, dropping the small jar of sweet-smelling lotion on the bed near their hips on the way.

Gareth didn't need any further invitation. Freeing his cock from his leathers, he scooped a dollop of lotion onto his fingers, quickly coated his cock, and reached in to stroke her anus. She had grown used to this over the past days and her body accepted him readily enough as he pressed forward, seeking the heaven of her tight ass.

Belora squeaked as he joined her.

"It's just me, my love." He bent to whisper in her ear, finishing with a sharp nip to her earlobe that made her squirm.

"I didn't think you'd make it in time." Her breath came in pants as both men moved in her, driving her lust higher.

"I ran all the way here." He pressed in, feeling Lars' hardness through the thin barrier of flesh that separated them. He also felt the explosion that was nearing in Kelvan's body as the dragons began to reach the limits of their flight. The dragon's lust pushed him, as he knew it pushed Lars, to heights no human male could achieve. It was a gift of their partnership with the dragons that they could reach such peaks and for such long, nearly endless moments.

He felt it coming and knew Lars would go with him when the dragons reached their zenith. It was up to the two human men to make sure Belora went along with them. He used his teeth to nip at her neck while Lars sucked her nipples.

"Now, Belora! Now!" He called, just as Lars bit down on her nipple and the dragons burst together into the sun. He emptied himself into her ass as Lars' cock pulsed in her vagina, their ecstasy echoing the long plummet to earth of the dragons. It went on and on, holding all of them in its grip while the pleasure wracked their bodies. Belora's climax rolled on and on, her inner muscles milking both of their cocks and he was glad to know that she was with them every step of the way.

Finally, after long, long moments of tight muscled ecstasy the dragons began to come back to themselves. They pulled apart and beat their wings just in time to save them from crashing to the ground, releasing their human partners from the rigor of their pleasure. Lars relaxed within her cunt as Gareth felt himself easing in her tight, tight ass. Belora was nearly unconscious from the pleasure and the men settled her between them as they each found the energy to pull back from her luscious body.

Gareth looked down at himself in disgust. He hadn't even managed to undress. His pants were open just enough to release his cock and his shirt was hanging wide, but he had his boots on in bed. Too bad he didn't have the energy to remedy the situation. Later, he thought. He'd get the damned boots off later.

Adora took Jared's advice and spent her evenings sewing a set of clothing for herself out of the incredibly soft leather he had given her. It was the softest hide she had ever felt and every time she stroked it as she worked, she thought of the tall, strong man who had touched her slumbering heart with the gift. Remembering Kelzy too, she used two of the precious, incredibly strong dragon scales, sandwiched between two layers of hide to make protective soles for a pair of soft boots that laced up her legs and held the leggings close to her body.

The outfit was somewhat indecent, fitting so closely to her skin and emphasizing the curves of her womanly form, but she couldn't resist the soft swish of the leather next to her skin and the warm feel of it between her legs. It reminded her that, although she had a grown daughter now mated and probably starting a family of her own, Adora herself was still a young woman. She had seen only thirty-eight winters and could still have more children of her own, if she really wanted to do so.

She had not even given thought to such ideas. Before meeting Jared, that is. Suddenly, she felt alive again as a woman. She experienced strange feelings in her body that she had not felt in years. Actually, she was not quite sure she had ever felt the way she was feeling at the moment. Jared had awakened something within her that she had not even known existed and she really wanted to see where it would lead, but she was scared.

Jared was not very encouraging. Although he had given her the specially treated leather and been so incredibly thoughtful about her safety, he had given her no outward sign that he was interested in her as a woman. In fact, he had done quite the opposite. He had been polite to the extreme at all times, but somewhat distant. He had not been rude exactly, but not warm either. Still, there was something about the man and his quiet strength that appealed to her. His thoughtfulness was even more attractive, and the fact that he was gorgeous and superbly built didn't hurt either, she thought with a wry grin as she finished off the last seam on her new outfit.

She had pants, boots, a shirt, and a small head covering that would protect her from the worst of a skith venom spray, should she be caught in a dangerous position. Personally she thought she would never need such protection, but she was a practical person and knew well the value of being prepared for all contingencies. Plus, the leather was so scrumptious that she could not resist making a complete set of gear for herself from it.

The design for the clothing was from her own imagination and perhaps a little strange looking, but very functional if she did say so herself. She had used the precious dragon scales to reinforce certain parts of the outfit like the knees and arms and to add a bit of decoration around the neckline. Kelzy's sparkling blue-green looked beautiful against the soft brown of the hide.

Gareth and Kelvan had dropped in to check on her briefly on their way home from patrolling the border the day before, but she had not seen her daughter for a few days. It would be a few days yet until Kelvan was free from his duties long enough to fly Belora and Gareth over for a visit, and Adora looked forward to it already.

But today was the day to replenish her herb stock, so Adora found herself on the deer trails in the forest near her small home with a sack of herbs she had already collected and more to gather. The first inkling she felt that something was wrong was when the birds grew quiet. Since Jared's warnings, she had learned to be even more observant of her surroundings than she already was. The birds going quiet could mean nothing, or it could be something quite dire. Adora cocked her head, listening, and felt the little hairs on the back of her neck creep up in alarm when the sounds of the forest did not resume after a reasonable amount of time.

Rising slowly, she collected her satchel of herbs and headed quietly for her house. She had enough herbs for one day and the unnatural quietness of the forest was getting to her. Moving as softly as possible, she retraced her steps back to the track just above her cabin, but stopped dead when she saw the huge, brownish slithering tail disappear inside her cabin's front door.

A skith!

And it was in her house. Probably lying in wait for her to return.

Skiths were large, dangerous predators that hunted with cunning though their mental capacity was nothing like a dragons'. Still, they were formidable foes when pushed into the open. Normally inhabiting the rocky outcroppings to the east, wild skiths did not, as a rule, prey on humans, preferring easier prey like livestock or wild beasts. The new king of the land to the east, however, had pushed the skiths beyond their normal hunting grounds and somehow gotten them to act as a first wave of his army. How he had done that was anyone's guess since skiths could not be reasoned with, yet he had succeeded.

Adora pulled the hooded head covering up over her head, well aware that there could be more where that one skith had come from. She wore her new suit of clothes as she had every day since it had been made, but she could not return home. Her only hope was to head for the village. If there was a skith here already, they may have gotten to the village or were heading there. She had to warn the people.

Moving lightly on her feet, Adora slipped through the forest toward the village but on the hill before the small town, she stopped to take stock. She could see even from this distance that the skiths had already been there. Their great bodies had pulled down several houses and the acid stench of their spray drifted on the wind, burning everything it touched that wasn't stone.

The village was empty, the people either dead or long gone, running for their lives. She could do nothing there, she knew. Even worse, she realized as she observed for just a moment too long, a few of the skiths were still there!

One sighted her, and with a deafening scream, alerted his comrades. With a shudder, Adora ran back into the forest, hoping to lose them, but the skiths, though legless, were fast on her track. She ran and ran, but soon realized the skiths would outdistance her easily, closing her in from both sides and she would be trapped.

Adora thought back to Jared's advice. She had to find a sturdy tree that she could climb. Preferably one with a very leafy canopy that might shield her from at least some of the spray they would no doubt shoot up at her in their hunting frenzy.

There! Just ahead, she found a sturdy oak that reached at least thirty feet or more up into the sky of the forest. Scrambling, she jumped for the first limb and climbed as fast as she dared, out of breath from running but unable to stop even for a moment. The skiths were coming fast now and she had to get out of their range.

Too late, she realized as she felt little pelting impacts against her lower legs and she smelled the unmistakable scent of burning leather. She looked down briefly. Two skiths slithered around the base of the tree, trying to reach up and grab her back with their strong jaws, spitting venom as they snarled at her. She looked back up and climbed higher. The leather Jared had given her was protecting her for the moment, but she didn't want any more of the venom to hit her. She was not sure if the leather would stand up to a second barrage of the deadly acid.

She settled in the tree as high up as she could go and took a second to look down. More skiths had joined the first two and their writhing bodies tumbled and climbed over each other, trying to extend their reach. She knew they were relentless hunters. They would not give up for days and she did not think she could last more than a few hours clinging to the spindly branches near the top of the tree. The situation was desperate.

Adora closed her eyes and felt tears gathering as she prayed. She prayed to the Mother of All and then she turned her thoughts to her dear Mama Kelzy. She reached out, as she never had before, and tried desperately to send her thoughts—her final words of love—to the dragon who had been such an important part of her childhood and who filled her heart still.

Mama Kelzy! If the skiths get me, I want you to know I love you. You are the mother of my heart. Adora's arms started to tremble as her strength and the burst of adrenaline started to fade. *Tell Jared his leathers worked. He's a beautiful soul and a good man. I'm going to hold on as long as I can and then I'm going to jump from this tree. I only pray the Mother will let me die in the fall so I won't feel anything when the skiths take my head and tear my body to ribbons. Tell my baby I love her.*

Adora returned to her prayers, focusing her thoughts and trying to steady her shaking limbs. There was nothing to do but wait now. She had to hold on as long as possible, and then, she had to end it with what dignity she could.

In the Lair, Kelzy trumpeted distress, her mind panicked, but clear in her orders. She called Jared to her and launched into the air even before he was fully seated. Her distress called to two other dragons as well, her son Kelvan and his mate Rohtina, and their knights soon flanked her wild flight toward the forest.

What is it? Jared asked his dragon partner quietly as they flew desperately for the forest. He deliberately included both of the other knights and their dragons in the conversation, linking them the way knights in battle were linked.

Adora! Kelzy's voice was panicked, almost irrational. *Skiths have her surrounded. She's in an old oak tree, but her strength is failing. She doesn't know I heard her! She doesn't know we're coming.*

We'll get to her in time, Kelz. We must. Jared's voice was grim and he bent closer to the dragon's neck to reduce wind resistance. Every second counted. *I want you two to fry the skiths and keep them busy while Kelzy and I get Adora out of that tree.*

Yes, General Armand. We're with you.

Lars was always the more correct of the newly formed pair and the respect in his thoughts for their commanding officer translated to steadfast devotion, trust, and a willingness to follow their commander, General Jared Armand and his partner Kelzy to the ends of the earth and beyond. Rohtina seconded her partner's words with a roar as Kelvan followed suit. The younger dragons headed a little lower, diving to gain speed as they headed for the location Kelzy shared with them in her mind. They would go in first to occupy the skiths while Kelzy and Jared tried to hover long enough to get Adora.

We're almost there, Kelz. Try to bespeak her. She might hear you now. Jared used his hands and strong legs to stroke Kelzy's tense shoulders, hoping to offer what comfort he could to calm her so they could act rationally and deliberately to rescue the woman that had become all too important to him in such a short time.

Adora, child! Hold on. We're coming! Kelzy's voice boomed through all their minds. She was using all her strength to try to make Adora hear her over the distance that separated them and it was forceful indeed.

Mama?

The single word was weak, but definitely there. The small group flying desperately closer felt heartened.

Hold on, child. Jared and I will get you. Hold on!

I see her! Kelvan reported from just slightly ahead of the others. *It'll be a tough grab, Jared.*

Jared looked over the position of the small woman in brown. He felt some satisfaction as he recognized the leather he had picked out and given her. She had done as he'd suggested and made a rather unconventional suit of clothing for herself. It may just have saved her life, he realized as they drew nearer and he could see the acid streaks on the lower half of her body. He ground his teeth at the thought of her being hit by skith venom.

I see what you mean. Get to work on the skiths and I'll figure a way to get Adora.

Yes, sir.

The two younger dragons swooped down through the leafy canopy and soon roars of flame were heard along with skith barking and bellowing. The knights too were employing their slings and even their swords as they got close enough to engage the slithering skiths. Jared left them to it, trying to figure a way to get Adora out of that tree and onto Kelzy's back with him, but it was not possible. She was positioned just wrong in the tree and obviously too weak at this point to move the great distance needed for him to be able to grab her.

Kelz, you have to snatch her.

No! I could kill her! It's too dangerous.

Making such a snatch in mid-air would demand all of the dragon's considerable skill as well as unflinching cooperation from Adora. If either of them moved at the wrong moment, Kelzy's dagger-sharp claws could rip her apart.

It's the only way. She trusts you enough not to move. You have to snatch her out of that tree.

They both heard a disastrous yowl of pain from below. One of the dragons was hurt!

It's now or never, Kelz. Those youngsters are good, but they can't wipe out the whole nest of skiths down there alone. For that matter, even if we helped, it wouldn't do much good. We need to get Adora out of that tree now. Do it, Kelz. Do it now. She's running out of strength.

Kelzy sent her thoughts to the woman in the tree. *Baby, I'm going to make another pass and reach out for you with my foreleg. Don't resist and try not to move, okay? Do you trust me, child?*

I trust you, Mama Kelzy. Whatever happens, I love you, Mama.

Oh, baby, I love you too. Hold still now. I'm coming to get you out of that tree. Don't move! Please, baby, don't move!

Kelzy made the final pass, glad to notice Rohtina was making her way out of the tree canopy, flying awkwardly but still under her own power. She was hurt, but she was clear of the skiths. Kelvan still fought below.

Kelzy concentrated all her effort on reaching out to her human child, snatching her out of the tree without hurting her. She reached out, timing everything as best she could in such bad circumstances and was gratified to feel Adora's waist in her grasp. She closed her talons as gently as she could and felt the small woman in her grasp flinch uncontrollably.

Adora! Are you all right?! Did I hurt you?

I'm okay. Thank you for coming for me.

Hold tight now. I'll have you to the Lair in just a few minutes. I won't let you go, sweetheart.

CHAPTER EIGHT

Jared reached over Kelzy's shoulder to look down at the small woman in his dragon partner's grasp. He could see the bright red of blood against Kelzy's blue-green foreleg but it was hard to see the jagged scrapes from the dragon's sharp talons against the brown leather that covered the woman.

A pain entered his heart as he saw her pale face, pressed tightly, trustingly against the dragon's muscular leg. She was so brave, so strong. This was a woman of rare character and ability, and she was fast becoming all too important to him. Either way, Adora would not be returning to her home in the forest. Kelzy and he would see to it that she stayed in the Lair.

This was a woman who needed to be protected and given the care she deserved. He wasn't looking for a wife, but he could not let her leave them again. She was much too precious.

How does she look? Kelzy's worried voice was for his mind alone.

He didn't want to worry his dragon partner, but neither could he keep the truth from her. *She's pale and weak. Your talons scratched her and she is bleeding a bit, but she's holding up well.*

Sweet Mother of All! Why didn't she tell me?

It doesn't look too bad, Kelz. Just get us to the Lair and we can fix her up, I'm sure.

If I hadn't snatched her out of that tree—

If you hadn't, he interrupted, *she would most likely be skith food right now. You did what you had to do and I'm sure she'll thank you for it, my friend. You don't hear her complaining, do you?*

She was ever a thoughtful child. She would never complain, even when she ought to.

Well, you can nag her about it after we get back to the Lair and the healers have a chance to look at her scratches. She's alive, Kelz. His voice dipped low, surprising him with the deep emotion he felt. *That's what matters most. She's alive and she'll live with us now.*

I should never have let her leave in the first place!

Neither of us should have let that happen, but we can and will stop her from going anywhere this time. I'll have her bound if I have to.

We're almost there, baby. Kelzy included all of them in her thoughts now as they approached the Lair. Kelvan brought up the rear with Gareth, both of them keeping close watch on Rohtina's injury as she struggled to fly back to her home.

Jared caught sight of the landing ledge and realized the younger dragons must have sent word ahead, because a contingent of people was waiting for them. Among them was Belora, wringing her hands with tears tracking down her pale face. Silla, the woman who acted as healer for the Lair was there too and it was to her side that Kelzy aimed her landing. She hovered a moment, allowing Jared to jump down and catch Adora as Kelzy opened her claws.

Adora was in a great deal of pain, but when she opened her eyes, Jared breathed a huge sigh of relief. She wasn't out of the woods yet, he knew, but she was conscious at least. Just seeing her beautiful eyes blink open reassured him.

"You shouldn't frown so hard, Jared. I'm fine."

"Then why are you only half-conscious?" His gruff voice was for her ears alone as he carried her away from the ledge so the dragons would have room to land fully. Belora was at their side almost instantly, making sure her mother was okay.

"I'm fine, baby," her mother assured her. "Just let me get bandaged up. You should see to Rohtina. She was hurt by the skiths, I think."

Belora gasped and ran for the ledge once more after kissing her mother and assuring her she would check on her as soon as she was patched up. Silla was there too, lifting the leather away gently and looking at the severity of the scratches. Jared looked too, frowning when he saw the deep gouges but silent as Silla made her own assessment.

"I can wrap them, but it isn't nearly as bad as it looks. A few weeks and she'll be good as new, I think."

Kelzy breathed a warm sigh of relief that washed over them all, bringing a smile to Adora's pale lips. "See? I told you it was nothing."

"Doesn't look like nothing to me," Jared grumbled, heading for the corridor with her still in his strong arms.

"I can walk, you know."

"I'm not letting you out of my sight until you're patched up and comfortable in bed. In your room. In our quarters." His eyes held hers as he laid down the law.

"Okay." She surprised him by placing her hand at the nape of his neck and stroking him gently.

"You're not going to argue about going back to your forest?"

Solemnly, she shook her head. "After what just happened? The village was destroyed. My patients are all gone—either dead or fled. There's nothing holding me there any longer."

Well, thank the Mother for that! Kelzy's disgusted voice floated to them as she followed close behind on their way to her quarters. *Not about the village— that's terrible, she clarified quickly, but about you staying with us now. We need you, girl.*

Adora chuckled and closed her eyes, letting her head drift to rest against Jared's strongly beating heart. He liked the way she felt against him, liked the trust she put in him by that simple gesture. Carefully he maneuvered her through the archways and into the room she had used before and placed her gently on the bed.

Kelzy's great head followed them into the small human-sized room to observe that he cared for her girl properly, he supposed. He didn't mind. He loved Kelzy and knew the dragon loved this small woman. They weren't bonded the way he and Kelzy had bonded, soul to soul, but their bond was perhaps even stronger. This was the bond between mother and child, as unlikely as it seemed. The unconventional relationship was just one more reason he loved Kelzy so deeply. She was a special dragon in every way, with a deep compassion and capacity to love that many others of her kind did not seem to possess.

Jared reached for the small buttons on Adora's clothing, undressing her with an efficient hand, over her weak objections. She was almost completely drained of energy. When his hands found the burn marks from the skith venom on her leggings and boots, he marveled at the way her unconventional garments had withstood the fierceness of the attack. When he removed her boots he noted the hardness in the sole and saw the flash of Kelzy's scales peeping through the burns, shaking his head at her ingenuity.

"Look at this, Kelz." He tossed the boots near to the dragon's head so she could inspect them. "Your little human daughter is a very bright woman."

Amazing, Kelzy agreed. *Why didn't we ever think of doing something like this? Incorporating my shed scales between layers of treated leather. It probably saved her from some serious burns.*

"Definitely. The scale stopped the acid. Even when the first layer of hide failed, the scale and the inner layer of leather were there to protect her. Her skin is unblemished, but the boots and leggings testify to the severity of the venom spray. She was hit pretty badly."

"Hey!" Adora protested when he pulled her leggings clean off, leaving her bare from mid-thigh to her wiggling toes. Jared simply lifted her legs, inspecting her skin minutely for any injury before pulling a blanket from the foot of the bed and tucking it around her.

"Your skin was protected by the leather, Adora. No burns on your legs from the venom, thank the Mother." He looked into her eyes as he reached for her tunic. Her hands came up to stop him, but he brushed them aside. "I have to clean and wrap those scratches." His voice was soft, but his tone serious and she let her hands fall away so he could do what he had to do.

He pulled off the ruined shirt as gently as he could, knowing by the way her breath hissed that it hurt her, but it had to be done. She was bare beneath the shirt and he was surprised for a moment at the sight of her lovely breasts spilling free of the form-fitting garment. She was built beautifully and quite the loveliest woman he had seen in many long years.

He stroked the side of her face with the backs of his fingers as he noted her discomfort. She was in pain and obviously shy. He had no doubt from her reactions that she had not been with a man since the death of her husband many years before. Jared thought that a crying shame. She was so beautiful, so vital. She deserved to enjoy life and love, not lock herself away in the middle of nowhere where no male could appreciate the beauty of her.

Not that he wanted to be that man, but he saw the value of her and knew she had been wasting her life away hiding in the forest. Here at the Lair, she would be appreciated for the jewel she truly was. He gritted his teeth and tried not to think about all the single men who would be beating a path to her door once they knew she would stay here in the Border Lair. Shaking his head, he concentrated on the task at hand while Kelzy kept the room nice and warm with her puffing breath.

He took a water jug from the nearby table and splashed a bit into the matching bowl, snagging a washcloth at the same time. Slowly and with great care, he cleaned the gouges on her back and side, being as thorough as possible before wrapping a clean cloth lightly around her middle.

Doctoring done, he stood from the bedside and helped her settle comfortably back before tucking the blanket around her. Kelzy stayed just where she was, even after he left the small chamber and he knew the dragon would watch over her human daughter all night. He shook his head as he reached his own room and tumbled into bed. It had been a long, eventful day.

"How bad is she?" Gareth called to Lars as soon as they landed.

Lars jumped off his Rohtina's back and rushed around to examine the damage done to her tough hide by the skith venom.

"Water! We need water here!" Lars began to panic as he saw how deeply the venom had penetrated Rohtina's golden-red hide. It wasn't easy for skith venom to penetrate dragon scale, but there were certain vulnerable areas on their bodies and she had been hit in one of them, just beneath her wing, in the supple crevice where it joined her body. The acid still smoked. Water would counteract that.

As the thought occurred, buckets began making their way to her side, a number of knights pitching in to help the wounded dragon. Lars directed them as Gareth helped and Kelvan used his great strength to haul a cistern of water up from the ledge below. He placed it near his mate and the process went much faster as the men could fill the buckets from a nearer source, splashing each one carefully to do the most good.

The ledges were built in such a way that the acid-laced water drained off, over the side of the cliff, well away from any place humans or dragons would come into contact with it. Besides that, the water had weakened the acid to the point where it was more or less safe. It would continue degrading over time all by itself, so the forest below would come to no harm from this emergency drenching.

Belora, help my mate. I beg you. Worry and pain filled Kelvan's voice, and it echoed through the minds of all present, making a few pause in surprise. Belora moved forward to face the green-blue dragon with the emerald eyes.

"I don't know what I can do, Kel. You know my healing talent has never been strong. But if I can help her, you know too that I'll do everything in my power to do so."

Kelvan bowed his great head. *Then go to her. Place your hands on her as you did with me and concentrate. Your power is greater than you know and perhaps the only thing that can save her now.*

Belora looked uncertain, but moved to the golden dragon's side. Up close now, she could see that Rohtina had used all her strength to get back to the Lair. She was badly injured and probably close to death from such extensive damage. The heart she had shown in flying all the way here with no complaint was amazing and Belora felt tears gather behind her eyes.

Gingerly, she reached out and touched the dragon's shimmering golden hide, now burnt brown and black in places, red in others where she bled heavily.

Concentrate, Belora, as your mother trained you to do.

Kelvan's voice in her mind encouraged her and gave her something to focus on as she gathered the energies that her mother had taught her to recognize, though they never seemed to do what she wished. She had never been a strong healer of humans, but Kelvan insisted that what power she did have felt good to dragons. She had to believe him.

You can do it, Belora. I have faith in you. You were meant to heal dragons. Not humans. Dragons. You are one of us.

There was no higher compliment a human could receive from a dragon and everyone within hearing distance heard and watched, with varying degrees of awe and suspicion. Belora forced all those watching eyes out of her mind as she focused the energy that was part of her. It leapt to life, as it had never done before, when she touched Rohtina's scarred hide gently.

Suddenly it was all clear. She knew what she had to do.

Belora placed her palms over the ridges of Rohtina's amber eyes, locking her green human gaze securely on the dragon's faceted orbs. Belora felt the power flowing through her as never before as she formed the connection with the dragon on several levels.

Belora screamed, feeling just the echo of Rohtina's great pain as her own, but after a moment it began to subside. She felt Lars and Gareth behind her, ready to support her if needed and her heart filled with love. The love too, transferred to the dragon and reflected back. Rohtina and she joined as one for a breathtaking moment out of time, then the power surged to life within Belora and poured out into the dragon. It went on and on until finally the spell was broken by Rohtina's blinking jeweled amber eyes. They sparkled with life and renewed vitality and a small tear leaked out one side, dropping down onto Belora's elbow, landing there and solidifying into a magical gem.

Thank you.

Dragons did not cry, but when stirred by great emotion, their magic could release itself in a tear that turned to a precious, magical gem. That Rohtina gifted Belora with the sparkling topaz jewel was amazing in itself, but even more amazing was the result of the magical healing. Rohtina was completely well. Not a scratch remained on her badly mangled hide. She was whole and healthy once more.

And Belora realized one other little thing that had seeped into her mind while they'd been connected.

"You're pregnant!"

Her whispered words were followed by a shout of joy from the watching knights. A dragon pregnancy or birth was always a cause for great celebration since there were so few each year.

I wasn't sure yet. Rohtina said shyly, the first hint of shyness Belora had ever seen from the magnificent golden dragon.

"Be sure." Belora removed her hands from Rohtina's eye ridges and cupped her rounded cheek. "I felt the presence of the dragonet within you. It is well and happy."

Praise the Mother of All that you were here, milady. Thank you for saving my mate and my child. Kelvan nudged her with his great head, moving closer to his golden mate.

"It was your faith that made me believe I could, Kel. I've never done that before in my life!" Belora laughed now in relief as the dragons surrounded her with their immense bodies and their love and joy.

Yet it is what you were born to do. Your power is the strongest I have ever felt, even though it's mostly untrained. You were never meant to heal humans, as your mother does. Your power is definitely more dragonish. I felt it that first night you sent your power to me. It's the most amazing thing I've ever encountered.

"It feels pretty amazing to me too, and kind of unreal, but I'm so happy you're okay, Rohtina." She stroked both long necks and smiled brightly as her own mates came up on either side of her.

"That was amazing." Gareth stopped in front of her and shocked her by kneeling. Lars did the same, grasping her hand and kissing the back of it with his eyes tightly shut against the emotions nearly overwhelming him.

"Thank you, my love, from the bottom of my heart. You amaze me."

"Why are you both down there? Get up." Her amused and embarrassed whisper brought smiles to their faces. She looked up and realized all the knights gathered were now kneeling and offering signs of respect to her.

"What's going on?"

"We honor you, Belora." Gareth explained softly. "It's well known that only those with royal blood have the power to heal dragons. From what we've all just witnessed, we know that you are of the line of Draneth the Wise. Somehow, some way, you are descended of kings."

"No way."

"Yes, my love," Lars squeezed her hand. "There's no other explanation. The Mother of All brought you to us in our time of need and now, with you here, we know our cause is just and our mission sanctioned by the Mother herself, for it was She that blessed Draneth and the dragons and brought them together. Just as She brought you to us."

"I can't believe this." Her eyes wandered over the kneeling knights in something like shock.

She swayed on her feet as the rush of energy began to leave her. Lars held tightly to one hand while in the other, she clutched the sparkling golden topaz dragon tear. It gave her some energy, but her strength was fast fading.

Gareth and Lars got to their feet and caught her as she began to lose consciousness. With deep concern, they carried her from the ledge to their apartments. They worried until Kelvan took a moment away from his recovering mate to reassure them.

The older dragons tell me that after a healing such as the one she just performed, it's normal for the healer to require a day of sleep to recover. Don't worry. She'll be all right tomorrow. It's just draining to do what she did, plus too, it was her first time so she's not used to the strain. She'll learn to handle the power with more finesse as she uses it. Just let her sleep.

Belora woke over twelve hours later, comfortable in her warm bed. She was naked under the furs with her two mates sleeping on either side of her. Gareth had his hand at her waist, one of his strong thighs between hers as he spooned her from behind. Lars faced her, his arm pillowing her head as he breathed softly into her hair, tickling her ever so slightly with his warm breath.

She looked out into the suite and saw Rohtina and Kelvan snuggling together in their wallow. Kelvan had one blue-green wing resting lightly over his mate and their necks were twined together lovingly. She felt a wave of love pass through her at the sight and realized that her small movements had woken her men.

Lars kissed her before she could even speak. It was a long, deep, hot kiss that spoke of love, commitment, passion, and joy. When he pulled back, he looked deep down into her eyes.

"Thank you, Belora. You saved us all when you saved Tina. I'll never be able to find the words to express—" he choked up a bit and she moved to kiss him, silencing his tumbling thoughts.

"I think I know what she means to you, at least a little. You don't have to thank me. I would do anything in the world for you, Lars, and for Kel and Tina. You all are my family and I love you." She kissed him once more and felt a stirring behind her as Gareth rolled her onto her back and loomed over her.

"And where do I fit into the equation?" The light in his eyes told her he was teasing. He knew full well where he fit in her heart and in her life, but it was good to say the words.

"You're the one who brought us all together."

Actually, I think that was my role. An amused dragon voice sounded in their heads as Kel brought his great head over to rest in the doorway, watching them. *After all, I'm the one who found you in the forest, milady.*

Belora sat up and regarded the dragon with some consternation. "What's with the 'milady' stuff, Kel? Why are you suddenly calling me that?"

Kel drew his head up to look down at the trio in the bed. *Because you are undoubtedly of the royal line. We dragons struck a deal with Draneth the Wise millennia ago and as his kin, you deserve respect.*

"How in the world do you figure I'm related to the king's line? I mean, I know that healing thing was awfully strange, but my mother heals people. What I did can't be all that different."

Ah, but it is. Rohtina's graceful neck lifted her golden head to rest near Kelvan in the doorway. *It's a gift of wizards alone and there's no true wizard blood left in this realm but for the royal line.*

Rohtina stretched to rub her sensitive neck scales along her mate's and all three in the bed felt the renewed arousal.

"We can argue about bloodlines later," Gareth grumbled, catching Belora about the waist and tugging her down on the bed once more. "For now, we have more important things to do."

Lars, not to be outdone, pulled her on top of him, using his powerful muscles to lift them both into a sitting position against the headboard of the huge bed. He positioned her across his lap so that she was straddling him while Gareth moved behind her. They felt the dragons withdraw to their large wallow, rolling and twining together as the heat rose between them.

The humans felt the same heat, sharing it with the dragons as Lars tested his mate's readiness with a few teasing, tantalizing fingers. He stopped, his fingers high up inside her, to look deeply into her eyes.

"Tina's pregnant."

"Yes, she is. So?" Her voice was more than a little breathy with Lars' fingers lodged inside her and Gareth stroking her breasts from behind.

"So you could be too."

Belora gasped as he rubbed that spot right up inside her that always made her squirm. "Mmm. Yes, I could."

"Would you like that? Do you want our baby?" His turquoise eyes sought her gaze, something deep inside, yearning in him. She could feel it.

She leaned forward to kiss him. "I want your baby. And Gareth's. I want a bunch of children with you both."

He sighed as he removed his fingers, caressing her as he moved her into position over his hard dick.

"Then we'd better get to work on them. What do you say?"

"Oh, yes," she breathed as he settled her down over his hard, solid length. He slid home as she writhed on top of him, her inner muscles clenching around him.

She could hear the dragons making a mess of the sand in the central chamber and knew they were nearing completion. It wouldn't be long now before both her men claimed her in perfect union with the dragons that shared their souls.

Gareth pushed her down onto Lars' chest and prepared her rear entrance. He bent over her, biting at her earlobe as he pushed himself home within her tight ass.

"If you have Lars' baby first, I want to be next."

"Yes. Anything, Gareth! I'll do anything you want."

"Now that's what I like to hear." He chuckled as he slid all the way home, the slow and easy passion the dragons were sharing this time having the same effect on the human side of the partnership. "You've had her pussy a lot lately, Lars. I take it you want to plant our first baby?"

Lars began to move in her body as soon as Gareth was fully seated. The men moved in rhythm, driving her wild as they timed their thrusts for greatest impact.

Lars grunted. "If you have no objection."

"Can you two discuss this later?"

The last word rose to a screech as she came hard around both of their cocks and they just kept pumping. She knew then that they'd bring her to orgasm multiple times before the dragons were finished with them. The frantic mating flights of the first few days had settled into long, drawn-out sessions in the sand that were echoed by the humans in hours of love play and the most incredible waves of pleasure she had yet experienced.

"Ssh, Belora, this is very important." Gareth's teeth teased her ear as he pumped steadily into her from behind. "Someone has to make plans here." He stroked her just a little more deeply. "Now what do you think about our first child being fair and blonde like Lars? Or would you rather have a dark haired tyke first?"

"Either. Both! I don't care!" She sobbed as she neared another peak, even higher than the last.

"Oh, but you must," Gareth chastised her as he rode her through another shattering climax.

"I want…" she panted to catch her breath and her scattered senses. "I want both kinds. Whenever the Mother grants it. I want both."

"Well, if that's what you really want, I suppose that's just what you'll get." Gareth stroked harder, his breath coming a bit shorter now as the dragons neared completion, urging on their knights. Lars too was pounding into her pussy now, stroking her higher and higher still.

"Sweet Mother, Gareth! You're right. Twins!" Lars pushed deeper now, his turquoise eyes bright with both satisfaction and hunger.

"Twins?!" she shrieked as she came yet again and still they drove her higher.

"When knight pairs mate with females of the royal line," he was panting, nearer now, "the Mother and Her magic often bless them with twins." He was close now and she climbed high once more. The dragons rolled furiously just outside the door, grunting and roaring just a little as smoke filled the air in the slight dome above their wallow. "One from each…" He dug into her as Lars did, both nearing their crisis point.

"Sweet Mother!" Lars swore as he started to come along with his dragon partner. Rohtina's cry sounded through the suite of rooms followed only a second later by Kelvan's harsh grunt.

Gareth came when Kel did and both knights filled her to overflowing as she screamed their names and convulsed between them. It went on and on as the dragons dragged out their pleasure. Gareth collapsed on them, squashing her for just a few moments between her men, a position she loved. Lars supported them against the padded headboard, his body spasming within her as the pleasure drained from him in long, hot waves.

When they finally found the strength to pull apart and settle bonelessly on the huge bed, Belora thought over what Gareth had said.

"Twins?" Her voice was soft and dreamy. "Truly?"

Gareth reached over to stroke her cheek. "It's more than a possibility. If you're of the royal blood—and I have little doubt you are—then the wizard magic is in your veins. You'll carry one baby from each of us."

"Oh, that would be so beautiful."

"I'm glad you think so." Lars leaned up on one elbow looking down at her, the love in his eyes shining bright in the dim room. "I want a big family. I want our children to have what I never did. I want them to belong to each other and to us."

Belora launched herself into her mate's strong arms. "That's the most beautiful thing I've ever heard." A tear found its way down her cheek and Lars bent to kiss it away. "I want the same thing."

"Then we're all in agreement." Gareth poured wine for each of them from the bedside table and passed the goblets around as they all sat up, some strength returning.

"I didn't thank you both yet for going to save my mother."

"Our children will need their grandmother. Especially when their parents want to spend some time alone." Gareth wiggled his eyebrows and chuckled, making them all laugh.

"No, I mean it. Truly. I didn't think I could love either of you more, but when you put your lives on the line for my mother, I knew that if I lost any of you—human or dragon—I never would be the same. I would never be whole again."

"But what about the king?" Lars spoke softly from the far side of the bed. "You'll have to go meet him and investigate where you come from. The royal blood is too precious to remain anonymous. What if you're a princess? Will you still want to live with us in this backwater Lair?"

She reached over to stroke his stubbly cheek. "Even if I were the queen, I'd never give you up. I love you." She narrowed her eyes in thought. "Though I suppose it is possible that I have some strange origins."

"Why do you say that?" Gareth moved up to support her from behind as they lounged on the huge bed.

"It's something Kelzy told my mother. She said that her parents weren't her blood parents, that it was obvious to Kelzy that my mother had been adopted."

"Adopted?" Gareth prompted her when her words trailed off.

"Yes, but she never found out from where, or who her real parents might be."

"By the Mother, then it's more than likely your mother's real parents were of royal descent."

"I guess that could be true." She shrugged. "And twins do run in my family. My mother doesn't speak of them much, but before me, she had twin girls. They were taken just before we moved to the forest when I was about five winters, I think."

"Taken? You mean they died?" Gareth had perked up and looked keenly interested.

"No, they're not dead. At least I don't think they are. They were stolen. It was horrible." She shuddered and leaned into Lars' supporting arm as both men moved closer at the first sign of her distress. "We were in a big town, at a market. Men rushed us. Big men. I remember one had a jagged scar on his face and was missing the two little fingers on his left hand." She shuddered and strong arms went around her, soothing her. "They hit my mother and grabbed my sisters. They were too strong for her and no one would help us. The scarred man tried to grab me, but my mother held me tight and started running. She ran and ran. They pursued us, but didn't catch her. She may be small, but she's fast." A small, sad smile lifted one side of her face. "She went back and tried to find my sisters, but they were gone. We left that day and never went back."

"So the reason she went to the forest, way out in the middle of nowhere was because she was hiding?" Lars puzzled through the situation with his calm logic.

"I never thought of that, but I guess it could be true. We didn't have any money and when we came across the cottage, it was empty. No one claimed it when we asked in the village and they welcomed the idea of having a healer move in closer to the village. Some of them even helped Mama in the early days, bringing her food and household items to trade for her herbal remedies. That's how we've lived for the past decade and more."

"How old were your sisters when they were taken?" Gareth's voice was calm but very serious.

"I was about five, so I guess they were about ten or eleven."

"Then they'd be in their early twenties now. Twenty-three or so."

"Yes, I guess so." She nodded, settling back into their arms. She saw the look of determination pass between her two mates and wondered at it.

"We have to find them." Lars' quiet voice made her sit up in surprise.

"What?"

"Your sisters. We have to find them. Royal blood is too precious, and women who potentially have the ability to heal dragons and be mates to our brethren are scarcer than even that. We have to alert the other Lairs to be on the lookout for your sisters. Dragons and their knights may be able to sniff them out, now that we know they exist."

Hope entered her heart. "Do you really think so?"

Lars stroked her cheek. "I believe it with all my heart."

"The Mother of All brought you and your mother to us, didn't She?" Gareth sought her eyes, his own smiling softly in the dim room. "Now that we know your sisters could be out there, we'll spread the word. Believe me, there's nothing a knight or dragon likes better than a quest."

All three of them chuckled at that and settled back in the huge bed.

"The Mother did indeed know what She was doing when She brought me to you." Belora's hands snaked out to either side to grasp her mates' hands tightly in her own, her thoughts spinning ahead to the possibility of finding her sisters. The future looked bright indeed.

BORDER LAIR

Dragon Knights Book 2

DEDICATION

To all the wonderful, supportive people on my discussion list, and especially Megan, Serena, Tam, Diana and Jess. Thanks for believing in dragons and believing in me.

PROLOGUE

The feminine moan of pleasure was music to Lord Darian's ears as he brought Varla to yet another peak with his tongue. She was greedy, but then, being the king of Skithdron's current favorite had to leave her cold. The lecherous bastard had become king after killing his own father—or so Lord Darian suspected—and didn't give a rat's ass about anyone's pleasure but his own.

"Are you ready for me now, Varla?" Darian looked down on the woman with little feeling as he rammed his cock into her.

"More than ready, my lord!"

The bitch was panting and practically tearing his skin off with those long red painted claws of hers. He moved her hands, grasping them tightly and holding them forcibly above her head, away from his skin. He'd be damned if he would wear her bloody marks after this bout. He was here for one reason alone.

Well, maybe two reasons, he admitted with a mental shrug. Getting his rocks off was part of the deal and a good reason to bed a willing wench, but the more important reason was this particular wench could grant him access to places in the palace he otherwise would not have. If he were seen coming from her chambers, so close to the king's own apartments, it would be more natural if he was her fuck for the night. If not for her, the guards would question his presence in the palace. If not for her, Lord Venerai would have him run out of the palace completely, denying him his right as a noble of Skithdron to serve at court.

Venerai was a viper. Climbing to the top of the pile of Lucan's sycophants by any means necessary, Venerai wanted all possible competition for the King's favor out of his way. That included Darian, though he had been more in favor with Lucan's father, King Goran, than with the current king.

But Darian was of royal blood, a distant fifth in line for the throne, and Venerai saw him as a threat. He went so far as to have Darian followed by an inept spy or two—spies he liked to send on wild goose chases, much to Venerai's disgust.

Darian would tire Varla out then go on his real mission of the night. He suspected some awful things were about to transpire but he had to have proof before he gave up his birthright. If he were going to forsake his country, his lands, his title, and risk his very life, he had to be damned sure of his information.

He rammed the wench harder as determination fed his strength. This final round ought to do her in, and then he could go on his little reconnaissance mission. First he had to fuck her into oblivion though and that was proving harder than he'd thought. Not only was she insatiable, but he just wasn't interested enough in her to make it really worth his while. Oh, she was a sweet release to his aching balls, but she failed to meet the strange yearning that had been building inside him for years now.

He really didn't know what he was looking for, but all the women in his life to this point were definitely not it. There was not one he would regret leaving behind if it did become necessary to leave his homeland. Not one he would consider asking to go with him. Not one he could love.

That was just a shame. How did a man pass thirty-seven winters without finding one single woman he could care for at least enough to make some small commitment? He didn't even have a steady mistress.

Was there something wrong with him? He was past the age where most men settled down with one woman and started reproducing, but he'd never found the woman he wanted to birth his heirs. Never found a woman he wanted so much he would pray to the gods his seed took root in her womb. He couldn't imagine ever finding such a woman among the many he'd tried on for size, but oh, how he had enjoyed the search.

Varla was a hot fuck and she writhed on his cock in a way that had him fighting to control his release, but she was just a means to an end. She had already been claimed by the ruthless bastard who now sat on the stolen throne of Skithdron. Darian might enjoy the pleasure of her body, but he felt nothing for the cold woman inside.

And he knew she felt nothing for him. Even as she came for the seventh time that night under his pounding, he knew she cared more for the sexual release than for the man who gave it to her. After all, she had already sold her soul to the devil.

After finally exhausting the voracious creature, Darian made his way to the king's study. Using all his stealth, he found the grim proof he had been searching for—and dreading—and his old adversary Lord Venerai was right in the thick of it. Darian's course now was clear.

In that moment, Lord Darian of Skithdron became a traitor. At least that's how King Lucan and his followers would see his actions. Still, Darian knew sitting by and doing nothing while a mad king herded deadly, venomous skiths toward innocent villagers would be a crime he could not live with on his soul. What the king had planned next was even worse, and his ultimate goal was completely insane.

But King Lucan was so far gone in his madness his plan just might work. Someone had to warn Draconia. The peaceful land had been a good neighbor to Skithdron for many generations, but it was all coming to ruin now with one crazy tyrant. Darian now knew beyond the shadow of a doubt, Lucan sought power through demented magics that drove him closer and closer to the edge.

Lucan had to be stopped and Darian was the only one to do it. For one thing, Darian had no immediate family against whom Lucan could retaliate. For another, as the former ambassador to Draconia, he had contacts in high places. If he could just get across the border and then across the lines to the Draconian side, he might have a shot at getting his message through to the people—and dragons—who needed most to know.

CHAPTER ONE

Adora opened her eyes slowly, her head tilted to the side as she lay on her stomach. She could just make out the huge form of Sir Jared, hovering over her, as he had for the past few days. His ruggedly handsome face carried a stark, broad scar down one cheek and onto his neck. The ragged mark of his warrior profession disappeared below the neckline of his shirt, making her curious to see just how far down it went on his broad, muscular chest.

"How are you feeling?" His voice was husky with disuse and she guessed it was late in the night.

"Jared, you should really seek your own bed. Sitting up with me does neither of us any good."

The knight favored her with a small smile as he poured a cup of water from the pitcher on the bedside table. Hearing the splash of water suddenly made her thirsty as her tongue moved around in a cottony mouth.

"Humor me, Adora. Besides, Kelzy wouldn't let me leave, even if I wanted to try." His gaze shifted to the wide archway, neatly blocked by the blue-green dragon's great head. Kelzy blinked at him sleepily—even the huge dragon showed weariness in the vigil she'd kept at Adora's side for the past few days.

Jared sat on the side of the bed with a gentleness she found astounding in such a powerful warrior knight. He was so big and muscular, so able to fight and destroy, but she had learned over the past days his magnificent warrior's body housed a gentle soul.

Because of the deep, slashing wounds that reached around from her back to one side, she had to lie on her stomach or the uninjured side and found it difficult to use one of her arms. Levering herself off the bed even to drink a glass of water was almost impossible to accomplish alone. Jared lent her his great strength every time she needed to rise and use the bathroom or as now, take a drink of water.

He slipped one hand under her torso from the uninjured side, his forearm settling intimately between her breasts as he spread his hand against the opposite shoulder. This odd position allowed her to use her one good arm to push herself upward while he held her securely, in case her strength gave out. As it was, her arm trembled as he held the cup of water to her parched lips. She wasn't entirely sure whether her weakness was from the injury or the mere proximity of the dashing knight.

It had been years since she'd been touched so closely by a man, and never by a man such as this. Jared took her breath away. A warm gust of air settled over her from the direction of the dragon in the doorway. Adora swiveled her head to look at Kelzy, but the motion caused her healing wounds to pull and she gasped. Jared reacted instantly, sliding both hands up her torso, supporting her, guiding her gently back to lie on her stomach.

"Easy now." Jared's voice was so warm and soft. It made Adora feel safe and protected. She tried not to think about the hand resting between her breasts as he lowered her slowly to the bed, nor the way he slid his rough hand out from between the sheets and her body, his strong fingers grazing the swollen sides of her breasts.

"Can you help me turn to lie on my side? My neck hurts a bit from sleeping in this position."

"So you admit you do need me here after all?" He chuckled and it warmed her heart.

Jared was always so serious that it was good to hear him laugh as he put his big hands on her once more. He handled her as if she were a priceless treasure but with a strength that would not be denied. Never had such a masterful man been so intimate with her body. Her long-dead husband's touch had been quite different. Jared was strong and sure, yet showed obvious care in the way he used his strength.

Adora liked the way he touched her. She liked him, if she was being honest with herself. Jared was a man among men, otherwise the dragon who had been like her surrogate mother would never have chosen him as her partner. Not only the dragoness, Kelzy, but King Roland himself entrusted a great deal to this man, for Adora had learned Jared was a general in the king's fighting forces. Jared and Kelzy were the leaders of this new Lair filled with dozens of knights and fighting dragons.

"I admit nothing." She enjoyed challenging him and smiled as Jared paused, his hands around her, his face very near.

"Adora…"

She felt his grip tighten on her and saw his face lower. She hadn't been kissed in far too many years, but still remembered the signs. She knew she could turn away—his approach was slow enough to give her time to call a halt if she wished—but she wanted his kiss. Suddenly, she wanted nothing more desperately in the world.

The moment his lips touched hers she knew why. His kiss was everything. Soft and gentle at first, firming to hard, demanding, male. Oh, so male, and so missed. She had missed this in her many years of widowhood. She had missed a man's strong hands molding her body while his lips and tongue plundered her mouth.

After the first few blissful moments, Jared's kiss turned molten and hungry. Powered by a lust that fired through his veins, he seemed to ignite as their lips came together for the very first time.

"Adora." He broke off the kiss but buried his hungry lips in her throat, nibbling at her soft skin.

"Jared," she whispered. His nipping teeth were just powerful enough that she knew he would leave a mark on her tender skin. The thought excited her. Never had a man been so hot for her, or she for him.

Interesting as this development is, Kelzy's dryly amused voice sounded through both of their minds, bringing them back to earth with a thud, *Adora's still hurt, Jared. Leave off before one of her wounds reopens.*

"Sweet Mother of All." Jared released her slowly. His blue eyes smoldered with something like shock laced with a bit of anger and frustration as he looked down at her. "Did I hurt you, Adora?"

She shook her head slightly, but his hand traced down her throat to the tender spot he had bitten, and their eyes locked and held. She suspected he had bruised her on purpose and she would wear his mark for a few days.

"Nothing significant." She tried to put his mind at ease about the love bite, but his expression went cold, and she realized her words might have sounded different than she meant them. She tried to find words to fix her error, but Jared was already on his way out the door. He was gone before she could speak and she found herself lying on her side, staring at the dragon in her doorway with mixed feelings. "I didn't mean that the way it sounded."

I know, my dear child. Jared is a hard man. His emotions are held close inside. In fact, I'm amazed he even let go enough to kiss you. He's not a knight to court the ladies. Let him be for a while. He has much in his past that he needs to come to terms with if he is to ever reclaim that portion of his life.

After long moments thinking on the dragon's words and that startling kiss, Adora finally slept.

The next day Adora woke to an empty chamber for the first time since she'd been hurt. Her back was on fire with pain as she slowly remembered the events that had confined her to the bed for the past few days. She'd come under attack by huge venom-spitting skiths while walking back to her forest home. Her little house in the woods was destroyed now, infested and torn apart by the giant snake-like creatures their Skithdronian enemies drove across the border.

Adora had only escaped them and their snapping jaws by climbing the tallest tree she could find. She'd known she was going to die, clinging to the top of a tree, her specially treated leather clothing smoking from the spray of skith venom that had hit her from the waist down.

A scream had sounded through her mind as she prayed to the Mother of All that her end would be fast and as painless as possible. Then Adora had sought the mind of the dragoness who had practically raised her. Her mind had sent out a call—much stronger than she realized—to Lady Kelzy and miraculously, the dragon had heard. Kelzy had summoned her knight, Sir

Jared, and two other fighting dragons and knights and raced to her rescue. It was Kelzy who had plucked her out of the tree with wickedly sharp claws.

And for that brave action, Kelzy was in torment now, Adora knew. The dragoness blamed herself for the scratches she had unwillingly inflicted on Adora's back with the razor sharp talons. Adora also knew the daring mid-air grab was the only way she could have been rescued from that tree without putting all of them in even more danger from the multitude of crazed skiths twining around its base.

Skiths were afraid of dragon fire, but had their own weapons and could fell a dragon with alarming ease. Lady Rohtina, the young golden dragon, had in fact been mortally wounded while providing cover for Kelzy's daring swoop. Thank the Mother, Rohtina had been healed of her grave wounds. She had managed to limp back to the Lair, at which point Adora's daughter, Belora, had been able to heal her. It had been a very close call though. One that drove home to all that war with Skithdron was coming fast, and this sudden invasion by venomous skiths was only the first wave.

Adora shrank back with a sigh as the cuts on her back protested. They had scabbed over for the most part but were still very painful. Kelzy's apologetic and remorseful clucking almost made it hurt more. Adora told the dragon over and over that she was not to blame but Kelzy would hear none of it. She was wracked with guilt over hurting her "baby" even it if had been the only way to save her life.

Kelzy's knight partner kept careful watch over her too. Sir Jared had barely left her alone, forever checking her wounds or seeking to make her more comfortable. Jared wasn't a chatty sort of man, but his steady, unsmiling presence had been oddly comforting. He was so solid and had such a pure heart. He had been hurt deeply—Adora knew with a certainty stemming from her own healing gift and intuitive nature—but he was a good honest man, though one who did not make friends easily.

He was also more ruggedly handsome than any man Adora had ever seen. Appearing only slightly older than she, he had short dark brown hair gone silver at his temples and striking deep ocean blue eyes. He kept himself neat at all times and commanded great respect from all the other knights as well as the dragons who lived in this new Lair.

Adora knew his bond with Kelzy kept Jared from aging as a normal man would. When dragons bonded with their knights, and by extension with their knights' chosen mate, the dragon magic worked to slow the humans' aging process considerably. Jared had partnered with Kelzy more than a decade ago and he probably hadn't aged much since, though his penetrating gaze reflected the wisdom of his years.

Adora dozed through most of the day, only waking when Jared came to bring her meals. He was distant today after their passionate encounter and made no reference to it, only staring long and hard at the purple love bite on her neck when he'd first seen her. Other than the leap of fire in his eyes when he saw his mark upon her skin, he had shown no emotion at all. Adora quickly gave up on the idea of trying to explain her hasty words of the night before. She was too tired anyway and in too much pain to sort it out now. She fell into a deep sleep that night without further complications from Jared.

CHAPTER TWO

The black dragon winged in under cover of darkness. No one saw him land except the few sentries posted to stand guard and lend assistance to any who should need it. Black dragons were rare. In fact, only the royal line could boast the starkly gleaming tar-colored scales that characterized this dragon, so it was understandable word of his presence in the Lair spread quickly.

The tall man who emerged from the shadows a few moments later—dressed all in black, with the same gleaming dark light in his hazel eyes as that of the dragon—strode forward confidently though he'd never visited this Lair before. The sentries bowed to him, as was his due, and received a regal nod in return.

He was not the king, but he was damn close. Prince Nico preferred to leave the political intrigues to his older brother while he pursued more…stealthy pursuits. As spymaster for the king, he was aptly suited to the task at hand. Nico had not arrived at this new Border Lair by accident. No, he was on a mission of the highest importance to the royal family. His mission would either bring rare royal blood back into the fold or expose an imposter.

The Prince of Spies. That's what the dragons laughingly called him and it was an apt title. He prided himself on his ability to get in and out of places with none the wiser to his presence, but the trip to this out-of-the-way Lair was official business.

Greetings, Lady Kelzy. What news do you have for me? Nico sent the message to the mind of the blue-green dragon whose glistening body was spread out in the wallow before him. He'd known the layout of the new Lair even before he left the palace and had made it his business to know where the leaders of this particular Lair lived. Kelzy's head rose up in surprise, swiveling on the long, sinuous neck to face him. Her aquamarine eyes glinted with happiness.

Nico! You're here already. I should have known you'd hear about the events of the last few days before we could send official word.

Prince Nico loved the easy manner of this particular dragon. She had taught him a great deal as a youngster and guarded him when he was still too young to protect himself. In a way, she had been like a second mother to him and his brothers, though she was just one of many dragons who served the royal family directly.

Her knight partner, though, was one of Nico's favorite people in the world. Sir Jared had taught him to fight and how to protect himself. He had also trained the young prince in the arts that helped him become not only a spy and reluctant politician, but a true diplomat when it was needed.

Prior to the tragedy that had taken his wife and child from him, Sir Jared Armand had been one of the old king's most trusted counselors. That one horrible event had taken the spark from Jared's eyes and sent him into self-imposed exile in the mountains. It was there Kelzy found him and finally claimed the man as her knight partner. The soul-deep bond between dragon and knight gave Jared renewed purpose, though he was still alone and would probably never marry again. The first time had undoubtedly been much too painful to bear.

Nico bowed in respect to the motherly dragon and smiled as she moved closer to him.

It's true then, what I've heard? You've found a mother and daughter who display the royal gifts?

Kelzy's great head bobbed in eagerness. *Both Adora and her daughter, Belora, are true healers. Belora healed a mortal wound to Rohtina, the dragon partner of Lars, one of Belora's mates.*

How did Rohtina come by her injuries?

You mean you don't already know? Kelzy's eyes snapped in humor at the Prince of Spies.

Actually, I can guess. Skiths? He fairly spit the name of the huge snake-like creatures that gave the neighboring kingdom its name. The king of Skithdron was using the skiths on the border—herding them and coaxing them across the border to destroy villages and towns in preparation for a large-scale invasion. The man was mad, Nico suspected. It was said King Lucan had spent too much time tampering with magics better left alone. Rumor had it dark magics had changed him and warped his mind.

Skiths were killing machines that slaughtered everything in their path. The only thing they were even remotely afraid of was fire and luckily the dragons had that in quantity.

The skiths attacked Adora. Jared and I had to snatch her from a tree. Rohtina and my son, Kelvan, engaged the skiths below. That's how Rohtina was so badly injured. She got too close to the skiths and nearly paid with her life.

Where is the woman now?

Kelzy's great head rotated to the doorway where she had been resting when he came in. The suite was arranged, like most sets of rooms in any Lair, around the central, heated oval sand pit that was the dragon's wallow. All the rooms flowed around the wallow with archways large enough for the dragons to lay their heads in if they so desired. In this way, the dragons and their human families could be together in all things.

She lives with you?

She is my daughter. When my last knight died, I went into the forest to recover. I met little Adora there. She was only a toddler when she first found my cave. I returned her to her family, but they couldn't hear me.

But she could?

Kelzy nodded slowly. They both knew the ability to hear dragons was passed from generation to generation. If the people who claimed to be Adora's parents could not hear the dragon as the child could, they were not her birth parents.

She spent most of her time with me until she was just coming into her teen years. That's when your parents were killed and your brother, Roland, took the throne. I moved back to the palace then to aid Roland in his new duties, but it became clear to me over time, that he needed wise counsel. When things had settled and Roland was steadier in his role as king, I set off on my quest, in search of Jared, I remembered him from when he'd served your father. He'd always impressed me as a strong warrior and never failed to give your father good counsel. I hoped he could be convinced to do the same for your brother. It took a while to find him, but when I did...

You chose him as your new knight partner. Nico finished her sentence with a respectful nod.

Kelzy's eyes dimmed with remembered sadness. *I lost track of Adora, I'm shamed to say. I went back to look for her years later, but she was long gone. Her family had moved and no one knew where they went.*

And you just found her again, after all these years?

Actually, my son, Kelvan, found her daughter. The girl was poaching in the forest and they argued over a stag. When she met my son's partner, Gareth, he knew he'd found his mate. We celebrated their joining shortly after. When my son met Adora that first day, she talked of the dragon she knew in her youth and he knew she was talking about me. He convinced her to come here for a visit and we were reunited. The dragon's jeweled eyes sparkled with remembered happiness. *But Adora is a dedicated healer and wanted to return to her hut in the forest so she could tend her patients in the nearby village. When the skiths overran the village, they nearly got her too.*

You said she climbed a tree to get away from them? She sounds like a brave woman.

Brave and ingenious! Jared gave her some treated leather before we left her in the forest and she fashioned it into the most remarkable garments. I asked Jared to give her some of my shed scales and she sewed them between layers of leather in her boots and in strategic spots on her clothes. She got sprayed pretty badly with skith venom, but not a scratch on her.

Then why is she recuperating? How did she get hurt?

That was my doing. I had to snatch her out of the tree and I clipped her with my talons. Kelzy seemed very upset by the incident. *I hurt my own girl! How could I have been so clumsy?*

It happens to the best of us, Lady Kelz. It's hard to be perfectly accurate all the time, much less under combat conditions, with such wickedly sharp talons. Don't be so hard on yourself.

You're a good boy, Nico.

The prince laughed outright. *Only you would have the nerve to call me that, Lady Kelz.*

At that moment, Jared emerged from the doorway Kelzy had indicated was Adora's room, surprising Nico. The older knight looked worn and tired, but there was a light in his eyes that had been missing for many, many years.

"Nico, my boy! When did you get here?"

A smile spilt the older man's face as he moved forward to catch Nico in a fierce hug. Jared was one of the few people in the world who would dare approach Nico and his siblings with such familiarity, but he was also one of the few people in the world who Nico actually loved as if he were part of his own family. Jared had been there for him after his parents' deaths, and for that he would forever love the slightly older, wiser man.

"I just got here a few minutes ago. Kelzy was filling me in on the history of your guest."

"Adora." The way Jared spoke the woman's name sent up warning signals in Nico's mind. There was something between them, he realized with a start, though he never thought Jared would heal enough to let another woman into his life, even just a little.

"You think she's of royal blood?"

Jared nodded. "I can't see any other explanation for what's happened. Her daughter definitely has the wizard gift. She healed a dragon's mortal wounds in front of half the Lair. They're all treading on eggshells around her now from what I hear." Jared chuckled, offering Nico a drought of mulled wine from the small kitchen area. "You'll stay with us, won't you?"

Nico took the goblet and smiled. "I'd enjoy that. If I'm here long enough."

Adora stirs. Kelzy sent her thoughts to both men. Jared instantly moved to the archway, a look of touching concern on his weathered face. Nico suspected the older knight was already half in love with the mysterious woman who could very well be a lost member of the royal family.

"Perhaps I can help?"

Nico didn't make the offer lightly. The royal line was said to be among the last of the wizard blood in this realm, and each of them had some healing talent. Nico didn't use his often, but it was there. He could do small healings, but his true magic was something far different. Still, if he could help this woman who clearly meant so much to two beings he valued so highly, he would do what he could.

Kelzy's glowing eyes pinned him. *Would you? Oh, Nico, I'd be forever grateful! We don't have another true healer in this Lair. Her daughter's gift only works on dragons, not humans.*

Nico knew the dragon didn't bother stating the obvious—that Kelzy's own magical healing ability, known as the Dragon's Breath, could not heal wounds made by dragons or that Adora's own healing skills were useless on her own wounds. It was a quirk of magic that healers generally couldn't heal themselves.

The prince followed Jared into the small guest room, noting instantly the unusual tenderness with which the older knight stilled the thrashing body of a small woman mostly hidden under the covers. Nico moved closer to stand on the other side of the bed as Kelzy's head filled the doorway, watching all closely. The dragon hovered over the woman as if she was truly her own dragonet, and Nico had to hide a smile at Kelzy's completely un-dragonish behavior. That was one of the many things he loved about this particular dragon. She never let anyone—be they dragon or human, prince or pauper— dictate her actions. Kelzy was her own dragon, through and through.

Nico could see the woman more clearly now and she was definitely a beauty. Only a little older than him, she looked somewhere near thirty winters or so. Though if she had a grown daughter, she must be a bit older than that. Still, she was a beauty. Her flowing hair was auburn in the dim light of the room and her features could almost be described as fragile though what he could see of her bare arms were lithely muscled and firm. Judging by the muscle, she had not lived a life of leisure, but she looked every inch the fair damsel. And she was most definitely in distress.

Jared soothed the woman and drew her onto her stomach, pulling the blanket away from her loose bandages. Three angry red, parallel furrows were partially covered by light swaths of linen across her back.

"Adora, wake up." Jared spoke softly near her ear and her head shifted sideways toward the knight.

Nico saw her eyes open and was stunned by the deep green reflected there. Most of the royal line had green eyes. His own hazel color was the exception rather than the rule.

"Adora, we have a guest. He has a bit of healing skill and is willing to try and help you." She looked as if she would have objected, but Jared placed a finger over her pouty lips, stilling her words. "Just lie still and let us do this for you. You haven't slept well and it pains Kelzy to see you hurting. Think of her before you object."

Nico sensed the resignation in the woman as she turned her tired green eyes to the doorway.

For you, Mama Kelzy.

Nico was amazed by the mental communication all three of them heard in their minds. Unskilled, but powerful, this small woman showed yet another of the gifts of the royal line. While knights could certainly communicate with dragons in such a way, it was a rare female human who could even hear dragons, much less send their own thoughts. All royals could do it, of course, but such a gift was rarer than diamonds among regular folk.

The woman settled down with a sigh, her magnificent green eyes closing as she trusted the men to do what they would. It was clear she had no doubts that Kelzy and Jared would protect her. She trusted them, which was undoubtedly why she didn't question his presence. That and her own pain and fatigue conspired to make his job easier. Willing patients were always preferable to those who were in too much pain to lie quietly. Nico's healing talent was small when compared to some of his kin, so it was important he be able to focus without too much distraction.

Jared stripped away the bandages with a gentle hand, and Nico was surprised by just how badly this little woman was injured. She had borne her injuries without much complaint from what he'd just seen and that was remarkable in his experience. He'd seen these kinds of wounds before and they weren't pleasant. The gouges were deep. Neat and clean, but very deep. Without help, they would take weeks to heal and scar badly, but he thought he could at least speed up the process, to help limit the scarring and take away the worst of the pain.

Focusing his energies, Nico reached out and touched the woman with just his fingertips. Then the strangest thing happened. A flare of light filled the small chamber as his energies met and reacted to hers. There was a moment of resistance, then a moment of pure bliss as the woman's magic welcomed his, aiding him in the healing and directing his meager skill with all the knowledge and power of a highly skilled healer.

Nico found himself wielding the strong healing power with ease. The serious wounds were no challenge to the incredible energy that echoed through him. When he sat back after a few minutes, all of them were smiling and Adora's back was whole and unblemished.

"Merciful Mother." Nico stared at her back in amazement. "That's never happened before."

Your energies recognized each other. They meshed so you could work together. Kelzy spoke softly to all of them. *This confirms it then. Adora has royal blood. This just proved it.*

Adora shifted in the bed, clutching the blanket to her nakedness as she looked at strange man at her side.

"Who are you?"

The rogue smiled and bowed, winking at her. "My name is Nico."

The Prince of Spies, Kelzy supplied with a dragonish cough of laughter. *We'll have to track down exactly where you come from, Adora, but this boy is probably a distant cousin of yours. Don't let the fact that he's a prince stop you from boxing his ears if he gets too fresh.*

"Prince Nicolas?" Adora's eyes widened even more as she realized the prince had just healed her and was even now watching her lounge, half-naked, in bed. Could this day get any stranger?

"I'll leave you to dress, milady. We have much to discuss as soon as you're ready."

The prince winked at her again and walked easily out the door, past Kelzy's bulky head, leaving Adora alone once again with Jared. She looked up at him, seeking answers.

"Did the *prince* just heal my back?"

Jared chuckled but nodded solemnly, his eyes twinkling. "Nico is an old friend, Adora. I've known him since he was just a boy. He's still a bit of a rascal, but a good lad. He came to see if you were what you claim to be."

"I don't claim to be anything!"

Jared shook his head. "That was a bad choice of words on my part. I should have said what you *appear* to be."

"Why?" A knot of fear settled in her stomach and unreasonable anger battled with panic just below the surface. "Just what do I appear to be?"

Jared eyed her bare shoulders, making her all too aware she was naked under the blanket. He stepped back and seemed to force his gaze to meet hers.

"Royalty, milady."

"You've got to be kidding."

He twisted his lips wryly. "Afraid not. Your daughter healed Rohtina's mortal wounds with nary a thought. Healing dragons—now that's a gift reserved to those of royal blood alone, Adora, and you bespeak dragons as easily as a knight. Kelzy heard you call her when you were hiding in that tree. Even I couldn't reach her over such a distance and we're bonded."

"It was an emergency. Sometimes people can do amazing things when faced with a life or death situation."

"That may be the case for others, Adora, but I believe you'll find no ready explanation for the way your magic sparked off the prince's just now. I think the magics recognized each other and that allowed him to use your knowledge and his gift to do a more thorough healing than that lad has ever been able to do before. He's not a strong healer. The most I expected was for him to be able to speed your healing a bit and maybe take some of the pain. Kelzy will back me on this."

Adora shot her gaze to the dragon whose head still filled her doorway. *What Jared says is true. Nico has never been a strong healer. His talents lie elsewhere.*

She stared at them both, speechless for a moment. Flopping her hands down on the blanket, she shook her head.

"I can't deal with this right now. I've got to get dressed. There's a *prince* waiting out there for me to make my *royal* appearance, for heavens' sake! Go away, Jared, and let me dress. I'll deal with all of this once I have some clothes on."

Jared moved toward the archway. "Your leggings were ruined but I found a few things that might fit and put them in the wardrobe for you."

"Thank you, Jared." Her voice went soft as emotion threatened to overwhelm her. "Once again, your thoughtfulness amazes me."

He just shrugged and left, but Kelzy stayed in the doorway as Adora stood. She examined her back as best she could in the polished metal mirror along one wall by the wardrobe. Her skin looked healthy and pink, without a scar in sight. Amazing.

Adora pulled on her own soft leather shirt, needing something familiar to help her deal with the upheaval in her life. She had to search in the wardrobe for leggings that would fit. There was a selection of both skirts and pants in the small cupboard.

Jared must have scrounged clothing from some of the younger boys who lived in the Lair to find leggings that would fit her small frame, and it was these she took from the closet. Adora was used to the feel of soft leather against her skin after having worn the unconventional outfit she'd made for a few weeks.

She needed comfort now. She couldn't worry about style. The reassuring feel of Kelzy's shed scales sewn into the layers of her tight-fitting top made her feel good. Adora only hoped her odd clothing wouldn't offend the prince. He was royalty after all.

More importantly, what would Jared think of the form fitting outfit? He'd given her the costly leather in the first place, way back when she'd stubbornly refused to leave her home in the woods. That such a gruff man would think of her comfort and safety still touched her deep inside. He'd surprised her with the gift, and the precious dragon scales that rightly should've been for his use as Kelzy's partner. Adora felt bad the outfit she'd spent so much time and effort to make was half destroyed now, but the leather top and matching leggings had undoubtedly saved her life when the skiths attacked. Only the specially treated leather and the few precious dragon scales had stood between her and their poisonous venom. She'd felt special wearing those clothes, because the leather and the scales had been a gift from the complex man who waited even now outside her door.

Would he be shocked by her appearance? Would he think her beautiful? It had been so long since Adora had cared what a man thought of her looks. The very idea of it made her heart speed and her palms sweat like a young, untried girl.

You're beautiful, Adora. You were always a pretty child but you've grown into a gorgeous woman, no matter what you're wearing.

"So now you're a mind reader?" Adora raised one eyebrow, turning toward the dragon hovering in her doorway.

We females always tend to worry about how we look to an attractive male.

"Kelzy! The prince is young enough to be my son."

Is not. Besides, who said I was talking about the prince? It's Jared I had in mind. And so did you.

Adora plucked up her courage and strode into the main room, finding the men at the edge of the dragon's wallow. Jared had installed a soft couch and chairs for human visitors' comfort. Being the one in charge of the Lair, Jared probably entertained knights who had to speak to him in privacy about one thing or another, she reasoned. Kelzy had told her all about Jared, and she knew the crafty dragon was doing all she could to promote a match between her and the slightly older knight.

For her part, Adora thought Jared was an amazing man, but wasn't quite sure she could handle *any* man in her life. Though if she had to choose just one, it would probably be Jared. Still, she knew he'd been hurt badly by the death of his wife and child. It was Jared who always backed off when they seemed to be getting close and she respected his right to do so. She wouldn't force herself on any man, even if they did live together at this point because of their close—but separate—ties to Kelzy. Kelzy wanted them both living with her and it was usually unwise not to give a dragoness what she wanted.

Adora squared her shoulders and strode with a confidence she didn't feel to where the men sat. Both had goblets of mulled wine in their hands and were talking easily. Her soft footsteps went unheard as Kelzy moved her great body in the sands, so both men started when she appeared before them. With a lithe grace, she curtsied deeply to the prince in the formal manner.

"Your majesty," she spoke demurely, "I humbly thank you for your healing skill."

The prince surprised her, standing to take her hand in his. He raised her easily to stand beside him.

"Then you feel better?"

"Much better, your majesty."

The prince sighed theatrically. "If you insist on calling me 'your majesty' then I'll have to call you 'milady' and we'll waste all our time on extra words that mean nothing in the grand scheme of things. It's all so tiresome." He sniffed with regal disdain, making Jared laugh out loud. "Please, call me Nico and I'll call you Adora, all right? After all, we're kin."

She gasped. "You can't know that for certain."

"Oh, I think it's safe to say that you have the blood of Draneth the Wise in your veins somewhere. Our magics would not have meshed in such an agreeable way had you not."

Adora swayed on her feet and Nico's strong arm steadied her, guiding her to sit on the couch. Settling her there, he pressed a full goblet into her trembling hand.

"It's impossible."

"No, I'm afraid it's not. I did some research before I left the castle, and it seems there are quite a few members of the various royal lines unaccounted for through the years. The most likely scenario is that you are the Princess Amelia Jane, who was stolen from her home the same night the rest of her family was killed. The baby princess was never found, though the rest of her family was left where they were slain."

Adora found herself reaching out for Jared, needing his strength as the prince relayed the sad facts.

"There was some talk at the time about a maidservant who'd gone missing as well, and many of the chroniclers believed the maid took the baby to safety, but she was never seen again." Nico sat next to them on the long couch, taking her other hand in his. "You would be about the right age to be little Amelia Jane, I think, though you look much younger than your thirty-eight winters."

Adora gasped. "How did you know my age?" Her eyes sought his, her confusion plain, then understanding dawned. "Oh, sweet Mother! The princess you mentioned. She would be thirty-eight?"

Nico nodded. "This year."

Adora felt a tear slide down her cheek, followed by another and another. Kelzy growled, crooning in her dragonish way as she had when Adora had been just a child, but it was Jared who pulled her close against his broad chest, comforting her with his warm strength.

"Do you have anything from your childhood, Adora? Anything that might tie you to your past?"

She sniffled, cuddling against Jared as if she belonged there. Turning slightly, she looked up at the handsome prince.

"Only one thing. It's not much." With shaking fingers, she reached into the front of her shirt, separating the seams she'd sewn between the layers, reaching for something only she knew was there, just under her heart. "I didn't even realize what it was until recently when Kelzy gave me her shed scales." She pulled out a gleaming black panel that was wafer thin and resilient as only true dragon scale could be. Nico went silent as she handed the evidence of her heritage to him. "But I've never seen a black dragon scale before."

Jared's arms tightened around her. Adora's breath caught in her throat as the prince turned the gleaming black scale over in his hands, studying it with an odd sort of knowledge. Kelzy's head loomed up over his shoulder, then suddenly, Nico spun to hold the deep black scale up to the dragon.

"Anybody you know?" Nico held up the scale like an offering as Kelzy reached out her long tongue, licking the black scale delicately with just the tip.

Not your direct line. Kelzy was more serious than Adora had ever seen her. *I think it likely to be from the line of Kent, but we need a dragon who knew one of them personally. I think Sandor served Prince Fileas when he was just a dragonet. He arrived at this Lair recently. I'll call him.*

While they waited for one of the older male dragons to make his way to them, Adora moved away from Jared's tempting strength. She sat up straight on the couch and tried to gather her scattered emotions. She felt shaky, but she knew Jared was there should she need him. It was a reassuring feeling.

"I never would have guessed you were over thirty, Adora." She felt Jared's hand stroking her hair softly and turned to look into his amazingly gentle eyes.

"I have a grown daughter, Jared. And I had twins before her."

"You must have been a child bride." Jared's teasing lightened her heart.

"Twins?" The prince turned back to her. "Where are they now?"

"I don't know. They were stolen from me when they were just little girls."

After the revelations of the last moments, it was devastating to think about the little girls she'd lost so cruelly. Adora gripped the cushions of the couch until her knuckles turned white. Jared must have seen her distress. He pried one hand up from its death grip on the couch and grasped it firmly between his own rough fingers. His silent encouragement meant the world to her in that moment.

"Girls?" The prince ran a rough hand through his hair. "Merciful Mother."

"What?" Adora's gaze went from the prince to Jared to Kelzy.

It was Jared who finally answered. "Royals, probably because of the wizard blood, have more twin sets than is usual. Twin girls are a rarity though. Few girl children are born to any of the royal lines, and only very rarely in pairs."

Sandor approaches.

A large, battle-scarred dragon with coppery brown coloring entered the archway leading to Kelzy's suite. He started in surprise when he saw the prince and bowed his great head in respect.

How can I serve you, my prince? The newcomer's voice boomed with resonance through the minds of all present.

Nico walked up to the huge copper dragon and held out the black scale. "Do you recognize this? Can you tell us who it may have belonged to?"

This new dragon repeated Kelzy's odd licking gesture and then his garnet eyes opened wide. *Fileas! This scale belonged to Prince Fileas.*

Adora was confused. "Fileas was a dragon?"

Nico turned back to her, his hazel eyes shining. "Yes, he was. As am I."

Jared stood at Adora's back, his presence reassuring as a black mist began to form in front of their eyes. Between one moment and the next the prince was gone and a sleek black dragon stood in his place. He was somewhat smaller than the other dragons, but obviously built for speed. He also had sparkling tourmaline eyes—eerily like the hazel gaze of Prince Nico.

The only black dragons are of the royal line. We alone have the ability to shift our shape from human to dragon, and it is that dual nature that solidifies this land's ties with dragons and humans alike.

"Prince Nico?"

"It's him, Adora," Jared assured her. She walked up to the prince and reached out hesitantly, but the black dragon moved forward into her touch with his sleek black-scaled head.

"Incredible." Her voice was a breath of a whisper. "You're dragon and human? Half and half?"

The dragon lifted one shoulder as if to shrug. *That's one way of looking at it. But Adora, if you are the daughter of Fileas as we believe, then half of you is dragon too.*

"Don't be ridiculous."

Kelzy claimed her attention. *Think about it, child. Why did you seek me out when you were just a baby? How did you even know where to find me? My lair was well hidden. None of the humans in the area knew I was even there until you toddled off to find me.*

"I can't shift into dragon form and fly away with you, Mama Kelzy." Her sarcastic tone was laced with shock and a bit of fear.

The very idea of Prince Nico being able to shift into dragon form tantalized her, though Adora knew in her heart it was impossible for her. Surely if that kind of power existed inside her, it would have made itself known long before now. Sure, she had a little healing talent, but most of the healing she did relied on skills learned through hard work and trial and error, not dragon magic. Or any other kind of magic at all, for that matter.

The black dragon moved closer. *Royal females generally can't shift, but they are usually healers of great skill and ability. Their dragon magic manifests itself in the healing arts—the Dragon's Breath made human, if you will. I understand your daughter is a dragon healer.*

The prince stepped back from her and the black mist swirled, leaving him human again, clothed all in black leather, before her. That was some powerful magic indeed.

"Sweet Mother! Belora." Adora's legs gave out and she found herself hoisted back onto the couch, wrapped securely in Jared's strong arms.

"She healed Rohtina," he reminded her gently.

At this point, the huge copper dragon craned his neck forward to lay his great head at Adora's feet. A rare tear sparkled in his deep garnet eyes. His tongue flicked out to touch the back of her hand and she started.

You are Fileas' daughter. You're little Amelia Jane. Thank the Mother that you've finally found your way home to us. The tear leaked out of his eye and tumbled onto her hand, a sparkling magical gem showing the great extent of emotion he was feeling. *I served your father when I was just a youngster. I was away when the attack came, on a quest issued by your sire, but if I'd been there, I would have given my life for his. He was a great man. You have his eyes, though you have your mother's smile and her beautiful hair. I stand by my pledge to your sire and I will serve you and your line all my days, if you will have me.*

Adora was moved to tears by the dragon's solemn pledge. She reached forward and touched his long snout, rubbing gently and feeling the magic inside her tingle in a way it never had before.

You're hurt, she thought, surprised when the dragon answered her.

An old wound, my princess. Nothing to worry over.

Wait. Adora felt the healing energy gather and suddenly overflow from her into the dragon, shining light all around them as her energy came alive as never before. She looked at the dragon's left foreleg and the awkward angle at which it was held. It had been broken sometime in the recent past and set badly.

He hid it well, but Sandor was in a great deal of pain that communicated itself to her when she touched him. Sometimes it was like that for her with human patients, but never had Adora felt such a response with a dragon. Then again, the only dragon she'd ever known before now was Kelzy and she'd always been quite healthy.

As they all watched, the magic flowed, and Sandor's leg straightened out, the lines of pain just visible around the dragon's eyes easing. Adora pulled away and felt the residual high of the magic already beginning to fade in her body. It felt much like it did when she did a complex human healing, but with so much more energy. It was very nearly overwhelming.

Adora sank back and Jared was there for her.

"Do you really have any more doubts about who you are, Adora? You're my cousin," the prince said, kneeling at her side. "You're Princess Amelia Jane of the House of Kent."

"That's not my name."

"It was." Nico shook his head. "But you never knew it, did you? You'll be Princess Adora from now on, of the House of Kent. Welcome back to the family, cousin."

Adora tried to focus but was fast losing energy. It was a phenomenon she knew well. She had overextended herself in healing Sandor, but it was worth it to know he was whole again and no longer in pain. She just needed sleep to recover.

Thank you, my princess, Sandor said gravely in her mind. I'm only sorry you tired yourself so on my behalf.

"I'm fine. I just need sleep."

Jared lifted her into his arms as she leaned back against him, cuddling close to his warmth. He felt so good. It was heaven to rely on his strength for just this short moment.

I'll seek you out when you wake, princess. I have no knight partner at present, but I would be your guardian as I was your father's before you.

"That's nice," she mumbled. "You're such a pretty copper color."

The dragon's voice rumbled comfortingly through her mind as she drifted into unconsciousness. *I match the lights in your hair, as I matched your mother's.*

Jared found himself again tucking Adora into the bed in the guest chamber that was now hers. Kelzy wanted her adopted human daughter close and Jared found himself wanting to keep Adora close for entirely different reasons. If he wasn't very careful, he could easily lose his heart to such an amazing woman. But his heart was too badly damaged to take such a chance again.

He realized, despite his best intentions, he had spent a great deal of time in Adora's room in the past few days, tucking the covers around this small, puzzling woman. No, he thought ruefully, make that this small, puzzling *princess*.

He could still hardly believe Adora was lost royalty. True, she was not in direct line for the throne. In fact, her family line was quite remote from the ruling line—only very distant cousins at best—but the fact they had bred true and the males of the House of Kent could shift to dragon form made them all princes and princesses of the realm. It was a closely guarded secret—and something of a legend now to the people of this land—that their kings were descended from dragons.

Few now knew how true the legend really was. Not only were they part dragon, but the males actually could *become* dragons when they chose. It was a very useful ability and one that allowed them to rule wisely over both human and dragon kind, giving them personal insight into both races.

Jared had been a knight for quite a few years, but before that had served in old King Jon's household. He knew the royal secret and had seen them shift back and forth from human to dragon many times. Each time though, it was still a bit of a shock. He could only imagine what Adora must have thought seeing the roguish Prince Nico shift not five feet from her.

Of the brothers, Nico was Jared's favorite, though he'd be damned if he'd ever let that scamp know it. Nico had been the wild child—the one who constantly needed supervision—and more often than not, it fell to Jared to get the young prince out of whatever scrape he found himself in at the time. Over the years, Nico had come to respect Jared's advice almost as a son would—or younger brother at least. Jared looked at Nico now and thought sadly of what might have been had his family not been torn apart by tragedy.

For years it had been hard to be in Nico's presence, but now after time and distance from the horrific deaths of his family, Jared found he missed Nico's peculiar brand of deviltry. He thought of the prince as he had thought of his son, with an almost fatherly regard and a fondness deeper than most.

"She's quite a woman." Nico's voice drifted quietly from the archway as Jared straightened up and moved out of the small room.

"You haven't met her daughter yet. She's just like her mother, only younger."

"Too bad she's already mated." Nico's eyes flashed with humor.

"You've got to be kidding me, Nico. You, interested in a woman of substance? What? Have you gone through all the whores in the kingdom already?"

Nico laughed, but Jared noted the slight echo of hurt in his eyes with some amazement. Could it be the rascal really was starting to think about settling down?

They went back to the sitting area and saw that Sandor had not left. The big copper dragon sat quietly with Kelzy, apparently deep in conversation, all but ignoring the humans. Jared was taken aback by how cozy the two dragons looked together, sharing the comparatively small wallow. It drove home the fact that Kelzy had lived a long and full life before choosing him as her knight partner. He'd never asked her about her past though, having been too wrapped up in his own misery in those days just after they bonded. Afterwards, he'd been too busy working towards the safety of the kingdom with war clearly on the way. Jared made a mental note to talk more to his dragon partner about her own life, just as soon as he found the time.

It was important to him that he give as well as take from this relationship and it suddenly struck him that Kelzy had been giving and giving to him for years. As far as he was concerned, she was the only reason he wasn't already dead. Since she'd come into his life, bonding with him on a soul deep level, he had a reason to live. Before that, in the dark times when his family was ripped from him, he had wanted nothing more than to join them in death. It was Kelzy who had given him a reason to go on. Kelzy had given him hope, companionship and a kind of love he hadn't ever expected.

"I won't dignify that little dig with a reply," Nico laughed, bringing him back to the conversation at hand with a jolt.

The prince was pouring more wine. He drank too much, Jared thought, but he knew that was just a symptom of unhappiness. Nico needed a wife.

"Nevertheless, I want to meet my younger cousin at the first opportunity." Nico turned to the dragons, lounging in the warm sands of Kelzy's wallow. "Lady Kelzy, on the way in I saw your son and a very pretty gold taking off for the moon. Do you think they're back by now?" His snicker was echoed by dragonish coughs of smoky laughter from the occupants of the wallow.

Are you asking if the human part of the family is recovered enough to speak with you? If so, I would say yes. They've been mated for a while now and are beginning to slow down and savor their moments a bit more.

"Good. I'm going to pay them a call."

I'll warn them so they at least have a chance to dress. Kelzy sent after the prince who was already on his way out.

Aw, Lady Kelz, you take the fun out of everything.

Jared went to check on Adora and found her tossing restlessly. She looked so fragile, so small, and so alone in the big bed. His heart went out to her as she moved in troubled sleep and he found his feet taking him closer, despite his intentions to stay away from her. Sitting on the side of the bed, Jared took her restless hands in his own, speaking softly.

"Hush now, Adora. Everything is fine. You are warm and safe, as is your daughter. I won't let anything happen to you. Be at peace."

Kelzy puffed warm air over them from the doorway, offering her own sort of comfort to the girl she had practically raised. He smiled over at the dragon. Her head lay in the archway, her neck stretching out from the heated sand pit that was her favorite place to rest. From that central wallow, she could crane her neck to reach just about any room in the roughly circular suite, ensuring that she was part of every facet of her chosen humans' lives.

Rather than intrusive, Jared had always found Kelzy's interest in his doings comforting. She was a friend, a companion, and a sounding board who lived, breathed, and cared deeply for him. He didn't question the bond between them. It was deep and it was real. It had formed that fateful day when Kelzy had found him.

Jared had been on the raw edge of despair for a long time after the loss of his wife and young son. The pain of losing them had almost driven him mad, but Kelzy's magical appearance in his life somehow made it just a bit easier to go on. Kelzy had found him deep in the mountains, hiding away from people and dragons alike.

Jared discovered only later that Kelzy had gone deliberately looking for him. Returning from a time of self-imposed exile while she mourned the loss of her previous knight, Kelzy had come back only after the old king and his wife were slain. Answering the call of her kind, Kelzy went back to the palace to find the king and queen dead and the youngster Roland being crowned king—without the benefit of one of the crown's top advisors. Kelzy had been one of the top-ranking dragons, well acquainted with the palace, the royal family and their advisors. She and Jared had always had a friendly relationship, if a bit distant in times past. But when she found him years later, so near the end of his sanity, only her claiming of him gave him reason to go on.

It was Kelzy who had broken the terrible news of the king and queen's deaths. It was Kelzy who had talked Jared into returning to the palace, assuring him that young Roland would need him, that his country needed him, that *she* needed him.

There was no greater guilt a man could feel than failing to protect his family, failing to be there when they needed him. Failing to help the young king—a young man he had known all his life—was something Jared could not allow on top of all the other tragedies in his life.

Kelzy had given Jared reason to live back then and he never regretted her interference. He loved her. But she was the last being he would love, he vowed. Loving came with too high a cost and he refused to hurt that way ever again.

So he couldn't love Adora, no matter how much he might crave her. She was light in the darkness, a gentle balm to his injured soul. Just having her in his home made him happy, but he refused to allow her into his heart. He refused to let the gentle feelings welling up inside him show. He couldn't give her the false hope that somehow they could be together. It would not be fair to her, and he didn't want to leave himself open for that kind of pain ever again.

For she would leave him eventually. It would hurt bad enough as it was, without letting the bond between them get any deeper. Still, he couldn't help but savor these few moments he had with her. He would not let himself love her, but he couldn't help caring deeply for the lost little woman who had shown him her bravery, her courage, her care for his best friend Kelzy and all the dragons he held dear, and her very human vulnerability. She was a rare treasure and he could appreciate her beauty—both inner and outer—from a safe distance. He hoped.

"Jared?" Her voice touched him as she blinked her wide green eyes sleepily. He turned from his contemplations to the woman whose hands he still held lightly within his own.

"I didn't mean to wake you, Adora." He tried to keep his voice low. "You were restless and I came in to make sure you were all right."

"I was dreaming. It was a nightmare." Her sleepy eyes grew frightened and huge as she remembered the vision that had disturbed her slumber. "You were falling. Jared, you were falling off Kelzy's back and you had an arrow through your chest. There was a lot of blood and you were so high." Her voice broke as real fear shivered through her small body.

He had no choice then but to pull her into his arms and comfort the trembling woman. She was so beautiful and so vulnerable in that moment. He couldn't bear to see this strong woman so afraid. Especially on his behalf. Especially when it wasn't even real.

"Ssh, Adora. It was only a dream. I'm here and I'm fine. Kelzy would never drop me. You know that." He rocked her as she clung to him, his voice crooning to her as if she were a babe.

"It seemed so real. Jared, what if it's an omen? What if—?" She broke off on a sob and clung to him.

He rubbed her back with one hand, his frozen heart cracking open at her distress. Without thought, he brought his head down to rest against her, cuddling into her warm neck, inhaling her delicious scent. He kissed her, placing soft little nibbles on her neck, just under her jaw and near the delicate shell of her ear. The shivers of fright changed to something more enticing. Biting gently on her earlobe, Jared felt her soft sexy sigh as she relaxed into his embrace.

"Don't be afraid, Adora." His whisper sent warm, moist air into her ear and she gasped. "It's only a dream."

"Jared."

Her gasping moan brought him closer to her lips, his arms shifting, drawing her nearer to his hard body. He wanted her desperately.

Giving in to desire, he brought his mouth to hers, sipping at her sweetness, drowning in her enticing flavor. This was what he wanted. This! He wanted her.

Aligning their bodies, he laid her back down on the bed, tearing away the covers that tried to get between them. He lowered his weight onto her carefully, his mouth following hers, surprised a little by her passion, but meeting it with an equal fervor. She was with him every step of the way, her little hands clawing at his shirt with a strength and enthusiasm he had not expected. It was devastating.

Impatiently, he ripped at the ties of his shirt, breaking their kiss only to tug the garment off over his head and throw it across the room. It landed somewhere near Kelzy's head. Jared looked up enough to see the jeweled dragon eyes blink open with surprise, then narrow in seeming satisfaction as Kelzy noted what the humans were up to. Jared was too far gone to care what conclusions his dragon partner jumped to though, turning back to whip off Adora's thin nightgown.

When she was bare, he moved back only a moment to enjoy the sight of her generous breasts, her soft skin, and her womanly form. Something was driving him to take her and make her his own. No matter how he fought it, the drive was there, pushing him beyond control.

"Adora," he gasped as she raised her little hand and caressed his muscular chest, following the line of his scar.

It flowed down from his face, over his pectoral muscle and past one hard male nipple, down onto his washboard stomach and lower, beneath the waistline of his leggings. He stopped her when she would have delved beneath and brought her soft hand to his lips, holding her gaze with his own.

"You are so beautiful." He put her hand on his shoulder, then pulled her soft body against his, meeting her halfway to the mattress. She was wonderfully warm beneath him, so enchanting. She was not shy, nor hesitant, but he could tell she hadn't done this in a very long time. Just the idea was entrancing.

Slowly, he rubbed his chest against her breasts, enjoying the way her eyes lit up and her body twitched in passion. He did it again, liking the drag of her hard nipples over his. Lightly, she traced the muscles on his arms and he felt himself weaken. She could easily turn him into her slave with just her touch alone.

He brought his hands to her breasts, pulling back only slightly to fondle and stroke her taut peaks. Her little gasps fired his blood and when he took her in his mouth and sucked, she bucked and moaned. He suckled her strongly, gauging her reaction by the way she moved in his arms. It had been so long since he'd had a soft woman writhing in pleasure beneath him. So long since he even cared who the woman pleasuring him was.

But he cared about Adora. No matter how hard he tried, he couldn't stop himself from caring at least a little. It was dangerous, he knew, but it couldn't be helped.

Firmly, he moved back from her, enjoying the view of her rosy nipples, still wet from his tongue and one of them holding the faint imprint of his teeth. He liked that.

Perhaps a bit too much. Alarms went up through his brain.

When she reached for him, he pulled back, but saw the need in her beautiful eyes and knew he couldn't leave her like this.

Gently, Jared pushed her back on the bed, lowering himself between her soft thighs. He wouldn't go any further than this, but he owed her something. He wouldn't leave her unfulfilled and needy. He would bring her pleasure and lull her back to sleep, then seek his solitary bedchamber. Even if it killed him.

And it probably would.

Sighing, knowing this was the one time he would allow himself to feel her feminine response, Jared lowered his head to her slightly rounded stomach, biting gently. Adora giggled and he pushed lower. The giggle turned to a gasp and then a moan as Jared brought his fingers and tongue to her secret folds. Gently, he probed, learning her body. He'd never wanted so badly to bring his partner pleasure before, never cared more for the woman's response than at this very moment. Adora was special.

Too special for the likes of him.

Jared parted her nether lips, blowing a current of air over her distended little clit. She sighed as her body trembled, hips moving in an uncontrollable rhythm. Covering her clit with his lips, Jared tongued her lightly at first, then more steadily as her temperature rose.

She moaned, her body thrumming against his lips as he took her higher. She tasted of warm honey and sweet woman, creaming over and over for him. Delving inside with his fingers, Jared curled just the tips, looking for that magical spot that would take her over the edge.

Adora cried out when she came, a sob of relief offered up to the night as he rode her through a glorious climax. Clenching around his fingers, Jared nearly died at the thought of how she would feel clenching just the same way around his cock. How he wanted to experience that! How he wanted to take her and make her his own!

But he couldn't. It wouldn't be right.

Adora deserved a whole man—one who could love her with a whole and unscarred heart. She didn't deserve a broken down, second-hand knight with ice in his veins instead of blood. He would not let her make such a sacrifice, but he would enjoy the few stolen moments this night gave him. Jared licked her widely with his tongue, lapping up every last bit of her excitement and taking it within himself.

He would never taste such ambrosia again.

After a while, she settled down and he found the strength to move away from her tempting thighs. He kissed his way up her soft body, pausing for a long tender time at her full breasts. Then he found her lips with his own and kissed her delicately as if he never would taste her again.

And he never would. He kept that thought foremost in his mind. Adora deserved better than the likes of him. Kissing her long and sweet, Jared cuddled her close as her sleepy eyes closed and her breathing returned to normal.

"Go to sleep, Adora."

"But what about—?" Her voice was already dreamy with satisfaction and the sound of it sent tingles down his spine, straight to his hard cock. But he wouldn't trespass further. She was too good for him.

He stroked her hair tenderly. "It was just a dream, Adora. Sleep now and have no fear."

As he smoothed his hands over her soft body and shining auburn hair, he could feel her drifting closer to the edge of peaceful oblivion. He felt good that he'd been able to soothe her, but knew she would be hurt when he turned cold on her in the morning light. Still, it had to be done.

Rising regretfully, Jared watched her sleep for a moment before finally steeling himself enough to leave her side. Kelzy was there, of course, partially blocking the door, staring at him with her wise blue topaz eyes.

It's for the best, he said, knowing she would understand.

I disagree, but you must be the judge of your readiness to commit to a woman, not I.

You're damn right about that, Kelz. The dragon sounded like she was humoring him, but he couldn't be sure. He was frustrated and angry that things couldn't be different. But they just couldn't.

Jared stalked past the dragon and made his way to the bathing chamber. Kelzy followed, watching as he tore off his pants, releasing his straining erection.

Adora would have welcomed that, she said, flicking out her long, thin tongue toward his cock, but not touching. *She hasn't had a man between her legs since her husband died. I think she's lonely.*

Lonely is no reason to climb in bed with me. She deserves better.

Kelzy shot a lick of flame toward the stone basin that was filling with water to heat it for him.

Again, I disagree. You're just what she needs, Jared. A man who will put her needs above his own, but I won't nag you.

Could've fooled me. He laughed without humor. *Now, can I have a little privacy to bathe?*

And polish your...sword? Certainly. The dragon left him with a broad-eyed wink.

CHAPTER THREE

Young Belora stretched, luxuriating in the feel of two strong male bodies, one on either side of her in the warm bed. She would never take for granted the love she had found with her two mates, Lars and Gareth. Nor would she ever take for granted the pleasure bond each of her knights shared with her when their dragon partners soared to the stars in a mating flight. When the dragons mated, the residual energy washed over their human counterparts in a wave of pleasure unlike anything she had ever known before.

Gareth was Kelvan's knight and Lars was partnered with the dragon's mate, Rohtina. She was wife to both men in the tradition of the Lair, since there were so few females able to live and communicate with dragons. That Belora was also able to heal dragons was a relatively new discovery and one that still had her puzzled.

The knights insisted she must be of royal blood but she had been raised simply in the forest. Belora had never been rich, but had always been happy with her mother and the simple life they led. Her mother, Adora, was a powerful healer and they made their living off the land and from the herbal remedies they traded to the people in the small village near their home. The place was overrun now by the first wave of the enemy invasion. Venomous skiths had decimated the village and destroyed the women's tiny house in the forest.

But her mates had saved her and rescued her mother from the skiths. For that she would be forever grateful. When the dragon, Rohtina, was mortally wounded, Belora's own latent healing ability seemed to come to life. Never before had she tried to heal a dragon and suddenly all the power she had ever wanted was hers to command. She'd used the magic to heal the beautiful golden Rohtina and discovered she was pregnant with a dragonet at the same time. It was a double miracle as far as Belora was concerned. She was so happy. Life couldn't get much better.

Uh, sorry to wake you all. Kelvan's voice sounded through all three human minds with some degree of urgency. *But you'll very shortly have a visitor.*

"Tell them to go away." Gareth threw a pillow out of the bedchamber toward the general direction of the dragons' wallow.

I can't. Kelvan sounded rather pained this time. *You have to get up and get dressed.*

"Who is it?" Lars asked, raising up on one elbow and scratching at his muscular chest.

"And what's the bloody rush? It's not even dawn," Gareth grumbled while Belora giggled.

She climbed over Lars, pausing to kiss him good morning before she headed first for the wardrobe and then small bathroom next to their bedchamber. She was just too happy to be grumpy in the morning. Her mates had made her the happiest woman in the world—repeatedly—last night. Humming a light tune, she dressed and moved into the small kitchen area to heat water for the tea she liked to drink in the morning.

The small fire she used for heating water had gone out, but with a quick look at the dragons, she got their help in lighting it once more. They were handy to have around, she thought with a grin, when one needed a light. She was still chuckling when Gareth came into the room, stretching and yawning. He grabbed her in a fierce hug, kissing the breath out of her as was his custom first thing in the morning.

Lars was just a bit more conservative. He stumbled in—still a little bleary eyed but his usual calm, quiet self. She knew well by now that still waters ran very deep indeed when it came to Lars. His steadiness warmed her as she set mugs of the strong tea she blended especially for them in front of her mates.

Belora noticed some activity out near the entrance to their suite and saw the dragons bowing their heads to a newcomer dressed all in black leather. He was a striking man, and more than a little scary. He moved with such self-possession, as did all the knights, but this was something more. This man prowled. It was as if there was a caged beast inside him, just waiting to be let out. She shook her head, smiling at her fanciful imagination as she nodded to Lars and Gareth.

"Looks like our guest is here. Do you know him?"

Both men turned and their eyes widened before they stood hastily. They bowed in respect as the man approached and he took it as his due while Belora stood dumbfounded.

"Your majesty." Gareth spoke for them all. "Welcome to our home."

"What do you know? Gareth and Lars, together again, I see. The Mother must have been sleeping on the job to allow this sort of pairing." The man's hazel eyes flashed, obviously teasing, and the knights relaxed in his presence.

Belora was intrigued.

"Congratulations on your wedding." The black clad man stepped forward, offering his hand in the knightly fashion, indicating he thought of her men more as contemporaries than underlings.

She liked that and found herself liking the tall man with the dancing hazel eyes almost immediately.

Both of her knights shook the man's hand with broad smiles, thanking him for his good wishes. They turned to her. Her mouth went dry for no reason she could discern. Again, Gareth spoke for them all.

"This is our mate, Belora. Sweetheart, this is Prince Nico."

Belatedly, she remembered to curtsy, but the prince's next words nearly threw her off balance.

"It's a pleasure to meet you, cousin."

"Cousin?" Lars was startled into speaking, his turquoise eyes wide with the shock they all felt.

Nico nodded. "Shall we sit? I have much to say and I'd like a chance to get to know your mate a bit better as well."

"By all means." Gareth gave the prince his own chair, pulling over another for himself and one for Belora. She brought the teapot and another cup, setting it before the prince, all the while marveling that a prince should be sitting to morning tea with her, of all things.

"I met your mother just a short while ago," the prince began. "I'm convinced that she is the daughter of Prince Fileas of Kent who was killed along with his entire family by our enemies many years ago. The only survivor of the massacre was his youngest daughter, the Princess Amelia Jane, who disappeared that day and was never seen again. Until now."

"Bright stars!" Belora's whisper reached the men, making them smile.

"I believe your mother is Princess Amelia Jane, though she will be known now as Princess Adora of Kent. That makes you Princess Belora of Kent and distant cousin to the royal line." The prince leaned back, apparently enjoying the stunned stares of the people around him. "And that makes you two…" He eyed the knights. "Prince Consorts."

"Holy shit." Lars and Gareth spoke at the same moment, clearly stunned.

Belora was overwhelmed. Her mind seized and her stomach revolted. Jumping up so quickly her chair crashed to the floor behind her, she ran for the bathroom.

She had never been so sick in her life, grasping the seat of the commode for dear life as her stomach emptied itself over and over. Dimly, she realized the bathroom was crowded with her mates and—horrors—the prince. Gareth wiped her brow with a cool wet cloth, which felt very good, while Lars held her, tying her hair back with a stray piece of leather. That done, he rubbed her spine gently. The prince watched with a pitying look, but there was a light in his off-green eyes that was more than calculating. He made her feel a little uncomfortable as he moved forward to squat down next to her.

"May I?" he asked both her and her mates as he stretched his hand near to her forehead. She nodded hesitantly, uncertain of what he intended, but one didn't say no to a prince, after all.

He touched her head and suddenly the knots in her stomach eased. She realized he was using his own healing energy to still her rebellious stomach. His touch soothed and within moments she felt much better, though still a bit too shaky to stand on her own. Lars helped her up, holding her against his chest as she faced the smiling prince. He had the most luminous look in his hazel eyes as he regarded her.

"Congratulations, cousin." His words were low, filled with emotion. "You carry twin boys and they will both be black dragons."

"Praise the Mother," Gareth whispered. He swayed for just a moment, seeking the stone wall for support.

Kelvan and Rohtina raised their heads in the archway and trumpeted their joy, nearly deafening all the humans present. Lars squeezed her close, his face buried in her neck as he kissed her.

"I don't understand." Belora looked up at the prince from within Lars' strong hold.

The prince laughed gently. "I know. Forgive me, cousin. This is just such a momentous thing. There are so few of us left. Every birth is a miracle to our line. Black dragons even more so."

"I still don't get it. Why are you calling them black dragons? I know that's the symbol of the king, but what has it to do with my...oh, sweet Mother, did you say I was pregnant?" Nico nodded and she felt tears gather in her eyes. "You felt them? Twins?"

"Yes, cousin. Two strong, healthy boys. One from each of your mates."

"Sweet Mother of All!" She turned in Lars' arms and hugged him hard, then reached for Gareth who still appeared stunned by the news. She embraced them both and her smile stretched from ear to ear.

"I take it the news is both happy and unexpected." The prince spoke once their rejoicing had died down a bit.

"Rohtina's pregnant too," Belora said, tears of joy nearly overcoming her.

"Then double congratulations are in order." The prince turned to the dragons and placed one hand as if in benediction on the young female dragon's head.

"Thank you for telling me! And for making me feel better too. My own small healing gift never works on myself."

The prince shook his head with a smile. "Such is the pity for most healers. But I understand your power is better suited to dragons anyway, which is a wonderful thing."

"Yes." She moved out of her mates' arms to face the strange prince. "We discovered it only a few days ago."

"So your mother told me."

"Oh! Mama's going to be so happy! And Kelzy!"

"All the dragons in this Lair will undoubtedly be happy to hear the news that your sons will soon be joining them."

Belora was puzzled by his wording. "Joining the dragons?"

"It's a gift of the royal blood we share, Belora. We are both human and dragon. That's why the females of our line can heal dragons when few other human healers can do so effectively. The males of our line take that one step further."

"How?" She was afraid to breathe.

The prince stepped back from her toward the dragons. Kelvan and Rohtina welcomed him with respect and a kind of deference she had never seen them display before.

"We *are* dragons."

So saying, the prince faded for a moment, a thick black mist swirling around his body. Belora recognized the tug of powerful magic on her senses. A moment later, a compact but still huge black dragon stood outside the archway between the other two dragons. The prince was nowhere to be seen. Or rather, he was there—incredibly—but in dragon form.

"Sweet Mother of All!" Belora strode forward, entranced by the gleaming black dragon. He was somewhat smaller than the other dragons, but he looked just as lethal, just as beautiful. She reached out to him and he craned his neck forward into her touch, allowing her to feel the shiny black scale of his neck and face.

Do you understand now, cousin?

Belora gasped as she felt the presence of the prince within the striking black dragon with the tourmaline eyes. No, that wasn't quite right. The prince wasn't inside the dragon, the prince *was* the dragon, and the dragon was the prince. It was simply amazing.

"My babies—?"

Your sons will be as I am, able to shift from human to dragon at will. I show you this so you will be prepared when they are ready. They'll probably begin to shift shortly after they learn to walk. They'll start flying around the same time Rohtina's dragonet will, I think, so they can all learn together. The Mother certainly knows what She's doing, doesn't She?

"I can't believe it."

Believe it. Your sons will bring hope to the dragons here in this Lair, which will shortly become key in our battle with Skithdron if I'm not mistaken. Just their presence will bring renewed hope for our land to the dragon population and the knights as well. I tell you this from my own experience. I've felt the power and the responsibility that comes with being of two worlds.

"Is it hard? I mean, it's such a responsibility. I was raised simply. You can call me a princess all you want, but I'm still just a peasant really. I always will be."

Then you might understand what it's like to live in two worlds as well, for you are a princess and apparently a peasant too. And to answer your question, no, it's not hard at all. It's the most amazing blessing of my life and I thank the Mother every day for allowing me such gifts. She was wise when She allowed the last of the wizards to form the pact between the dragons of our land and our ancestor, Draneth the Wise. He was the first black dragon, forged by magic and his own wizard blood, but each of us since has been truly of both races. It's how we can understand the needs of both humans and dragons and continue to guide both races in harmony and cooperation. It's a gift, Belora, a precious one.

His words touched her so deeply she felt a tear trickle down her cheek. The prince moved back and the black mist swirled once more, leaving him clad in black leather, human once again.

"Whatever doubt remained is now gone. You carry royal black dragons in your womb. There can be no doubt you are of the royal line." The prince moved forward, kissing her on both cheeks. "Welcome back, cousin, to our family. It's a happy day to have found you and your mother once again."

This time, she did cry—her emotions all over the place with the shocking news of her bloodlines and her pregnancy. Gareth and Lars came up behind her, their supportive arms around her, there for her.

"There's one other thing I have to discuss with you, Belora, if you think you're up to it." The prince looked uncertain for a moment in the face of her turbulent emotions and she smiled to reassure him.

"Anything, Prince Nico. You've given me such happy news."

They walked back toward the kitchen area and sat down once more. Nico reached out a finger to each cold cup of tea and warmed them with his inner fire. Apparently he didn't have to be in dragon form to call on his fire.

She would have to remember that for when her boys started to experiment with their own abilities.

"I don't mean to bring up bad memories, but I need to know everything you can remember about your sisters."

Belora gasped at the sudden change of topic. She had not expected it but realized it made sense that the prince would want to account for all the members of her line. The kidnapping of her sisters suddenly took on an even more sinister light in her mind. Had the kidnappers known their true identities? Is that why they had been targeted? She shivered and Lars and Gareth were there, putting one arm each around her at shoulders and waist, silent and supportive. Stars! How she loved them.

"As I told my mates, all I remember is that we were in a big town, at a market. My mother could tell you where exactly. A bunch of men rushed us. Big men. I remember one had a jagged scar on his face and was missing the two little fingers on his left hand. He hit my mother and the others grabbed my sisters. They were very strong and no one would help us. The scarred man tried to grab me but my mother held me tight and started running. She ran and ran. They pursued us but didn't catch her." Gareth and Lars moved their chairs closer. "My mother and I went back later and tried to find my sisters, but they were long gone. We left that day and never went back. We walked and walked, through forest mostly, and when we came upon the cottage, we watched it for a few days before my mother would approach."

"Sounds like your mother was taking wise precautions." The prince's voice held respect and admiration, which warmed Belora's heart.

"We didn't have any money or much to trade except my mother's healing skills. No one claimed ownership of the cottage when my mother asked in the village and they welcomed the idea of having a healer move in closer to them. Some of them helped Mama in the early days, bringing her food and household items to trade for her herbal remedies. That's how we've lived for the past decade and more."

"How old were your sisters when they were taken?"

"I was about five, so I guess they were about seven or eight."

"Then they'd be in their early twenties now."

"Yes, I think so."

The prince stood. "Thank you, cousin. I want you to know that I'll do everything in my power to find your sisters."

Nico went back to speak at length with Adora while Belora and her new family celebrated the two pregnancies—both human and dragon. Adora, after she woke, was able to fill in the blank spaces in what Belora had told him about the day her sisters were snatched from them.

It was a cold trail, over ten years old, but Nico was a man who prided himself on his ability to learn things that others could not discern. He had a place to start at least, knowing the town from which the children had been snatched. He would start there.

The black dragon winged away from the new Lair under cover of darkness, off on his quest.

Everything was not as it seemed in the royal palace of Skithdron. While on the outside, things looked much as they had during old King Gorin's time, on the inside, an evil pestilence roamed freely through the new king's chambers. Lord Venerai knew his friend and sometime lover, King Lucan, dabbled in magics not of this land—perhaps not of this world—and paid a high price for such power, but Venerai understood. He too, would do anything for power.

When Venerai received the royal summons to present himself in the king's private bed chamber, he prepared himself for a night of serving the young king's rather rapacious desires. But he found quite a different evening awaited upon entering the king's chambers. For one thing, Lucan was not as he had seen him last. Lucan greeted Venerai with inhuman, slitted eyes that reminded him of the almost reptilian gaze of a skith. Then, as Lucan shrugged off his robe, Venerai saw the changes that had been made to Lucan's once soft and pampered skin. Gone was the almost boyish pudginess, replaced by a sleek, *scaled*, lithe musculature that was startling to say the least.

Lucan's skin had an earthy cast and it rippled with scales in the candlelight. Venerai didn't know what to make of it and for once in his life of political intrigues and power struggles was at a total loss for words. The young king noted all with his new eyes and laughed, but Venerai didn't care. Lucan was dangerous now. Let him laugh. As long as King Lucan wasn't ordering his death, Venerai was pleased to serve as the king's fool.

As Lucan approached him, appearing to slither more than walk, Venerai held himself still. He started to notice changes in the room since last he had been summoned to pleasure the king. Desperately trying to hide his reactions, Venerai knew one misstep here could easily get him killed.

A ragged girl cowered near the foot of Lucan's bed, bound to its ornate golden post with a golden chain. She was dressed scantily, but dressed nonetheless, which indicated to Venerai that she was not there for the king's pleasure, but for some other purpose he could only guess at. The girl watched Lucan's back with hate-filled, startlingly green eyes.

Venerai also noted the large trapdoor that had been installed near the ornamental golden fountain at one end of the grand room. It opened and Venerai tried to hold his reaction back as three giant skiths slithered into the room, making their way to Lucan's side as if seeking their master.

Skiths were native to Skithdron, and gave the land its name. They lived in the rock formations that littered the land, menacing all living creatures. Most active at night, skiths would eat anything that moved and seemed to rejoice in ripping people's heads from their bodies. Skiths were truly evil creatures, with acid venom that could burn through just about anything. Only the stone walls that surrounded every village kept the people of Skithdron safe from the predatory creatures.

They slithered like snakes and had slitted eyes, but they were as large as dragons, though of course they couldn't fly, or even climb very well. Solitary creatures, Venerai knew Lucan had found a way to herd them before his armies. Just how he'd learned to control the creatures was a subject of much conjecture and Venerai almost feared he was about to find out the secret of Lucan's power.

The power itself was tantalizing to Venerai. The hideous creatures were not.

Lucan welcomed the deadly skiths with outstretched arms as they twined around him like puppy dogs. Venerai had never seen the like. It was a moment before Lucan turned back to him, his pet skiths standing tall, extending upward from the floor on their sinuous bodies, backing Lucan with their immense size and fearsome presence.

"You have pleased us greatly, Lord Venerai. You have always been a faithful servant."

Venerai bowed low, nearly scraping the floor, and dropped his gaze as the king demanded of his subjects. "Thank you, your highness."

"In recognition of your service to us, we have decided to raise you higher yet."

Venerai's heart stilled with a mixture of fear and anticipation. Power was what he wanted, but what price was too high?

"Come forward, Lord Venerai, and join with us. We promise it won't hurt…much."

Venerai stumbled forward as the king laughed.

CHAPTER FOUR

War came on a quiet day. The wild skith raids on border villages had diminished in the days just before Skithdron launched the entirety of their first wave. Venomous skiths were herded before the army, bringing utter destruction to anything in their path. Somehow the generals were able to direct the creatures, bringing their army up behind. They destroyed three villages completely before enough dragons raced to the incursion to put up a decent defense against the unprecedented swarm of skiths.

Flames flew everywhere as Jared arrived on the scene, swooping in on Kelzy's back to lead the dragons and knights in their forays against the lethal creatures. But the skiths weren't the only thing to worry about—as if they weren't bad enough by themselves. The army of men and horses just behind the skiths was armed with crossbows that could shoot small but dangerous arrows at the dragons. A lucky hit to the eye or some of the rare sensitive places on a dragon's body could do enough damage to take them out of the fighting. The knights, too, were vulnerable to the arrows so the danger was real, as all the knights knew full well.

They flew higher to avoid arrows as best they could, but in order to effectively fight, they had to make low flame runs. Though he hated to give the order, Jared knew the dragons' flame would be effective against the bowmen as well. Jared watched grimly as the new assault started to have some effect.

Suddenly Jared sighted a familiar banner as it dipped and rose once more with an additional white flag of surrender on its pinnacle. The lone rider made a break for the Draconian side, across the field of devastation, riding for the nearest dragon and knight—Kelvan and Gareth.

Kelzy, can you see? Is that—? Sweet Mother! Is that Lord Darian?

It is. The crazy loon. He doesn't see the skiths turning to chomp on him.

We have to do something. He's flying a white flag.

I see it, Jared. Kelzy made a swooping dive toward the man on horseback, who was almost entirely surrounded by venomous skiths, but another dragon got there before her. This copper dragon had no rider on his back and was acrobatic enough to scoop the man right off his horse a moment before the skiths reached it. The skiths feasted on the poor beast, rending the horse limb from limb with their razor sharp fangs.

Sandor! Good flying. Jared heard his dragon partner call to her friend. *Will you take him to the Lair while we finish here? Don't let him out of your sight.*

The copper dragon gave a smoky snort that clearly said he would never do such a ridiculous thing and turned for the Lair, the man clasped tight in his sharp claws. All in all, Jared was glad the other dragon had made the save. He knew Kelzy might have balked at snatching up a human since the last time she had done it—the guilt of inadvertently hurting Adora had bothered her for days and days. He didn't want to live through that again right now, though he was planning some drills with inanimate objects to sharpen her skills and build her confidence in snatching and grabbing targets as soon as they had a free moment. A fighting dragon needed to train constantly and keep all their skills as sharp as their talons.

When Jared and Kelzy landed at the Lair, they found a scene of chaos. Several knights shoved the Skithdronian man around, sneering and shouting angrily at him, though he did little to defend himself from them. Jared called for order and the knights grudgingly moved away, staring down the stranger with hatred in their eyes.

"What the hell do you think you're doing? Acting like a bunch of children in a schoolyard!" Jared admonished the knights, most of who were on the young side, he realized looking at them. Few had seen real fighting before. "This man came to us under a flag of surrender. You young hotheads should at least wait to hear what he risked his life and forfeited his country to tell us!" He noted a few eyes clouding with chagrin, but some were still defiantly angry.

"It's probably a trap, General," one of the younger knights yelled from the other side of the crowd now gathered on the wide landing ledge. "How do we know he's not some kind of spy sent to mislead us?"

"I know because I know this man. I've known him for years and have called him friend for just as long." Jared moved to stand beside the Skithdronian lord. Darian was a little worse for wear after the way he'd been greeted by the knights, and Jared was disgusted. Knights were supposed to behave better than this. "I lead this Lair until the king says otherwise and I trust this man. So you all had better just calm yourselves."

A dead silence fell then as the younger knights simmered. They didn't have to like his orders. They just had to follow them. He was the leader here and their job was to follow. Simple as that.

"Now, if you'll all get back to your duties, I'll talk to our guest and learn what news he gave up his home, his lands, and his title to bring us."

There was muttering and shuffling of feet but the knights dispersed, leaving a few curious dragons who were being tended by their knights for less serious wounds sustained fighting the skiths. Many were being doused with water to remove small spots of the venomous skith spray from their tough hides. It was best to do that here on the ledge where provisions had been made to remove the contaminated water safely, before the dragons moved around into other parts of the Lair and spread the noxious stuff around too much.

Jared turned to the man at his side, looking him up and down before reaching out a hand in welcome. Absently, he noticed Adora hovering near one of the injured dragons some yards distant, a strange look on her face as she watched them. She'd avoided him since that night he'd brought her to climax with his mouth and fingers, just as he had avoided her.

"I'm sorry for their behavior, Lord Darian. They're young and inexperienced with real war."

The other man sighed as they shook hands. "Would that I were the same, but I've seen too much in my years, Jared. I don't blame them."

Jared growled. "I do. I command here and their ill behavior reflects poorly on my leadership. I apologize."

"No problem. I didn't expect to be welcomed with open arms, but I had to come. I thank the gods that I got through and that you're here, of all people, to hear what I have to say."

Both men's expressions grew grim. Jared realized many ears were craning to hear what they would say to each other.

"Come with me where we can talk privately. I'll also ask our healer if she will see to your wounds, if you like." He looked over at Adora and with a slight motion of his head asked her help. She waved a hand and nodded in agreement, and he knew without words that she would join them as soon as she finished her work with the badly injured dragon. He could count on the fact that she was a truly dedicated healer to bridge the icy gap that had grown between them since the night he had lost control of his senses.

Jared winced as he watched his old friend limp down the corridor with him. Kelzy followed behind with Sandor. The break from his own people, the skith attack, being snatched up by Sandor and flown here in the dragon's fist, and the beating from the young knights had left Darian with a pronounced limp and assorted cuts and bruises. But true to his character, he didn't complain. Jared respected the man. Always had. Of all the Skithdronians he had met as counselor to the old king, this was the man he'd dealt with the most, and the most successfully.

Darian winced with every step but couldn't complain. He was alive and luckier than he had a right to be. He'd hoped to get to someone in power who might believe him and take his message higher, but he never expected to see his old friend, Lord Jared, riding atop a dragon. When Darian had lived near the palace, serving as the newly appointed ambassador from Skithdron to the old king's court, he and Jared had formed a close friendship. As a bachelor, he was often invited to spend holidays with Jared and his family.

Darian knew the new Skithdronian king had been behind the attack on Jared's family but didn't know how in the world he would ever break such news to his old friend. Besides, that was in the past and Lucan had gotten his wish—Lord Jared, the keenest of the old king's advisors had been a broken man after the deaths of his young wife and child. He had left the old King's service and retreated into obscurity for a long time. In fact, Darian would bet none in Skithdron yet realized just who commanded the dragons on this part of the border.

Jared led him to a large chamber that had at its center a massive oval pit filled with sand. The dragons who followed close behind made for the sand pit and sank in with what Darian would have sworn were dragonish sighs. They rolled slightly in the abrasive sand, which seemed to brighten their iridescent scales to a glossy shine even as he watched.

"Be welcome in our home, Lord Darian. As you can see, everything is designed around Lady Kelzy's comfort here." The other man gestured toward the beautiful blue-green dragon he had been riding.

Darian knew enough about dragons to make as deep a bow as he could manage toward the large heads that watched him carefully.

"Thank you for your hospitality, Lady Kelzy." He turned to the copper dragon then. "And thank you, sir, for your timely rescue."

You're welcome. Though I've yet to decide if you were worth risking my neck for.

Darian's eyes widened as he heard the booming voice echo through his mind. It could only belong to the huge copper dragon whose garnet eyes twinkled down on him with a sly sort of merriment. Tentatively, Darian sought the way to the dragon's mind with his own thoughts.

I can only hope that after you hear what I have to say, you'll be convinced.

The dragon gave a smoky chuckle and turned back to the sand and his grooming. Apparently neither Jared nor the female dragon was aware of the silent communication that had just taken place between Darian and the big copper.

"Sir Sandor," Jared spoke again as he led Darian to a long couch, "is an old friend of Kelzy's. He's newly arrived to our Lair and without a knight at present." Darian sat with only a small grunt of pain but Jared grimaced when he looked at him. "Our most gifted healer will see to your wounds as soon as possible."

"Don't worry about me, Lord Jared. There are things I need to tell you. Things you need to hear—"

At that moment, he broke off speaking as the most beautiful woman he had ever seen walked through the main archway. She spared a smile for the dragons and it lit her entire face. Even from a distance he could see the glint of deep green in her wide eyes and it drew him in. She was a goddess come to earth and he would gladly worship at her feet, if she would but let him.

The very idea of it shocked Darian right down to his toes. He'd long ago given up on finding a woman to share his life. No woman had ever evoked such a violent or immediate response in him. Darian knew deep inside, just from looking at her, this was a woman he could spend the rest of his life with.

As simple and startling as that, Darian knew he was looking at his destiny. Never one for overly romantic thoughts, Darian was laid low by the seductive sway of the woman's hips, the gentle glide of her dainty feet across the stone walkway.

The woman turned her head, spotting them, and it was as if his prayers had been answered when she made her way directly to the couch where he sat. As she drew closer, he could see she was no young maiden, yet there was a freshness about her that made her appear much more innocent and younger than the wisdom in her startlingly beautiful eyes betrayed.

Jared stood stiffly and Darian noted the longing that entered the other man's eyes as he gazed on the beauty who approached. Darian realized Jared was not unaffected by the woman's grace. The knight wanted her, it was plain to see, but Darian questioned whether Jared—after the devastating losses in his life—would ever act on it. Darian's eyes were drawn back to the stunning woman and he noted more than a flicker of interest as she looked at him. But the dewy admiration in her eyes was for Jared alone as she passed him.

There was something there, on both sides, but he knew Jared was probably too wounded emotionally to be a good match for this delicate flower. If Darian could, he would have her—take her and cherish her in the way she deserved to be cherished. He knew in his heart he would be better for her than pining away after Jared—a man who might never be heart-whole again. Darian would make her forget the impossible longing for Jared that showed in her every movement. Darian would teach her the delights she'd find in his arms and the love he would give freely, if she would but accept it.

"Princess Adora of the House of Kent." Jared made formal introductions, but Darian could see from the woman's start of surprise that she wasn't comfortable about something. "May I present Lord Darian Vordekrais of Skithdron, former ambassador to our land during old King Jon's reign."

The woman stopped in front of him and smiled, nearly taking his breath away.

"I'm not big on formality, milord. I'm a healer and would help you if I could. May I?"

"Princess Adora, you may do whatever you wish with me. I'm yours to command."

The woman blushed so prettily at his daring words he almost wished he could spend the rest of the day making her smile, but he had come here for a reason. He had to get his message out and Jared was just the man to use his information.

She directed him to lie back on the couch, pulling a wicked looking knife from her waist and setting to work cutting her way through the ruined leather boot and leggings that contained and constricted his swollen foot, ankle, and leg. She was efficient and so gentle he felt little pain.

Darian shook himself, focusing on his task. No matter the distraction of the woman tending his wounds, Darian knew he had to deliver his message. He'd given up his home and country to deliver his warnings, and they had to be heard as soon as possible.

"Jared, you've got to get word to your king. Lucan has gone completely 'round the bend."

The knight dragged a chair closer and sat, leaning forward to catch every word. Darian also noted the dragons had craned their necks over near them and listened intently as well.

"I've heard rumors about him, Darian, but nothing concrete."

"Jared." He grabbed the man's wrist, trying desperately to make his old friend understand the urgency of his news. "I've seen it now with my own eyes. Lucan has sunken into dark magics that have twisted him into something not quite human. He keeps skiths as pets and trains them. They are far smarter than I ever gave them credit for being. Jared, the ones he trains go out and teach the others. They're learning to hunt in packs, in orderly groups, to work together. What you've seen so far on this side of the border is nothing. Lucan had them test and train on some of our own villages. Every human and animal for leagues around the villages of Vorkrais, Hemdan, Pennrin and Sokolaff are now gone. Skith food."

The woman gasped, drawing his eyes. She was white with fear and Darian regretted immediately putting such a look on her lovely face. He let go of Jared's wrist and—almost without realizing he was doing it—moved to cup her cheek, offering what comfort he could from such dire news.

"I'm sorry, Princess, to have distressed you. I should have waited to speak."

"No." She surprised him by reaching up and taking his hand in her own. He felt a spark between them and his gaze was glued to hers as she spoke. "Jared needs to hear what you have to say. I thank you for your selfless act in coming here, breaking with your people and subjecting yourself to the Lair's questionable hospitality." She made a face at his swollen and bruised leg. "It's just that I was chased by skiths not too long ago and almost didn't make it."

His hand tightened on hers. "Thank the gods you got away. I would hate to think of what could have happened." Darian fought back the amazing attraction that flowed between him and this woman. He had a mission to complete. He had to impart his information. Only then could he concentrate on the gorgeous woman who ministered so tenderly to his wounds. "Jared, Lucan has found a way to communicate with the skiths and I believe he's made some kind of bargain with them."

"Sweet Mother of All!" Jared rocked back in his chair.

"As you probably know, wild skiths are solitary creatures. They hunt and live alone, usually in wilderness areas. They aren't much trouble unless you blunder into their territory or they try to take up residence near a village or something. But Lucan, he's organized them! They're working together, fighting together, living and hunting together. I've never seen the like. He's formed an army of the creatures, and they're coming this way. They will kill every man, woman, and child in Draconia, sweeping through your lands with the help of the human army Lucan has at his command, until they take it all." His voice rose with the passion of his words. "Jared, Lucan doesn't want to just conquer your land, he wants to destroy it utterly. He plans to kill every last human and dragon and allow the skiths to breed and multiply to numbers we have never before seen."

"That's insane." Adora's shocked whisper brought his eyes back to hers.

"Sadly, you're right. Lucan has gotten involved in sinister magics that have warped his mind. It is said he drinks skith venom and bathes in blood. He's consulted a foreign witch who some say managed somehow to allow him to communicate with the skiths. They say that's how he's been able to convince them to do things they never have before. He can control them."

Jared's scarred face was very grim. "I can't thank you enough for risking your life to come here and tell me this. You have my guarantee of sanctuary and a place in my House for as long as you need it."

Darian realized it was a generous offer and more than he had expected when he set out on his dangerous quest. To have the protection of Lord Jared's ancient and distinguished House meant quite a bit in this land or any, for that matter.

"I am deeply honored, Lord Jared, and thank you."

He hissed then, involuntarily, when the woman shifted his injured leg. All eyes moved down to appraise the damage she had revealed by removing the boot and cutting his legging up to mid-thigh.

"You won't be running anytime soon, but slow walking with a stick to help support you is allowable. I'll do what I can with poultices and what healing energy I can spare." She shook her head sadly. "I'm sorry to tell you I must save most of my energy for the dragons."

He was shocked. "You heal dragons?"

The princess nodded, her gentle hands already ministering to his painful leg. He waited patiently, amazed at the tingle of her healing gift when she put out a tiny bit of energy to mend his abused muscles. With that little head start, he knew his healing time would decrease significantly.

She swayed just a bit when she stood and it was Jared who caught her, betraying his concern over the small woman. He steered her to a chamber in the suite, disappearing inside with her for a few minutes while Darian fought off sleep. There was more he had to tell Jared, but he hadn't the heart to speak the worst of his news before the tender creature who had done her best to heal him.

When Jared returned, his expression was thoughtful.

"Tell me the rest."

Darian chuckled wryly. "You know me too well, old friend." He settled back against the arm of the couch. "Lucan has been sending envoys to that heathen Salomar in the north. They are working together to develop weapons that will take down dragons. I saw some drawings of one briefly but it was too fast for me to get much detail. What I did see, though, gave me nightmares." He sat up, his eyes narrowed. "I've since learned that Lucan is sending massive shipments of diamond blades from the mines in the south to Salomar. I fear the worst."

Both men knew that a diamond blade was just about the only thing that could slice through dragon scale as if it were butter. Jared sat heavily in the chair at his friend's side.

"This is bad, Darian. Very bad."

"I know. It's why I came. You have to warn your dragons, Jared. I believe the human army will try to use their new weapons to drop the dragons from the sky and let the skiths do the rest. I wouldn't wish that sort of death on even my worst enemy, and I've never considered the dragons of your land or any of your people to be my enemies or the enemies of Skithdron. It's Lucan who's started this war and as far as I'm concerned he is the real enemy here."

Jared stayed by Darian's side, talking quietly and thinking through the dire news until the other man fell into a restless sleep. Adora had been more worn out than he liked her to be in healing the dragons who had come under attack that day. She had dropped off into an exhausted sleep moments after he'd put her to bed and would sleep for many hours yet.

He covered Darian with a blanket where he lay on the couch. He didn't have the heart to wake the injured man just to move him to a bedroom. Tomorrow was soon enough.

Jared wanted to seek his own bed, but he feared sleep would not come so easily to him. Not after what he had just learned. He stood, stretched, and walked over to the edge of the dragon's wallow. Kelzy and Sandor lay side by side in the large tub of heated sand, each looking at him with troubled jewel eyes.

You heard?

We did. It was Kelzy who answered into the minds of all three.

We must send word to the king right away, but we need more information if we're to train against this new threat.

Sandor elevated his head so that he was on a level with Jared's eyes. *Though I have no knight partner at present, I wish to stay in this Lair and train with your ranks, Sir Jared. Kelzy and I have worked well together in the past. I would do so again, if you agree.*

You're most welcome to stay, Sir Sandor. Right now, I think we need all the help we can get. Thank you for volunteering.

Sandor settled back down beside Kelzy as if he meant to stay right there in her wallow with her, but Jared didn't question it. His mind was too preoccupied with more desperate concerns than where a new dragon chose to sleep. If Kelzy didn't throw him out then who was Jared to say anything?

On his way to his own chamber, he stopped to look in on Adora. He almost wished he could talk to her about these troubling developments, to share his burden with her in some small way. Such thoughts were dangerous and skated too close to intimacy for his comfort, but they would not be denied. Adora was a bright, intelligent woman and he valued her insight. That's all these strange feelings were about, wasn't it?

He shook his head in disgust at himself as he walked silently away from her doorway. He was a damned fool. Already half in love with the woman and unable to work up the courage to do anything about it. Too afraid of being hurt again to even try.

"How are you feeling, Lord Darian?"

Adora sat beside the man's bed the next day, as soon as she finished checking on the dragons who had been hurt the day before. Jared had given him a room on the other side of the suite from hers that was similar in design and layout. There were several of these guest chambers in the large suite since Kelzy and Jared were the leaders of this Lair and often entertained guests and visitors.

"Much better today. Thank you, Princess."

"Please, call me Adora. I didn't grow up as a princess and I don't think I'll ever get used to the idea."

His blue eyes twinkled as he smiled at her. "Far be it from me to argue with royalty. I will gladly call you Adora if you will call me Darian, or Dar if you prefer."

She couldn't help but smile. This man was charming, that was certain, and so handsome he was almost hard to look at. Straight white teeth shone in contrast to his tanned skin. He had hair black as a raven's wing and startling, almost ghostly, blue eyes that smiled easily and sincerely at her, though he was still in a bit of pain, she well knew.

She busied herself looking over his leg injury. It was still swollen, but healing nicely now that he was off his feet. "Well then, Darian, how are you feeling?"

"Much better now that you're here."

She laughed. "Much friskier too, I see. Were you born a flirt or did you perfect the art over time?"

"Actually..." His eyes grew serious. "I've been a confirmed bachelor all my life but I think that's about to change."

"What makes you say that?" She dared not look up to meet his gaze as she changed the dressing on his leg wound.

It had been so long since a handsome man had flirted with her, Adora couldn't be certain she wasn't reading something in to Darian's words that wasn't truly there. Certainly Jared had paid quite a bit of attention to her—and reminded her what pleasure truly felt like—but it felt almost as if it were against his will, or his better judgment at least. By contrast, Darian was very honest about his desire to make her smile. In short, he was a flirt and she almost didn't remember how to deal with a man on that level. Still, it was exciting to try.

Darian's hand covered hers, forcing her gaze up to his. Even the air stilled, waiting as their eyes met.

"You, Adora. You're the reason." There was no easy smile now, no sign of amusement. No, this was a man puzzled by his own reactions but willing to risk...to trust. What she saw in his earnest face nearly stopped her heart for a moment.

"I don't understand it, but I think I'm falling in love with you, Adora. It's like my heart was waiting for you all this time, and now it sees what it's wanted all along." She was at a loss for words but he wouldn't release her hands. His eyes implored hers. "Say something, sweetheart. Let me know if I at least have a chance."

"A chance?" she repeated, stunned witless.

"A chance to win your love. I want you, Adora. My life is a mess right now. I have little to offer, I know, but my heart is pure and it's yours if you want it."

"Darian, I've been alone a long time."

"Don't say no only because you're frightened. I'll do all in my power to alleviate your fears. Just say you'll give me the chance to try to win your heart. Give me hope, Adora. I beg you."

Her eyes grew moist as he held her gaze, tenderly stroking her hands. She realized in that moment, regardless of her growing feelings for Jared, this man was open in a way Jared could probably never be again. This man, brave enough to leave his life behind for the good of her people, was offering his heart on a platter—and it touched her in ways she didn't quite understand. She barely knew him but she knew his nobility—his courage and his honor— and admired him greatly for it.

Could she know his love as well? She wasn't sure, but a part of her really wanted the chance to try. Another part of her longed for this kind of offer from Jared, but sadly knew it might never come. Should she turn down her chance with Darian because of the attraction she felt for Jared that might never be realized? Or should she take the chance of getting to know this sweet, noble, handsome man who seemed so ready and open to her?

Something about him had fascinated her from the start. He was good looking, yes, but there was also something in his make-up that spoke to her on a much deeper level. He had an energy about him that drew her in and she was powerless to pull away.

"I'm not saying no, Darian. I'm saying…maybe, I guess." She smiled crookedly. "I was married young and lost my husband young as well. I raised my daughter alone, on the run. I haven't had a man in my life, or in my bed, for a very long time." She blushed a little at her own boldness but she wanted to be frank with the man. She owed him her honesty at least, as he was taking the risk she would refuse him outright. "I honestly don't know if I'm ready for that again. My children are grown and I'm at a crossroads in my life. But I like you, Darian, and I'm willing to call you friend. Perhaps lover, but friend for now. Is that all right?"

He beamed at her as he brought her hands to his lips, kissing them soundly.

"It's wonderful, Adora. For your sake, I'll try to control myself, but you're damn near irresistible. You're a special woman and I'll do everything in my power to remind you of that every day."

She felt her cheeks heat with a blush at his impassioned words while his gentle smile warmed her heart.

That night, after all were abed, Adora went to check on her new patient. Darian was restless, his swollen leg healing well, but still a bit uncomfortable at just about any angle. She caught him trying to reposition it on a little mound of pillows with a frustrated expression on his face.

"Can't sleep?"

She advanced into the room, her voice calm as she moved to his leg and gave just a touch of her healing power to ease the ache.

"You shouldn't spend your energy on me, milady."

She sat on the side of his bed. "It's nothing to me if it will help you rest, Darian. I meant to do a more thorough job of your healing before, but I was too tired that first night because of all the energy it took to deal with the dragons. Let me do what I can for you now, all right?"

Darian lay back, watching her every move as she placed her hands on his leg. The warmth of her power swept through her fingers and into his injury, mending the strained muscles and tendons, coaxing the fluid swelling the area to recede. It would take a while to do so, but she knew he would be out of pain now, and probably good as new by morning.

She smiled as she lifted her hands away. It hadn't taken all that much energy after all, and he would be fine now. She was glad of that.

Darian reached up and stroked her cheek with the back of his fingers. "You're a compassionate woman, Adora, and a beautiful soul." His gaze searched hers. "Why did you come here, to me? Couldn't you sleep either?"

This was it. This was her moment of truth.

"No, I couldn't sleep. I kept thinking about what you said about…us." She sought reassurance from his almost ethereal, sky blue gaze. "You got me thinking, Darian, wanting things I haven't wanted in a very long time."

His hand turned to cup her cheek, then moved down her neck to her shoulder. He sought permission before moving further.

"Do you want me, my love?"

"I want—" She sighed as his hand moved lower, parting her robe. She was bare beneath it. Her voice trembled as she forced the words out. "I want you, Darian. I want to be a woman again."

"You've always been that, Adora. You are a desirable, beautiful, brave woman."

He sat up to meet her as she sat on the side of his large bed. With gentle hands, he pushed her robe from her shoulders and moved to meet her lips with his own, taking her in a tender kiss that spoke of desire, passion, and respect. He deepened the kiss and she went with him, following him back down to the bed, her robe hanging open so that she was bare to his roaming, worshiping hands.

Darian kissed her, steadily increasing the pressure on her lips, delving his tongue into her sweet mouth to catch her breathless sighs as his hands caressed her breasts, tweaking the hard nipples, luxuriating in the softness that was Adora. He moved one hand lower, up over her back under the satiny robe and down to her taut butt. She had a muscular body from living off the land and working hard all her life, but she was supple in the places that really counted. Womanly soft and womanly warm, Darian thought, and more welcoming to his lonely soul than any woman had ever been.

She sighed as he rolled her gently on the large bed, pinning her beneath him, the pain in his leg forgotten in her enticing arms. He tugged the robe down over her shoulders, trapping her arms in the thin fabric.

"Say you want me, my love, my beautiful Adora."

"I…" Her breathy voice trailed off as her luminous eyes met his. He watched carefully for any sign of fear, but found only an almost maidenly hesitation that soon disappeared as she made her decision. "I want you, Darian. Make love to me."

He smiled at the soft look in her eyes. She was such a wonder to him, reaching out for what she wanted, what she needed.

"I need you so much." Darian's voice whispered through the dim chamber.

He nibbled on her neck, kissing his way across her body, down to the sweet valley of her thighs. He lingered there, spreading her legs, licking at her tender folds, noting every reaction and cataloging every shiver of delight he brought her. It made him feel so good to see her writhing in passion beneath his hands and mouth. He paused only to pull the long, borrowed sleep shirt over his head and toss it across the chamber, reclaiming his place between her legs with a barely repressed growl of need.

Biting gently, he focused his tender assault on her clit until she came apart under his mouth. She gasped as her body shook through a long, powerful orgasm. This little woman was so needy. He loved the idea that he was one of very few men to bring her such joy—for he could tell this beautiful, shy woman was not too free with her charms—and vowed in his heart this would not be the last night he would pleasure her. He would have her in his bed come morning and every day thereafter, as soon as he could convince her to tie her life to his. She deserved better, it was true, but he was just selfish enough to take her and claim her and spend the rest of his life dedicated to her happiness. He knew he could bring her that at least, if with nothing else but his body, his hands, and his clever tongue.

Darian had never fallen in love before—never felt such immediate, stirring desire for a woman in his life before—but he knew this was the real thing. With a conviction in his heart, he made plans to make her his own. He knew he could no longer be complete without Adora, and only Adora. No other would do ever again.

He moved back up her trembling body, plying her with kisses as he went, bringing her back up to an even higher peak of desire before claiming her mouth and rolling so she was on top of him. He positioned her beautiful, slender but muscular legs on either side of his hips, encouraging her to cocoon his aching cock in her tender folds. Her eyes met his as she gasped and pulled slightly away.

He dragged the satiny robe down her back, throwing it across the chamber to join his sleep shirt. She was beautiful in the dim light of the chamber, gorgeous to him in all her feminine glory.

"Take me this first time, my sweet Adora." He cradled her head in his hands, stroking her hair as he looked deep into her mesmerizing green eyes. "I know it's been a long time for you. Take me at your own pace."

She smiled down at him, repositioning herself with slow movements that drove him wild. She was so soft and wet for him. He wanted her badly, but didn't want to hurt her with his eagerness, so this was the only solution for this first time. Later he would take her the way he needed to, claiming her and pounding into her without mercy, without restraint.

She moved on his cock so tentatively it was killing him, but this time was for her. She would be tight and tender from so many years of denial. It was like taking her virginity, in a way, and he felt like a king that she would give such a gift to him.

Adora rose up and positioned him with her small, trembling hands, nearly making him come right there, but Darian held on, gritting his teeth as he watched them join for the first time. Adora sank down on him by slow degrees, taking him a little way, then bouncing back up, only to go a little lower the next time. Within a few agonizing strokes, she was seated fully upon him and Darian was well on his way to heaven.

He placed his hands on her hips, stroking upward to pull at her hard little nipples. She shivered in response, her wet pussy tightening on his cock and driving him higher. He pinched her nipples harder and was rewarded with another little spasm of her inner muscles around him.

"Do you like it a little rough, Adora?" His eyes dared her to tell the truth he could read from her responses.

"I don't know." Her eyes were wide with surprise, and he tugged again, just a little more harshly this time on her nipples, testing.

"I do." His grin widened as he brought one hand down to slap her ass. She jumped, yelping breathlessly as her pussy spasmed and creamed around him. "You've got an adventurous soul, my little love."

She sighed and shivered as she began to move on his hard cock. "I never did before." She gasped as he used his hands to pinch her bottom. "It must be the company."

"Are you saying I'm a bad influence on you?" His hands encouraged her to speed her pace with gentle slaps to the fleshy part of her ass. He knew she liked it from the way she smiled and squirmed in delight on his cock, sending him higher as well. "If so, I'll have to remember to influence you more often." Darian emphasized his statement with a gentle but firm slap right over her straining clit and she took off for the stars, coming around him and gripping his cock so tight with her inner muscles he thought he would go off with her.

But he had bigger plans for his adventurous little love. As she came down from her peak, he rolled her beneath him again, never leaving her body for one moment. He couldn't bear to part from her even for a second.

"Are you back with me, sweetheart?"

"I'm with you, Dar." Her voice was breathy and divine. It fired his senses.

He dipped down to capture her smiling lips with his own. He had plans to tire her out and ride her until she couldn't walk straight tomorrow, but he wouldn't take her any further if she had gone as far as she could go. He measured her response to his kiss, the tightening around his still hard cock and slippery wetness told him she was ready for more.

"Hang on," he warned, bringing his hips down forcefully into the warm cradle of her thighs. Her eyes jolted open, but her sexy lips curled with delight, reassuring him it wasn't too rough. He would rather die than hurt her.

Darian kept careful track of Adora's responses and pounded more heavily into her tight sheath, reveling in her closeness, her warm body, and her heavenly scent. She was all woman and all his. He loosed the need raging within him and brought himself hard into her again and again, feeling at last her pulsing pleasure as he too was overcome. That final blast of pleasure just went on and on and on.

Darian stiffened above her, tensing in every muscle as his cum shot deep within the only woman he would ever love. The idea was startling, but oddly comfortable. She felt so right in his arms, in his heart. He loved her truly and deeply, he knew in that moment. And he would never love another.

When it was over and he could move once more, Darian kissed her thankfully as she began to relax into a boneless, trusting, exhausted sleep beneath him. He rolled off her, tucking her close to his side as he lovingly arranged the blanket over her luscious, bare body.

A movement near the door caught his eye and Darian looked up only to find Jared staring back at him. The devastation in Jared's lonely gaze chilled Darian to his core. He opened his mouth to speak but Jared was gone before he could find the right words.

Darian looked back at the bed and realized Adora was fast asleep. She didn't know Jared had seen them together. She didn't realize how deeply they had hurt him. Perhaps that was for the best. Darian would find the right thing to say to Jared tomorrow. He hoped.

CHAPTER FIVE

The next morning Adora was up and out of bed before Darian even woke. He dressed and stepped out of the small chamber, leaning just a bit on the walking stick Adora had left for him, in search of breakfast. He found Jared sipping strong dark tea, standing over the cook fire in the small kitchen area.

Jared eyed him hostilely, but said nothing. Still, the tension was thick between the two men as Darian poured out a mug of tea for himself and found an apple to munch.

"Jared." Darian tried to find the words to broach the subject that was clearly standing between them. "I'm sorry if I hurt your feelings, but I couldn't help myself. When I first saw Adora I realized very quickly that she's different from any woman I've ever met before."

"You're damn right she's different." Jared was going to be belligerent about this, he realized. "She's royalty, Dar."

"She's also a warm, mature woman with a woman's needs. She needs love, Jared." Darian tried to speak gently, not wanting to rile his old friend.

"Love? Is that what you call it? Because all I saw last night was you nailing a willing wench." He shot Darian a look of disgust. "How could you?" Jared's deep voice was hoarse with emotion, accusatory and gruff as he glared at Darian. If looks could kill, he'd surely be dead.

"Look Jared, don't jump all over me for this. If you wanted the woman, you've more than had your chance. She cares for you. Don't you think I saw that right away? But I also saw you, in denial, ignoring her. You were hurting her with your indifference, man. Don't fault me for stepping in and making her happy where you've only made her miserable, longing for things you won't give her. She needs someone to care for her and make her feel wanted, cherished, and loved. She's lost her home, Jared." He shook his head. "That's something I have a little experience with as it happens. She needs someone to hold her and make her feel safe and needed."

Jared rocked back on his heels, deflated. "Damn it all to hell and back again." He ran a frustrated hand through his hair and sat hard on the sofa. "You're right, Darian. I'm an ass."

Darian sat down in the nearby chair, watching his old friend closely. Jared sighed hard and shut his eyes tight for a quick moment, the pain of the past hours clear on his face. Darian sensed a break in the wall surrounding his old friend and took the chance to get everything out in the open.

As gently as possible, Darian spoke into the heavy silence. "Ana and James are gone, Jared."

Jared sucked in a sharp breath as every muscle in his body tensed. Darian's heart went out to the man, but this needed to be said. Jared was living in a world of hurt, much different from the carefree, jovial man Darian had once known. He owed Jared his support and help in becoming that man once again. No one should live with the kind of burden Jared kept firmly planted on his shoulders.

"I know that, Dar. I don't need to be reminded. I live with the guilt of their deaths every day of my life."

"Guilt?" Darian was truly puzzled. Jared opened his eyes and ran a hand over his rough face.

"I should have been with them, Dar. I should have protected them. Instead I was off serving my king while they were murdered in their beds by greedy thieves in the night."

Darian was silent a long moment. Could that be what Jared really believed about the attack on his family? How could the man not know the truth of those dreadful days? No wonder he was so changed. Jared blamed himself for something over which he'd had no control or responsibility.

Darian knew he could relieve some of that guilt and perhaps focus the anger of this brave man on something more productive than wallowing in his imagined sins of the past. Darian weighed his words carefully, then finally spoke, albeit a bit hesitantly.

"Those were no simple thieves, Jared." He leaned forward as Jared listened intently. "I found out not long ago that your family was targeted by Lucan. Even back then, he had designs on the throne of Skithdron and worked to throw your country into chaos. You were too close to King Jon and his sons. Too protective. Too smart. Lucan needed you out of the way. He succeeded when he ordered his assassins to kill your family. You left the king's service and his way was clear."

Jared was as near to tears as he'd come since that day he had learned his wife and young son were dead. To learn finally who was responsible was both a terrible shock and, oddly, a relief. Jared felt like the weight of the world had been lifted off his shoulders. It focused him. As did his anger.

Jared's anger was slow to build, slow to burn, but once it got going, it was an unstoppable inferno. He felt the fire rising in his veins, but he needed to have all the facts before he would decide on a course of action. The wisdom of his years had taught him to think before loosing the rage within him. While it was still possible to reason somewhat clearly, he needed to hear everything Darian knew.

"Are you sure? The Lucan I met years ago was a sweet child."

Darian scoffed, "He's a maniac, Jared. I believe he killed his own father. Do you think ordering the deaths of an innocent woman and child would bother such a demon?"

"Sweet Mother of All."

Jared staggered to his feet, emotion overwhelming him. He fought down the sizzling anger, but it bubbled up from within, threatening to break him into a million pieces, never to be reassembled. All the years he'd wasted, blaming himself for something perpetrated by an enemy.

Certainly, he still felt remorse over not being there to defend his family when Lucan's assassins came to call, but knowing their deaths hadn't been random violence somehow made it easier to bear his own guilt. The assassins would have waited until he was gone from home to hit their targets, no matter if he were down the road or in another country. When Skithdronian assassins targeted a person, they didn't miss.

Now Jared knew where to place the blame for his family's demise, the anger and shock of it boiled through his veins like acid. Lucan had won. He'd succeeded in taking Jared from the work he loved for his king and his land, and nearly succeeded in taking Jared's life too. If not for Kelzy, he would have killed himself in his grief long ago. Only the dragon had saved him, bringing him a new purpose.

But Jared's family wasn't the only one to pay the price for Lucan's political designs. No, the old king and his wife had been murdered too. Soon after Jared left the court because of the tragedy in his life, King Jon and his Queen had been killed, forcing young Roland to assume the throne long before his time.

Like patterns in the sand, the lines of deceit were becoming clear. Jared's mind spun as he realized the depths of Lucan's treachery. His family's destruction was just the beginning of the devastation Lucan had visited upon the people of Draconia. Jared had felt terrible guilt at the deaths of the king and queen, thinking if he'd only stayed at court, he might somehow have prevented their murders.

But Jared had been in too much pain at the time. He'd carried his grief with him every day—for his wife and son—but also for the king he had served and loved as a brother. So much death. So much treachery!

Jared's hands balled into fists, his thoughts boiling up until he thought he might explode. Blindly, he moved toward the door. He didn't know where he was going, but he had to do something. He had to loose the anger, grief, sorrow and overwhelming pain in his soul for all that had been lost. So damn much destroyed! So much pain. So much waste.

Suddenly, Kelzy was there, her warm breath bathing him in comfort as the years of sorrow engulfed him. He reached out to the one living being he'd allowed himself to care for and wrapped his arms around her neck. Jared buried his face against her gleaming hide as the emotion welled up and over, pouring out of him with the tears he'd never allowed himself to shed before. He cried for the family he'd lost. For the king. For the years of desolation and pain.

Darian came up behind him and put a strong arm around his shoulders as Jared wept for the first time in many, many years. Jared barely registered his old friend's presence, but he felt the warm support of Kelzy and Darian, needing it as never before.

Adora found them like that when she walked into the suite a few minutes later. Darian caught her eye and motioned her over, his expression solemn as he supported his old friend with a brotherly arm around his wide shoulders. She looked up into Kelzy's aquamarine eyes and the dragon explained what had happened in her silent way.

Adora felt tears well in her own eyes as she thought of how badly this news had affected the strong man who held a piece of her heart. She reached out, coming up on his other side to offer what comfort she could. Her healing gift reached out to his pain as she put her arm around his waist and snuggled into his side.

A moment later, she was whirled around and grasped tightly in his embrace as he let go of Kelzy, only to cling to her instead. She was shocked, surprised, and so touched she gave freely of her healing energy, wishing only that she could heal his shattered heart. She looked up into Darian's sad eyes as Jared choked out broken, nearly silent sobs, his face hidden in her neck as his strong arms engulfed her. She saw sorrow, love, and approval in the eyes of her new lover as she held the other man. It was confusing, but it felt right.

It's as it should be, daughter. Kelzy's voice was gentle in her mind as her breath puffed over them with comforting heat. *Do not fear your feelings for either of these men. They are your destiny.*

Both of them? But how?

The idea of her daughter having two knights as husbands was still uncomfortable, but she sort of understood the necessity with the way the men were bonded to mated dragons. This, however, was something else altogether. Only Jared was bonded to a dragon and Kelzy was unmated. If Adora was mated to Jared, she would eventually be expected to take the knight of Kelzy's dragon mate as her second husband, if such a thing ever occurred.

Because of the bond dragon and knight shared, when dragons mated, their human partners were inevitably caught up in the sensual frenzy. It was a sacred rule that fighting dragons never mated while their knight partners had no mate. The frenzy as the dragons joined would drive an unmated knight insane and a casual sex partner just would not do. The depth of feeling—the love—had to be there for the mating frenzy to be sated, for it was deeply emotional as well as intensely physical for both the dragons and the humans involved.

Don't ask how, child, Kelzy counseled her, still sending warm breaths of cinnamon-scented air over them to offer what comfort she could to her heartbroken knight. *Just accept it will be so. The Mother and we will make it so. We see the way both these men feel about you and how you feel about them. This is the turning point, I think.*

Who's 'we'? She had a sneaking suspicion, but the idea was too wild to even contemplate.

Leave that to us, child. See to Jared now. This storm was a long time in coming and he will feel shame for his actions if you give him half a chance. Best to take him to your bed now and take his mind beyond the grief of the moment. Give him something much more pleasant to focus on.

You want me to sleep with him?

Isn't that what you've wanted for weeks now? Kelzy's voice was sly with the knowledge only another female could understand.

Well…yes, I suppose so. But he doesn't want me. Not really.

Nonsense! The man loves you.

Adora gasped. *Are you sure?*

I know my knight. He's stubborn, but he loves deeply and true. He has a good heart that has been badly hurt and he takes too much responsibility on his solitary shoulders. He needs you, Adora. He needs your strength and your love.

But what about Darian?

Child, the Mother of All knows what She is about. Look at Darian. I think he understands. He knows how much Jared loves you and needs you. He loves Jared like a brother and hates to see him hurt like this. I think he'll understand. He will help, I think. Take him with you and see where it leads.

But he's not a knight. He doesn't expect to have to share a woman with another knight.

He's a man, child. I don't know of too many human males who would turn down a threesome when offered the chance.

Adora smiled just slightly, shyly, as she met Darian's eyes over Jared's broad shoulder.

She saw warmth there—the warmth of care and love, but also the warmth of desire. Darian had shown her just last night she was not as dead sexually or emotionally as she'd thought. He had given her a boost of confidence along with his tender and commanding loving. She knew he cared for her and was fast falling in love with him as well, but her heart also wanted Jared. Adora had wanted him almost from the first moment she'd seen him.

Jared needed her so badly, she knew it in her heart, and this breakdown only proved it further. He needed love and support. He needed to let people close to him, not just dragons. For the past years, only Kelzy had managed to breach the defenses around his heart. But those walls crumbled and crashed as she and Darian supported him in his soul-deep grief.

Darian moved slowly, coming around her, holding her gaze as long as he could until he was behind her. Sandwiched between two hard male bodies, Adora swept her hands down Jared's back as his weeping began to ease. He was so silent, so needy, but so resolute. Jared straightened by degrees, his warm lips nuzzling into her neck as he moved, perhaps unable to meet her eyes while his own were red from grief too long denied. Or perhaps because he was finally giving into the attraction between them.

As he moved, so did Darian, reaching to clasp her waist, moving his already hard erection against the soft globes of her ass. So Kelzy had been right. Apparently getting Darian to share wouldn't be such a hard thing after all. Or rather, there was a hard thing involved, but it was a good, hard thing she would see was put to good, hard use. She could hardly wait.

Smiling to herself, Adora tugged at Jared's leather shirt, pulling at the laces as he worked at hers. Darian was already stripping down her leggings and baring her legs. Kelzy watched all with apparent approval, puffing her sweet breaths over them to keep them warm as they bared themselves and each other.

Adora couldn't believe she was acting so wanton. Her only lover before last night had been her husband. They had been married young, just teenagers fumbling in the dark until they got the hang of meshing their bodies together, but this was something else entirely. Darian had shown her things the night before that she never would have imagined and she sensed she was in for another breathtaking lesson here.

Jared seized her mouth with his own, his lips demanding as never before. Her clothing was gone and she pulled at Jared's with his enthusiastic help. Soon he was bare too, but she didn't get the chance to step back and enjoy the view of his masculine body. No, he was too eager. He kept her close, kept his lips fused to hers as his hands roamed, learning and claiming first her breasts then the smooth expanse of her abdomen and lower, to cup the wetness between her squirming legs.

Darian was busy too, ridding himself of his clothing and dropping to his knees behind her. His lips left a trail of kisses all the way down her back and up her thighs until he reached his goal, between the soft cheeks of her ass. He gripped her cheeks and squeezed, apparently enjoying the soft flesh, leaning forward to nip and suck, leaving his mark on her and licking the momentary, exciting pain away with his clever tongue.

It was Darian who eased her to the floor, his strong arms taking her weight as Jared refused to let her go. Having two sets of masculine hands caressing her body was an enticing, exciting, amazing experience. The approval she read in both their faces when Jared briefly let her up for air gave her the confidence to reach up and run her hands over Jared's chest and down to his straining cock. He was so hard, so ready, and she knew this first time would be fast.

That was fine with her. She would do anything for him. She realized in that moment that she loved him—truly, deeply and without reservations.

"Come to me now, Jared. Make love to me."

He growled as he bore down on her. Thankfully Darian had made a bed of sorts out of the pile of their discarded clothing. Kelzy helped by scooping a mound of warm sand from her wallow. Darian had covered the sand with clothing until Adora lay on a squishy sort of bed that was much more comfortable than she would have expected.

Jared looked down at the woman waiting for him—her soft thighs spread, her beautiful green eyes wide with acceptance of whatever he might do…and love. He could see the love shining in her eyes and knew he felt the same. He could no longer deny his need for her and her beautiful, open, healing heart.

He settled between her legs, unable to help himself. He kissed her tenderly, then pulled back for one last moment of sanity to look down into her beloved face.

"I don't want to hurt you."

"You won't." Her simple acceptance of him and all he was humbled him.

"I love you, Adora." He held his breath. Leaving his heart out in the open like that was a risk.

She touched his rough cheek, her smile generous. "I love you too, Jared."

Her words touched a place deep in his heart he'd thought was gone forever. But suddenly she was there, in his heart, and he knew she would never be removed. Kissing her sweet lips reverently, the heat between them rose once more to a fever pitch.

"I need you now, Adora. I'm sorry, I can't be gentle."

"I don't want you to be gentle. I want you, Jared." She emphasized her demand with an erotic pulse of her hips that brought his hard cock within the hot warmth of her waiting sheath. And he could wait no more.

With a groan, he buried himself inside her, glorying in her heat, her warmth, her wetness, and her love. He was so far gone in his desire he barely heard her answering sighs of pleasure as he pumped hard and fast into her, straining against the force that pushed him onward, holding out to make this first time last as long as he could, but it was a losing battle. He had waited too long to accept the reality that she was his, and all too soon he felt his balls clench and his entire body tense as he erupted within her, showering her with his tribute, bathing her womb in his essence, making her truly his.

Jared collapsed on top of her, eyes opening slowly to stare down into hers. He kissed her then with a gentleness that had been near impossible only moments ago. Adora sighed into his mouth, her hips quaking in the last rolls of orgasm. Jared felt a sense of relief that he'd somehow managed, even in his blind desire, to bring her pleasure.

He kissed her neck, her shoulders, working his way down to the tips of her breasts and she sighed. A rustle of leather off to his side registered just barely in his preoccupied mind and Jared looked up.

There was Darian, trying to squeeze a painfully hard erection back into his leggings.

"Where do you think you're going like that?" Jared was sated enough to have regained a bit of his usual good humor.

Darian started, his eyes meeting Jared's with regret. "Look, you two obviously need some time alone—"

Not alone! Kelzy insisted. *He's part of this, Jared. Make him see.*

Jared looked up at the dragon who had witnessed all and a rueful smile twisted his lips.

"As my dragon partner reminds me, Darian, you're responsible for this. I know you love her too." Jared finally found the strength to lever himself off her luscious body. Caressing her as he got to his knees, Jared removed himself gently from between her slippery legs. How he hated to be apart from her! But things had to be settled between all three of them. He had to make Darian understand the complex feelings he himself couldn't quite figure out, but accepted nonetheless.

"I was jealous as hell when I saw you with her last night, but I know what I saw. There was love there, in every moment. On both sides." He leaned down to kiss her flushed face.

"You saw?" She flushed red with embarrassment.

He winked at her. "I saw all right. Didn't sleep at all for thinking of how he must feel, locked deep inside your beautiful body." Jared kissed her softly. "Now I know." Their eyes held for a moment, her blush fading as her breathing sped up again. "And I also know he's part of this, Adora, in your heart." His gaze shifted to Darian, still standing in indecision, his clothes clutched in his hands.

He saw how Darian watched Adora and how she returned his loving gaze. There was love there, without doubt. Adora would not give herself without it.

Darian shook his head and resumed dressing as Adora sat up on the makeshift bed. "I should go."

"No. You shouldn't." Jared's voice was firm but held more than a hint of frustration. How could he explain something he didn't understand himself? "Look, Dar. It's the way of things for knights to share. If there's love, then

there's nothing wrong with us both being with Adora, as long as she wants it."
He looked over at the startled but smiling woman. "And I think she wants it."
He nudged her knee with his own. "Am I right, darling?"

Adora was confused, but her heart knew what it wanted. Her heart
wanted both of them, with her, forever. Her pussy wanted both of them too. It
was a scandalous, exciting thought.

"I…" She searched for the right words. "I don't understand it, but…I
want you both. You're both in my heart." They stood and Adora went first to
Jared and then to Darian, taking each of them by one hand. "I need you
both." Blushing uncontrollably, she kissed Jared, then Darian, leaning into
Darian a bit longer, convincing him with her mouth, her naked warmth, and
her soft sighs that she didn't want him to leave.

When he released her, there was a tentative smile in Darian's sparkling,
light blue eyes.

"Are you certain, Adora?"

She laughed. "I'm shocked by my own behavior, but I know I want and
need you both. As crazy as it sounds, I love you both. Please don't make me
choose between you. It would shatter my heart." Her eyes grew serious.
"Unless the thought of, um…sharing…hurts you. I wouldn't want to cause
either of you pain."

Jared smiled broadly at her. "I didn't ever expect to have a woman to
love in my life again. You're a miracle to me, and as a leader of knights, I'm
used to three-partnered relationships. I see everyday how well they work out.
Darian and I have known each other for a very long time. We respect each
other as warriors and statesmen, but more so as friends. You'll get no
complaint from me."

Darian's head tilted as he seemed to think carefully about his answer.
Adora held her breath and waited to see what he would say. He was from
another land, after all, where traditions were probably much different. The
Mother only knew what he had been raised to expect… Adora realized in that
one tense moment she would never be truly happy unless she could have them
both. It was that simple and that amazing. She had never thought to have

even one man in her life again and now she felt incomplete without two. She was getting greedy in her old age, she thought with an inner chuckle.

"I don't understand this at all, but I need to be with you, Adora. More than I need to breathe." Darian moved a step closer and caressed her cheek with the back of one big hand. "Jared and I have been good friends for a very long time. He's like a brother to me, and if I had to share with anyone, it would be him. I don't pretend to understand how these three-partnered relationships work, but I'm willing to try, if you truly want this."

She took his hand and turned it to press a tender kiss to his palm. Their eyes locked and held as she smiled.

"I truly do. I want to try." Joyous tears slipped down her face as she looked up at him. "Darian, I love you."

"And I love you, Adora." A kiss sealed his words as he pulled her body into his embrace. Adora pushed at his hastily donned leggings until he was naked once more.

"Let's move this into the bedroom," Jared suggested. "I believe we have some unfinished business to attend to."

Tugging on Darian's hand and catching Jared's in her other hand, she led them both toward the largest bed in the big suite. It happened to be in Jared's chamber. Jared winked at her as he caught her up in his arms, strode through the archway and deposited her on his wide bed.

"As my lady wishes, of course."

Darian knew he couldn't go slowly this time. He needed her too badly. Watching Adora make love with Jared, instead of defusing his desire, had only made it rise impossibly higher. A look of understanding passed between the men as Jared stepped back, motioning Darian to take the lead this time. With a nod of thanks, Darian knelt down on the bed beside Adora. She was eager for them both and her responsive little body only made his passion climb higher than it had ever been before.

"How do you want it, sweetheart? Slow, fast, gentle, rough?" Darian whispered as he nipped her tender throat on the way to her sensitive breasts.

"I want what you want," she answered with little guile.

He loved that about her. She was fully a woman, yet so innocent. He would bet her husband, gods rest his departed soul, hadn't taken her beyond basic lovemaking. Darian relished the thought that he could teach her a thing or two about giving and receiving pleasure. There was so much he wanted to experience with her, so much he wanted for her to experience.

"Then hang on for a wild ride, my lovely."

He bit softly at her slight belly, winking up at her as he licked down lower, over her distended clit. A second little nip there as he tested her readiness had him smiling. She was gushing and so responsive to his every move. She was more than ready for him.

Moving with some urgency, yet caressing her skin at every turn, Darian positioned himself under her. He had something in mind and, glancing over at Jared, was pleased to note the fire in the other man's eyes as he watched Adora. It boded well for Darian's plans. Catching Jared's attention with a patting motion on her beautiful fleshy ass, Darian raised one eyebrow at the knight. Understanding flared as Jared licked his lips, seemingly mesmerized by the sight of Adora's womanly body swaying seductively with her passionate motions.

"How about we all do this together?" Darian made sure his voice was pitched loud enough so that Jared would hear his question to their woman.

"Is that possible?" Adora sat back, looking down at him with questions in her lovely green eyes.

He chuckled. "You're a healer, woman. You should know there's more than one place a man can pleasure himself and his woman."

She blushed so prettily he reached up and kissed her, the muscles in his abdomen rippling and contracting as he sat up under her slight weight. Pulling back, Darian watched her eyes carefully for any sign of fear, but there was none. No, his little adventuress was curious and more than a little excited if he read her right.

He looked over at Jared and caught the other man's eye once more. "What do you say?"

Jared's cock was hard as stone watching Adora climb all over Darian's firm body. The other man was damned near perfect. No huge, ugly scar marred his skin and Jared remembered how his handsome face and perfect teeth had been sighed over by the ladies of the court. He could understand why Adora might fancy Darian, but he couldn't fathom why in the world the woman would want him as well.

He was scarred badly, his face nothing to write home about. His body was rough, hair flying whichever way no matter what he did to tame it and starting to go grey now just at the temples. He was no longer the handsome lord he'd once pretended to be. He was a rough warrior now, through and through. Yet, the magical light of passion tempered Adora's sultry green gaze when she looked at him.

Apparently love truly did make one blind, for she looked at him with the eyes of love—the same way she looked at Darian's perfect features. How had he gotten so lucky? Why had the Mother blessed him so well? Jared would never know, but he would spend every moment proving to Adora that her love was not misplaced, demonstrating over and over how much he loved and cherished her in return.

When Darian's raised eyebrow challenged him, Jared was more than up for it. He searched around the sparse room, knowing he would need something to ease his way inside Adora's unused channel. The curiosity in her eyes told him she had never done this before—never taken a man's cock up her pretty ass—but he knew she was game to try. He didn't want to hurt her, so he'd make sure she was well prepared. The only problem was, Jared was totally *un*prepared. He had nothing to use as a lubricant to help ease his way past her tight muscles.

Look in the top drawer of the table at the side of your bed.

Kelzy's voice came to him seemingly out of the blue. Turning, Jared spied Kelzy's large head watching all from the archway. He should have known his dragon partner would be watching over him and the small human woman she thought of as her daughter.

Jared moved to the nightstand and opened the drawer. Inside was a large tub of a pleasant smelling herbal concoction tucked neatly into the top that he'd never seen before.

He looked back at Kelzy suspiciously. *Where did this come from?*

I asked Belora to put it there.

You were awfully sure about this then, huh?

I hoped, Kelzy clarified. *I prayed to the Mother that you three would come to your senses and see what was right in front of you all the time.*

Without comment, Jared scooped out a bit of the salve and went back to the lovers entwined on his bed. Adora was impaled on Darian's cock, riding sinuously while Darian held her to a slow pace. The other man knew what was coming and he was coaching her into the experience, thoughtful and tender as Jared looked on approvingly.

Jared caught Darian's eye as he positioned himself. Nodding to each other over Adora's shoulder, Darian reached down and pulled her luscious cheeks apart, helping Jared in his quest to teach her this new pleasure.

He slathered her little hole with the herbal mixture, probing gently at first, then more insistently as she responded with soft sighs and hungry moans to his moves. He sank two fingers into her, stretching gently, urging her to relax as he worked his way inside. A third finger slipped in and after a bit of stroking in and out, he figured she was as ready as he could make her.

As gently as he could, he positioned himself at her opening, pressing steadily inside. She accepted him with surprisingly little fuss, her body shivering just a bit as she was stretched in this new way for the first time.

"Is it all right?" Jared asked, bending to nip the lobe of her ear.

Adora moaned. "It feels so strange! So good. Oh, Jared!"

He smiled and sank completely inside her. Once there, he just waited a moment, both to let her adjust and to savor the feeling. Jared could feel the ridge of Darian's cock through the tissues separating them. Jared knew the other man felt her pussy tighten impossibly around his own straining member, just as he felt the flexing inside her ass. He caught Darian's eye and they began to move in her. This was a true partnership—the goal of their work to make the woman between them experience the ultimate in pleasure.

They were both dedicated to their work.

While Adora whimpered in mounting pleasure, they each worked their cocks in and out of her, in rhythm. She strained between them, coming to peak after peak as they rode her through the pleasure right into another wave of ecstasy.

"Are you with us, love?" he heard Darian ask her. She moaned in reply as both men chuckled, but the time was drawing near.

Jared sped up, knowing Darian would feel and understand the need for urgency. Together they rode her higher and higher. Jared loved the way her fingers clutched at his hands and arms and her mouth sought purchase on Darian's sweat-slicked skin. She was close to total meltdown and together, they were going to take her there.

"Now, Adora! Now!" Jared called out as he bucked into her, ramming high and tight. He felt Darian do the same as her body convulsed around them in the biggest explosion yet. Adora screamed as she came, over and over, hard and fast, and Jared finally gave himself permission to let go.

He pulsed into her ass, filling her with his cum, knowing that at the same time, Darian was filling her womb with his own tribute. It was an amazing feeling and one he never thought he would know. To love and be loved and know that should he falter, there was a partner there, ready and willing to help him, even as he would do the same. Together they would cherish and love this little woman who gave so much of herself to them both, and she would never be in any danger as long as one of them lived.

Pulling from her as gently as he could, Jared took only a moment to clean up before returning to the big bed, claiming one side of her luscious, sated body for himself and falling into a deep dreamless slumber. The crisis was past. There was only the future to look forward to now and it looked bright indeed.

CHAPTER SIX

Before the others rose the next morning, Darian walked through the halls of the Border Lair, needing to exercise his healing leg. The Lair was a truly magnificent feat of architecture and magic, combined to form a place that was hospitable for man and dragon alike. There were few women and children about, but there were some. Most smiled and nodded as he passed, friendly but reserved. It was, after all, quite early in the morning, so everyone kept their voices down to avoid waking those who needed more sleep.

Darian followed most of the early risers in the general direction of the great hall. There, he found quite a few people gathered, eating breakfast. Some knights were clearly just coming off duty, dressed still in their leathers, and some were freshly shaven, in a rush to get out on their own patrols.

All of them eyed him suspiciously, though none bothered him as he ate a small bowl of porridge one of the smiling women had spooned up for him. There were those who didn't view him as the enemy, but they appeared to be few and far between. The disgruntled looks shot at him from all around the hall made Darian feel rather conspicuous. Rather than tempt fate—and the angry knights eyeing him hostilely—he finished his meal, then stacked his used bowl and spoon in the area set aside and walked quietly out into the hall.

That should've been the extent of the excitement, but Darian didn't count on the foolishness of youth. A few of the younger knights followed him, walking beside and behind him in the wide hallway as he headed for the landing ledge. It was on the way back to Jared's suite and Darian had wanted to get a bit of fresh air before returning, but the younger knights changed his plans.

They followed on his heels, slowing their pace to match his as they neared the wide landing area. All his instincts went on alert. These knights apparently had some kind of problem with him and they undoubtedly wanted to be heard—or worse.

Normally Darian was light on his feet and good with his fists, but the recently healed injury put a little cramp in his style. Even so, five against one weren't the greatest odds—even for him. And to top it off, Darian didn't really want to fight with these lads. He hadn't the heart for it. The Draconian knights had every reason to despise Skithdron after the unprovoked attacks on the border. Skithdron was in the wrong here and these young hotheads saw him as the enemy, no matter that he'd sacrificed all he owned and all he was to come here and warn the Draconian side of worse things yet to come.

To them he was simply an enemy.

Darian sighed as he stepped out into the open landing area. They would act now, if at all, he knew. They didn't disappoint him.

"We don't want you here, Skithdronian scum."

Darian turned to face the speaker, his back to the wide expanse of the landing ledge. There were seven of them now. Apparently two more had just flown in from patrol and joined with their fellows against the enemy in their midst. Darian had to forcibly hold back a sigh.

"I have no quarrel with you, sir knight." Darian did his best to keep his tone civil, but firm.

"What if we have a quarrel with you? Skith bastard." Another of the young fools found the nerve to speak, buoyed by his compatriots.

"Go back where you came from," yet another of them sneered.

Darian didn't want this to turn into a fight. These men were all younger than he was, big and battle-trained. But Darian had skills that—even with his slightly swollen leg—assured him he could at the very least hold his own. Still, he didn't want to harm any of these youngsters. He thought it wouldn't be a good idea to repay Jared's welcome by disabling five or six of his knights on his first full day in the Lair.

"Look," Darian held up his hands, palms outward in a gesture for calm, "I don't want any trouble."

"Then leave," came the quick reply.

Darian was at a loss as to how to defuse this situation. The young knights were attracting attention and others were coming over, some to join and some to simply observe. He became aware of dragons too, pausing to see what their human counterparts were doing, and one dragon in particular, came up behind him, settling at his back.

Almost dreading what he'd find, Darian craned his head around to find the huge blue-green dragon, shockingly, standing behind him. It was Kelzy, and she clearly showed her support for Darian, eyeing the knights arrayed against him—no, *them*, now—with a baleful glare.

He hadn't dared expect any assistance from the huge dragon, though he thought she was coming to like him a bit better as she got to know him. Still, this sort of show of support was completely unexpected and oddly humbling. Darian didn't know Kelzy well, but knew in his heart she had to be a special dragon indeed to gain the trust of Jared, a man he'd known as wise and honorable to the core.

The young knights didn't back down, but they stopped threatening Darian physically, and before he knew it a full-fledged confrontation was in the works. He cursed himself for going out into the public areas of the Lair alone as other dragons came over to see what Kelzy was doing. Suddenly his morning walk had become an international incident.

"Oh, great," Darian mumbled to himself when a slightly rumpled Adora and Jared elbowed their way through the massive group now gathered around him and Kelzy. He should've realized the dragon would call her partner.

Darian would rather not have forced Jared's hand this way, especially not after the momentous events of the day, and night, before. He had no idea if Jared would be welcoming or wounded this morning. The chances were good either way after the emotional upheavals of the night.

"What's going on here?" Jared demanded of his knights while Adora stood back, watching with wide, nervous eyes.

One of the ringleaders stood forward from the sizable throng that faced him now.

"We want him gone, Jared. He's Skithdronian scum and probably a spy."

Jared stared at his knights in deep disappointment. He thought he knew these men. He thought he knew their hearts, but apparently he'd been wrong. They didn't know him well enough to trust his judgment and really, when had he ever opened up to them? It was his own fault.

Sadly, he shook his head. There was nothing he could say. Leaders led by example, not by making speeches. Jared took the time to look each and every one of his knights in the eye. He noted the ones who stood against him directly in defiance of his leadership and those who merely watched from the sidelines. Gareth and Lars were nowhere to be seen, though he would have hoped those two, at least, would have stood with him and trusted his judgment.

Saying not a word, Jared turned his back on the doubters and strode forcefully to Darian's side. Clapping him on the back, Jared demonstrated his support of the Skithdronian lord who had become more than a brother to him, more than just a friend. This man was part of his family now. No matter what complications might arise from it, he would be there for Darian.

Kelzy moved away, surprising Jared, but it didn't change his mind. He would stand with Darian against all comers. Alone if need be.

But they weren't alone.

A moment later, another dragon loomed behind them. It wasn't Kelzy and for just a second Jared feared some new form of attack, but when he looked up, his mind spun as his thoughts sped. The looming presence could only mean one thing. He just hoped his old friend was ready for what was to come. Oh, the Mother was having a grand joke on all of them today. Her influence was clear in this new development. Jared just hoped Darian would understand what Fate had in store.

The huge copper dragon loomed over Darian's shoulder, a solid presence, somehow even more comforting than Kelzy had been. Sandor's voice boomed through Darian's head as it had only once before. But this time, he felt a thickening of the connection, an opening of the pathway that led from the dragon's mind to his own.

I claim you as my knight partner, Sir Darian, former Lord of Skithdron. You have proven yourself worthy and if you will have me, I will be your companion and partner for the rest of your days.

"Merciful gods! What are you talking about?"

"You heard him?" Jared asked loudly. Darian was puzzled. Why would Jared ask such a thing? It was plain they'd all heard the dragon speak.

"Of course I heard him."

Lord Darian has always had the ability to hear me It was just untapped. I have spoken to him before.

"Is this true?" Jared wanted public confirmation for some reason.

Darian nodded. "He spoke to me once before."

"Then it's his right to choose you as knight partner. Our law says any male who has the ability to communicate with dragonkind may be claimed if he is deemed worthy by the dragon who wishes to partner with him."

"What are you talking about?" Darian looked from the astonished knights, to the huge copper dragon, to Jared and back again. Something cold and nervous settled in the pit of his stomach, while at the same time, something eager and joyous wanted to shout from his heart. Could this huge dragon really want him? Could this ancient and wise creature really see anything of value within a man who'd turned traitor to his own country?

I do claim you, Darian. If you will have me, I'll be your dragon partner for the rest of your days and you will be my knight.

"Me? A knight of Draconia?" Darian could hardly believe it, though something deep in his soul wanted desperately for it to be true.

You have already proven yourself willing to put your life on the line to warn the humans and dragons of this land of grave and serious danger. You are a brave and honorable man. There are few knights here who are your equal, Lord Darian. Accept me as your partner and we will continue to do good work for the humans and dragons of this land.

Darian considered the copper dragon's words for a long silent moment. The boy who never aged within his heart was jumping up and down in excitement. Sandor was such a noble being and it was such a rare and splendid thing to even hear a dragon speak, much less want to be your partner for life. Darian knew he'd be a fool to pass up this magical opportunity. If he didn't accept the dragon now, he'd live with regret for the rest of his life.

Still, agreeing to be a dragon's knight partner wasn't something to be undertaken lightly. Darian ran through the various possibilities in his mind but there was really only one answer for the dragon's request.

"All right." Darian breathed deeply, his chest expanding with excitement and joy. "I accept. And I'll do all in my power to live up to your high opinion of me, Sir Sandor. I only hope you know what you're doing."

The dragon chuckled smokily. *Trust me, my friend. Let it be your first act of faith in our new partnership. To make this official, you must accept me like this, Darian, mind to mind. Follow the path I have forged between us.*

With the bright wonder in his heart spilling over into joy, Darian followed the path in his mind used only once before. It was wider now, more direct and easier to access. It felt as if the connection had always been a part of him and it gave him just a bit of insight into the soul of the incredible, magical creature who had just managed to alter the course of his life forever.

I accept, Sir Sandor. I will be your knight partner for the rest of my days.

Sandor turned and trumpeted his joy skyward, a noble acknowledgment of the newly made knight. All the other dragons followed suit, welcoming the new knight with a huge crescendo of sound that shook the very mountain itself.

Adora wept openly as she watched it all. First Jared had made her proud, his noble heart beating true as he stood up for his friend against the younger knights. She knew Jared's honor demanded he stand for what was right rather than bend to pressure and she loved him deeply for his nobility and honor.

Then Sandor arrived, making such a public display of claiming Darian for his knight partner it took her breath away. Adora suddenly realized exactly who Kelzy's co-conspirator had been all along. All they needed now was for Kelzy and Sandor to declare themselves mated and it would all be tied up with a nice, neat bow.

Adora was about to confront Kelzy with her surmise when Gareth and Lars strode in, having learned from their dragons what had just transpired. Without a word, they went to stand firmly at Darian and Jared's sides. Even their dragon partners, Kelvan and Rohtina, lumbered over to stand with

Sandor. Kelzy moved to stand beside her son, Kelvan, and Adora finally saw the resemblance that had escaped her before.

Kelzy, is Sandor Kelvan's father? She sent the question privately, amusement lacing her tone.

It took you long enough to figure it out. And here I thought you were such a bright child.

Sandor is your mate, then? That's what you were talking about when you said the Mother of All knew what She was doing, wasn't it?

Sandor came to the Lair to meet Kelvan's new family, but when he first saw Darian, he knew he had found his next knight partner. Kelzy bowed her great head in acknowledgment and Adora suddenly knew what she had to do. Moving to stand before the two men she loved, Adora reached up and kissed them both, deeply, in front of the entire Lair.

"Do you trust me?" she asked both of them as quietly as she could.

Both men nodded.

"Do you love me?"

Again, they nodded and their eyes were filled with the flames of their love as they looked at her. Adora offered up a silent prayer to the Mother of All, then turned to face the doubters who still stood against them.

"I am Princess Adora of the House of Kent." There were a few surprised looks from those who hadn't ever heard public acknowledgment of her royal status. "I claim these two brave men, these knights, as my mates and Prince-Consorts. They deserve your respect, and if you don't like it, you may take it up with my cousin, the king."

So saying, Adora linked her arms through both of her men's and walked regally through the throng, which parted as if by magic in front of them. The dragons followed behind as they promenaded out of the area, leaving stunned silence behind.

When they reached their suite, both men turned on her.

"What did you just do, Adora?" Darian eyed her with suspicion, then turned his gaze up to the copper dragon who stood next to Kelzy trying to look innocent. "And you! What was that all about, Sandor? I'm no knight. I'm not even Draconian."

I beg to differ. Every action you have taken since I've known you has been more than worthy of a knight. You are an honorable man and one who puts the good of others above his own. Those youngsters could learn a few things from you, Sir Darian.

"I agree with Sandor," Adora said with some conviction as she moved to stand with the copper dragon. "He is after all, Kelvan's father." She looked accusingly up at the dragon, but her smile softened the teasing. "And Kelzy's mate."

"Sweet Mother!" Jared sat heavily on the sofa. "You two were planning this all along."

"Planning what?" Darian wanted to know.

"Last night, and now Sandor claiming you…it's all so they can be together."

At this the dragons appeared to take offense, rearing their great heads.

So you three can be together, you ungrateful swine, Kelzy berated her knight. *We saw right away that you three belonged together. You need each other. You were made for each other. Sandor and I have been mates for many years, it's true, but we will outlive you all many times over. How could we sit by and watch you waste even one more of your precious years when love was looking you in the face and you were turning away? Ungrateful—*

Now, Kelzy, he's just young. He'll learn. Sandor's deep voice sounded amused to all three humans.

"Young?" Jared was clearly upset. "I've already lost a wife and son." His voice broke on the words as his emotions threatened to overtake him. "Or did you forget?"

No, we can never forget them. Nor will you. Kelzy had calmed in the face of Jared's sorrow.

Adora went to him and took him in her arms. "Nor *should* you, Jared," she said. He held her fiercely.

"I don't deserve you, Adora."

Now that's the first sensible thing you've said since we got here. Kelzy's tone was teasing in all of their minds.

Jared kissed Adora deeply then, as if he needed to feel her in his arms, grounding him in the changing situation.

"We have little choice, I'm afraid. We've been outmaneuvered by generals greater than ourselves." Jared smiled briefly up at the dragons.

Darian gave Jared and Adora a lopsided grin, his eyes somewhat uncomfortable. "I can hear them in my head."

Adora chuckled and reached out, pulling Darian into the embrace as Jared shifted her around in his arms.

"And so you should, *Sir* Darian." She kissed him soundly. "Sandor couldn't have chosen a knight who couldn't hear him speak, now could he?"

Darian shook his head, smiling faintly. "I guess not. I still don't quite believe it. Or understand it."

All you need to know for now, Darian, is that by choosing you, I've fulfilled the Mother's design for us all. It was fated that you three join and that by doing so, reunite me and my mate. Sandor's deep voice was wise and gentle. *The rest will come to you in the fullness of time, my friend. I believe you still have a role to play in protecting our world from King Lucan. He threatens to upset the balance of Nature with his evil plans and the Mother of All must have some purpose for you left to fulfill. Believe in that, believe in yourself, and believe in me. You will never be alone again, Darian, as long as any of we five here now, live. We are a family.*

There was a mating feast, of sorts, held that night in the great hall of the Lair. Many were still injured from the battle and many others were on patrol. The merriment was low-key, but the congratulations were heart-felt from most of the revelers. Some still eyed Darian with suspicion, but most of the younger dragons had been trained by Sandor or Kelzy, or both, and trusted in their judgment. With encouragement from the dragons, most of the younger knights were willing to give Darian the benefit of the doubt.

Surprisingly, Darian was familiar with the traditional mating feast dances from his years spent as ambassador to Draconia and was able to dance easily with Adora and Jared. It was Adora who had a tough time keeping up with her newly claimed men. Certainly, she had seen her daughter learn the steps to the odd three-partnered dances favored between the mated sets of knights and their ladies, but she had never performed the steps herself.

At the beginning of the dancing, when the patterns called for her knowledge and input, she stumbled, but either Jared or Darian was always there to catch her. As the night wore on though, the dancing got hotter and the men did most of the work. By the time they got around to the traditional mating dance, she had little to do—and little to wear—as the men tossed her around between them, holding her close, kissing her deeply, and fondling her nearly naked body.

She was all too ready to leave for their suite when the dragons took to the sky in their first mating flight in years. She knew Kelzy and Sandor were eager to renew their relationship and her men were even hotter than they'd been the first time the three of them had joined in passion. That first time had been a catharsis for Jared and even for Adora in a way. They'd worked through all their old pains and offered them up on the altar of passion, wiping away past hurts and forging new ties that were stronger and deeper than anything any of them had known before.

This time the joining would be joyous. This would be a mating, a claiming, a joining of pure hearts and souls. There would also be the frenzy of the dragons, influencing the men and probably Adora as well, as closely bonded as she was with Kelzy, not to mention the unpredictable influence of her own royal blood.

The closer they danced, the higher their passions rose, and when Kelzy and Sandor trumpeted as they took to the sky, Jared picked Adora up bodily and made straight for their bedchamber, Darian following close behind. Other mated pairs and threesomes headed out of the main area as well and Adora had only a glimpse of her daughter and her two mates leaving before she was out of the great hall.

Jared was kissing her even before he placed her in the center of the large bed in their suite. Darian undressed her and himself in between biting kisses to her backside and her hips. For her part, Adora pulled at what remained of Jared's clothing, removing the loincloth with eager hands as she began to feel the echoes of the dragons' passion through the bond she'd formed at a young age with Kelzy and the bonds that were even now strengthening between herself and her chosen mates.

Darian was nearly beside himself and she knew he would find this night the hardest to deal with of the three of them. He had only bonded to Sandor hours before and hadn't had any time to get used to the dragon who now shared a connection to his soul. Jared had been partnered with Kelzy for years now, but had never felt the intense mating heat two grown dragons could create. He would have a little more chance of tempering it, but Adora knew she was in for a wild ride that night.

She wouldn't have it any other way.

Darian looked at his new lover and realized she was his home. Adora was comfortable in a way he had never before experienced. The moment she touched him, he'd known that she was the last woman he would ever desire and the only woman he would ever love. It was that sudden, that harsh, and that true.

It's like that for knights, Sandor had told him earlier that day when his thoughts turned once again to Adora. *Lest you doubt you are truly a knight, you should know most knights recognize their mate the moment they lay eyes on her. It's part of being a knight and joining with my kind. We too know our mate the moment we see her and for us, there is usually only one mate for all our many years.*

Sandor's words came back to Darian as he looked at Adora now. She was it for him. He was certain of that as he had never been certain of anything in his life before. This was love—plain and oh, so simple. There would never be another woman for him. Only Adora.

He couldn't get enough of her. He couldn't get close enough and couldn't seem to control himself when he touched her. He felt her fire, her steam, her desire as if it was his own, but then perhaps it was the dragons' fire he was feeling. Darian shook his head to try to regain some sense of normalcy, but it would not come.

He was linked to the soaring dragons as they circled and dived, climbing higher in their joy before joining and taking that dangerous plummet to earth as they pleasured each other only to separate at the last possible moment of freefall. To do it all over again.

Adora was on the bed now. All three of them were naked and wanting. Darian tried to cool his ardor to give his beloved Adora a chance to catch her breath. Struggling for control, he sat back, but she would have none of it. Adora rocketed up, grabbing him by the ears so that he had no choice but to follow where she led.

"Come into me now, Dar. I need you and Jared both."

"I don't want to hurt you. I'm just barely in control here." The admission was ripped from his soul, but her smile made everything all right.

"I don't need your control tonight, Darian. I need you. I need your passion, your lust, your cock. And your love."

Freed by her harsh gasp of excitement, Darian watched as Jared pulled her back on the bed, mounting her swiftly. He moved in time with the dragons Darian could feel in the back of his mind.

Jared's hard cock slid home as he rolled beneath her, pulling her ass cheeks apart, making room for his partner in this strange marriage. Darian prepared her, entering slowly but steadily, using the special ointment Adora had placed on the nightstand before they even left for the feast. She'd apparently known what to expect from this night and she was getting it in spades, he realized as he slid home within her.

When they were both seated fully, Darian met Jared's eyes over Adora's shoulder pressing deep within her. With a nod, they began to move, slow at first, then getting longer and stronger as the frenzy grew within them all. Dimly, he heard Adora's panting cries of ecstasy as she came to peak after peak between them. Darian felt the powerful contractions of her orgasms around his hard cock, but he couldn't come until the dragons did.

Higher they flew, the dragons and the humans locked in coital bliss. As the dragons began their freefall, so too did their human counterparts, both knights spurting their cum deep into the woman they both loved, adored and cherished with all their hearts. She was claimed—filled and marked for all time by the hard, merciless loving. As she smiled lazily at them, Darian knew she loved every minute of it.

The dragons rose again, only an hour later, searching for the stars as their bodies joined, beating wings into the night. First though, the men treated Adora to a long soak in the heated tub where they teased her mercilessly. They lifted her out, stepping free of the huge tub and drying her inch by precious, tantalizing inch, licking her flame higher.

Darian caught Jared's eye as they brought Adora back to the bed. Both men could feel the dragons taking off for the stars and they knew their time of rest was almost at an end.

"Are you up for something a little different, my love?" Darian whispered in her ear as he ushered her toward the bed, his legs right behind hers. He rubbed his chest against her back, his arms caging her breasts as she giggled like a young girl.

She turned in his arms to place a teasing kiss on his lips. "Anything you wish, Master."

Darian growled. "Mmm, I like it when you call me that." He nodded to Jared as the other man finally noticed the cords Darian had left out before joining them in the bath. "Have you ever been tied, Adora? Will you trust us to see to your pleasure completely? Will you let yourself be helpless in our arms?"

She looked uncertain at first as her gaze moved between the two men, but then she smiled and the twinkle in her eyes brightened his soul.

"I trust you."

Darian kissed her deeply, backing her onto the wide bed as Jared prepared the soft ropes Darian had scrounged earlier from elsewhere in the large suite. While Darian held her arms up, Jared tied them tightly together above her head, using one rope to secure her to one corner of the large bed.

Darian lifted his head to survey the work and nodded with a broad grin. Jared had done this before, he could tell. It amazed him that they were alike in this way, but he didn't question his good fortune. He had work to do before the dragons took him beyond reason and into their own brand of wild lust.

Adora lay diagonally across the wide bed, hands bound together, then secured to one corner. They could maneuver her easily into just about any position either of them could dream up.

Darian flipped her over onto her knees and elbows, positioning her just so as he surveyed the enticing sight her spread, wet pussy made against the bedclothes. Jared slid beneath her upper body, seating himself within easy reach of her mouth. Darian realized Jared was letting him have her pussy for this round and thanked the other man with a sly grin as he slid his fingers into her slick well.

The dragons rose now, their passions echoing through the knights as both his and Jared's rods stiffened beyond bearing. The level of arousal he felt was inhuman. It was but an echo of the immense desire filling the dragons and influencing their bonded knights to be more than men in those moments. It was humbling and invigorating at the same time. Darian saw the incredible need he felt reflected in Jared's expression and knew they were both caught up in their dragon partners' lust.

"Suck him, Adora. Take Jared in your mouth and swallow him down."

That she complied so eagerly pleased him. He liked directing her actions in this way and would heartily enjoy it when Jared and he reversed their roles, he knew.

He lay down on the bed and pulled her down slightly so that her pussy rested over his mouth. He used his tongue to sink deep within her tight hole, licking upward, spreading their combined moisture and making little circles around her sensitive clit. He felt her tremble against his mouth and he knew she was close.

So was he for that matter. The dragons neared their zenith and he just had to be inside his mate before the passion overtook him completely and drove him mad. With a growl, he lifted her hips, rose up, turned and sank home within her in one smooth but forceful motion. If she could have screamed with her mouth stuffed fully with Jared's cock, he knew she would have in that moment. As it was, she made a sound deep in her throat that both knights enjoyed.

Darian knew from Jared's gasp and the way he clenched his fist in Adora's auburn tresses that her vocalization had reverberated through his shaft. For his part, Darian just enjoyed hearing the proof of her enjoyment as they both possessed her.

He began shafting in and out, his rod harder and stiffer than it had ever been before. Darian began to realize just how fully the dragons affected both he and Jared in ways he never would have imagined, allowing them both to bring Adora to peak after peak before coming themselves.

But this wasn't one of those times. This time was hard and fast, harsh and earthy. Darian plowed into her, slapping her ass just once as she tightened on him, coming for him nicely before he totally lost control as the dragons did.

After that, he lost all rational thought, driving home within his new mate the only goal.

"Adora!" he shouted as all of them neared the stars with the dragons.

Darian's eyes shut hard and every muscle in his body tensed as he joined with Sandor in a hard, long release inside the warm welcoming depths of his mate. He felt what the dragon felt in that moment, sharing in the glory that was the physical expression of love no matter the species. He felt the pleasure multiplied through him and Sandor and through Sandor to Kelzy and to Jared, magnified and sent back to him. It was a true sharing, a completion and a new start for them all.

Darian realized in the aftermath that he was linked with Jared through the dragons, but Adora had a direct link to him as well, somehow. It was a phenomenon he vowed to explore further now that he'd decided to make his home in this land and among these people.

This was his home now. Wherever Adora, Jared, Kelzy and Sandor were. Without all four of them, he would no longer be content or complete. They were his family.

As he came down from the fast, hard high, he realized the dragons were plummeting to earth in the freefall of their spent passion, their wings outstretched at the last moment to prolong the pleasure and allow them to glide on the wings of love for a long, satisfying moment. They were basking, as he was too, in the glory that was his mate and his new family.

CHAPTER SEVEN

As leaders of the Lair during a time of war, there was no long honeymoon for Darian, Jared, and Adora—or the dragons. They were back to work the next day, yawning a little, but with wide, satisfied grins as they went about their business.

As a previously mated pair, Kelzy and Sandor were better able to manage their frequent urges to couple, though they did catch their human partners off-guard a time or two over the next few days. Each time though, the men raced to their suite, throwing off clothing as they ran, only to find Adora waiting for them already naked on the bed. She welcomed them both with open arms...and legs. They varied their positions, but the love between them never varied, never altered, never changed, except to grow deeper and surer with each passing day.

Darian was a novice when it came to fighting from atop a dragon but proved himself an able student and an innovative strategist as he trained with Sandor each day. His added insights into the workings of the Skithdronian army were invaluable as they prepared their defenses. Darian had spent most of his younger days as a warrior before becoming an ambassador, so fighting and training was nothing new to him. Nothing, that is, except flying on the back of a huge dragon. Now *that* was new and absolutely thrilling.

Sandor was a great teacher and Darian learned as much and more from just watching the way Jared and Kelzy worked together. The four of them were a fighting team now, since the dragons were mates, and would fight side by side. They trained together, lived in the same suite, and shared the same wife. It wasn't as Darian had always expected his life to work out. It was much better than that, actually. Though he still believed in the gods of his culture, he had to admit this 'Mother of All' his new family believed in certainly did know what She was doing when She brought them all together.

Still, Darian felt his years when he returned to the suite late at night after a full day of riding patrol and drilling with Sandor, Kelzy and Jared. Jared just laughed at him and shook his head but Adora was more sympathetic. She went to him while he soaked in a hot tub of water in the bathing chamber. She had an herbal mixture for his bath and later gave him a rubdown with a warm, fragrant massage oil she'd prepared to relax his overstressed muscles.

After such delicious treatment, he was ready for the dragons to take off for the moon and drive him and his mate to a frenzy of pleasure. Darian positioned himself under Adora this time, where he wouldn't have to put any extra stress on his already abused muscles, but when she took Jared and him both into her beautiful body, he forgot all about his aches and pains. The only ache he felt was one at the center of his heart for this lovely, giving woman who had become the center of his universe.

The skirmishes continued over the next few days but the reconnaissance reports indicated the Skithdronian army was massing just over the border. They were waiting to start the second wave of attack, Darian surmised, for something…or someone.

The answer came the next day when their patrols reported movement on the border. Skiths slithered across the already destroyed fields and farms, heading for the few villages that remained populated after the first round of attacks. Jared was a sight to behold as he decisively took charge of the Lair's fighting forces, marshalling the knights and dragons to mount an effective defense against the renewed attack.

When the first dragon fell, all trumpeted in horror and sadness. It was a youngster named Jizra with an equally young knight named Bennu who fell first to the new, deadly weapons Skithdron had unleashed. Diamond tipped bolts took him down, and the deadly, horrifyingly organized skiths did the rest. Both knight and rider were lost in a matter of moments.

Jared called a retreat to reorganize and Kelzy sent out the message through the dragons. They fell back to a rocky outcropping, Darian silent as he thought through what he'd seen of the Skithdronian lines carefully before voicing his observations.

"I think they were waiting for the weapons to arrive before they launched the second wave. We have to assume there are more of those catapults and diamond bladed bolts. I also have a suspicion about who now leads this army."

"Who?" Jared's voice was grim as he looked over the stunned knights who were finding places to rest a moment until the order came to regroup.

"Venerai. An old enemy of mine. His symbol is a white skith on a field of blood red. I think I caught a glimpse of his banner toward the back ranks. He's one of Lucan's *pets*." He practically sneered the word. "Jared, if he's here, we also have to look at the skiths. I don't think these are wild skiths. These are the trained ones. Did you see the way they went after poor Bennu and Jizra? They're organized, working together."

"So we'll have to expect some kind of coordinated attack from them as well, I gather."

Darian nodded grimly. "I want Venerai. If we take him out, there's a good chance the skiths will lose their cohesion. From what I was able to learn before leaving the palace, the trained creatures only respond to certain favorites of Lucan's." Darian felt the anger burn through him for the evil Lucan had loosed. "I want to try for Venerai."

Jared nodded. "Then I'm with you."

Kelzy, tell Kelvan and Rohtina to take point with the majority of our forces, Jared ordered.

Darian knew that meant Gareth and Lars would lead the attack with their dragon partners. They were all excellent warriors who worked so well as a team they were nearly unstoppable.

"I'm with you, Dar. If you say we can end this by getting this Venerai, I believe you."

Darian didn't know he'd been holding his breath until that moment. He was touched and gratified to know this man, this friend, this new brother trusted him enough to place his very life—and those of his people—on the line.

"Thanks, Jared." Darian nodded around the knot in his throat that threatened to choke him.

With a silent signal, Sandor and Kelzy took Darian and Jared into the sky. Using the other dragons for cover, they worked their way higher and higher until few on the ground could see even the dragons' large bulk against the bright sun. Coming out of the sun, they used it to their advantage to drop down steeply behind the enemy army. Darian guided Sandor to the disguised command tent he knew would house the opposing general.

With a rending tear, Sandor burst through the thick canvas of the huge canopy followed closely by Kelzy, both spewing flame as they went. Darian dropped to the ground, clutching his sword, still better suited to fighting on the ground than on dragonback. Besides, he was looking for someone.

While the dragons created a ring of fire around them, Darian sought and found his target. He bounded over to stop Venerai from slithering away.

"Stand and face me, Venerai!"

The bold shout brought the man's head whipping around and Darian couldn't suppress the gasp of surprise that sounded from his throat.

"Darian? You dare come here?" The words hissed through the altered face, no longer quite human. Darian could see the slitted eyes that looked like a wild skith's, the dark mottling of the man's once golden skin. He almost looked...scaled.

"I've come to kill you, Venerai, as I should have long ago." Darian felt a presence at his side and knew without looking that it was Jared, come to back him up if need be.

"And who's this? Is that the old troublemaker Jared of Armand?" Darian was surprised Venerai would recognize Jared. He didn't think Venerai had ever been dispatched to Draconia, but then Venerai had worked behind the scenes for Lucan for years.

Venerai sneered at Jared as he drew his sword. "I thought I'd done away with you when I killed your wife and that pathetic whelp of yours."

Darian had to hold Jared back, so great was the anger coming off his fighting partner.

Don't let him rile you. This man is evil straight through. Kelzy cautioned them both. *Sandor and I will hold the ring around you as long as we can. None will be able to see or interfere with what transpires within.*

I suggest you kill him quick, though, Sandor put in. *They're bringing up reinforcements and we won't be able to hold them off forever.*

"Fight me like a man, Venerai. Or maybe you're no longer a man, are you? You look like a fucking skith." Darian grimaced as he stalked Venerai, sword drawn and ready. "What the hell happened to you? Or is it your true nature finally coming out after all these years?"

Darian circled the other man, noting Jared coming up behind to block and guard. They already fought well together, like brothers. He knew he could trust Jared to kill Venerai, should he fail, and take care of Adora. It was a secure feeling, though he vowed to himself not to fail. He had waited too long for this.

"No, Darian, this is how Lucan rewards loyalty." He raised his arm, allowing the wide sleeve of his shirt to fall back and reveal deep acid burns in his skin, scaled over with reptilian looking skin. It was disgusting and downright scary. "I am one with the skith and they are one with me."

He lowered his arm and suddenly there were skiths attacking the dragons from all sides. Sandor bellowed in pain as some of their venom singed one wing, but he flamed even higher, crisping the skiths that dared to answer their new master's call. Kelzy fought on the other side of the ring, and though they drew in toward each other, lessening the space they must keep aflame, they held off the skiths and roasted every last one.

"Your pets can't seem to overcome our partners, Venerai. Or were they your cousins? No matter, they're dead now."

Venerai's eyes narrowed as he charged with his deadly sharp blade, his animal rage momentarily overcoming his human intelligence. Good, Darian thought, that's just the reaction he wanted, but Venerai had the strength of ten men and the sinuous motion of a skith. It was difficult to anticipate his moves and Darian paid the price a few times in shallow cuts to his exposed body. The areas where Adora had incorporated dragon scale into his leathers were holding firm, protecting him, but there were too few precious dragon scales and too much of his large body left vulnerable to this almost inhuman attack.

Jared jumped between Darian and Venerai and took some of the blows, allowing Darian just a moment to regroup. Jared had a fire in his eyes that Darian well knew was the light of revenge. His new fighting partner finally faced the man who claimed to have killed his family and he wanted justice. Darian vowed he would get it this day, no matter the cost.

With renewed effort, Darian rejoined the fight. Whatever had been done to Venerai, it made him stronger than either Darian or Jared and it took both men to fight this one deranged, half-skith-looking monstrosity. They managed to push him back, but only just barely, each knight suffering shallow wounds that hurt fiercely and bled enough to be downright annoying.

You must end this now, boys, Sandor advised them, *before they get those giant crossbows into position. They're setting up the machines too far away for us to flame before we take to the sky.*

We hear and obey, Darian sent with just a touch of wry humor to his new dragon partner, *but this son of a skith has changed since I knew him and not for the better. I should have killed him years ago.*

The Mother of All knows that's true. Sandor continued to flame all who dared come near the wall of fire he and his mate kept going around them. *Get your asses in gear, knights! We must end this with haste.*

Jared saw his opportunity a moment later. The grotesque creature before them was starting to weaken as his eyes showed pain. He didn't understand where the pain came from since neither of the knights had managed to score any major hits on the bastard, but Jared knew that look could not be manufactured. Venerai was trying too hard to hide it.

With a flourish, Jared moved in and struck at the joint where Venerai's arm met his body, double striking to the knee with the same complex, arcing sweep. Venerai went down hard on one knee. Darian came up behind and ran his sword through the vulnerable part of Venerai's plate armor, near the waist, putting the enemy general in the perfect position for Jared's next powerful swing.

"This is for Ana and James," he whispered, one final time recalling the happy young boy and laughing woman who had shared his life and died by this enemy's hand. With one final motion, he separated Venerai's head from his body, killing the bastard who had killed his family. Justice had finally been served.

Both knights panted, their breathing harsh, as Darian searched the enemy general's pockets for any bit of intelligence that might be helpful to their side. Jared slung the evil bastard's head into a sack. He would take it and burn it to be certain no sort of evil magic could ever bring this bastard back to life. Jared never would have believed such a thing before, but then he had never seen the kind of magic that would turn a normal human man into the grotesque monster they had just faced. Lucan had access to powerful, demented magics, and Jared wasn't taking any chances.

Darian scanned the area, taking anything that might be of some kind of use to the Draconian cause, then ran for Sandor's side. He saw Jared do the same, tying something to the pack around Kelzy's neck that they used sometimes during battle. Within moments they launched skyward, the dragon wings beating with all their might for the high ground that would mean their safety from those dragon-killing weapons below.

They were almost out of range when a simple arrow screamed out of the sky from below, jamming itself through Jared's chest. The shock of it sent him scrambling for a hold, but he tumbled off Kelzy's back and went plummeting toward the ground at an alarming speed.

Jared! Kelzy's distress trumpeted over the field of battle.

Without pause Darian and Sandor, both of one mind, turned and dove, positioning themselves beneath the tumbling warrior. Darian reached upward, his own position increasingly precarious as he caught Jared and settled him onto Sandor's broad back, holding him tight.

We've got him! Kelzy, we've got him! Darian's thoughts were stronger each day he worked and trained with both dragons and he knew Jared's partner would hear him.

Flying as fast as he could, Sandor raced for the Lair, his mate at his side. *We'll save him, my love. He's a strong human, in the prime of his life. Adora will not let him die.*

Adora was beside herself when Sandor landed at the Lair. Jared had lost a lot of blood and she feared the arrow might have pierced his heart.

"Thank the Mother!" she cried as she realized the arrow had not hit either his heart or his lung. It had gone through the muscle near the shoulder joint and it looked a lot worse than it really was. She sobbed as Darian helped her break off the arrow and pull it through cleanly, then got herself together enough to continue his treatment.

Jared stopped her with a hand over hers when she would have healed him as fully as she could, draining herself in the process.

"Don't you dare, my love. I need you beside me, talking to me, caring for me. Not unconscious from exhaustion that could put you in danger."

She smiled at him and it was a watery smile. "Let me just do a little, Jared. Just start the process. We can do it a little at a time over several days. That way I won't be drained and you won't lose any of your ability to use your shoulder fully."

"You drive a hard bargain, my love, but I agree as long as it puts you in no jeopardy."

She kissed his cheek, his lips, and his brow. "None at all. I promise. Jared, it hurts me to see you injured. Let me do this for you."

He pulled her head down with his good hand, kissing her soundly. "All right," he whispered as he released her. "Do your worst."

She laughed as she knew he had intended and let the healing energy flow through her fingers and into his shoulder. She concentrated on knitting the tears and rejoining the muscle and blood vessels that had been disrupted by the arrow. Once this part of the healing was accomplished, she knew he would rest easier and there would be little lasting injury from the wound. Adora sighed as she felt the first ebb of her power. It was enough for now. She'd promised him not to tire herself too much and she knew he'd be watching closely for any sign of fatigue, chastising her lovingly if he suspected she was the least bit tired.

Adora pulled back and Jared sat up, gingerly at first. Then a broad smile crossed his face and he tumbled her into his embrace, kissing her soundly.

After a long, joyous moment, he moved back, keeping her on his lap while he searched around them.

"Darian! Thank you, brother, for the good catch, and you, Sandor. I can never repay either of you for saving my life."

"Think nothing of it." Darian winked at his fighting partner. "I expect you'll do the same for me someday."

Jared laughed shortly, then his eyes sharpened. "How goes the battle?"

Darian's broad smile was answer enough, but he stepped back to let Gareth and Lars move closer. Both younger men were flushed with excitement, fresh from the battle and high with their victory. Gareth stepped forward, the usual spokesman for the duo.

"Whatever you two did, it did the trick. Just before Sandor and Kelzy burst into the sky, the ranks of skiths lost focus and started to scramble. They turned on the Skithdronian army and started fighting them as they fled across the border for their home rocks. Their forces, both skith and human, are in retreat, running for the border as fast as they can."

A cheer went up from the knights surrounding them now and all were smiling. Adora put her hand over Jared's shoulder when he tried to stand, she and Darian supporting him as he faced his warriors.

"You've done well this day, my lads!" Again they cheered as he buoyed their spirits. "Send out patrols to watch the retreat and make certain no stragglers remain on our side of the border. Gareth and Lars, you're in charge of the patrols for now. I have some recuperating to do with my family."

Many of the knights stepped forward to pat him on his good shoulder as he passed. Adora noted that just as many offered congratulations and a respectful hand on the shoulder to Darian. All of them talked about the brave and magnificent save Darian and Sandor had performed by plucking Jared out of freefall and flying hell bent for leather back to the Lair. They'd saved Jared's life and unwittingly earned the respect of many a knight that day.

When they reached their private suite, Darian and Adora helped Jared to bed. Adora undressed him, surprised to find his cock hard and wanting as she uncovered it.

"What's this?" she teased, dipping her head to kiss the tip of his erection.

"It's what always happens when you touch me, my love." He reached for her hand, pulling her onto the bed. "Dar, she's wearing too many clothes. Can't you do something about that?" Jared's deep blue eyes twinkled up at her as the knights amused themselves with a lighthearted seduction.

"Are you sure you're up to it, Jared? You just almost died."

He dragged her down for a deep kiss. "No better time to reaffirm life than when you've almost lost it, Adora. The question is, are you up to it? You expended a lot of energy healing me. Do you need to rest, or can I make love to you first?"

"As long as I can sleep sometime tonight, I'll be just fine." She tugged his head down to hers. "Make love to me, Jared. I'm so grateful you're alive." She kissed him deeply, cooperating with Darian as he moved around them to remove her clothing. When she was bare, Darian turned to leave. Adora stopped him with an outstretched hand.

"Where do you think you're going?" Jared asked, his voice rough with desire and strong with the vitality of returning health.

"You should celebrate together."

"Not without you," Adora said softly.

"I thought we'd settled this already." Jared sighed loudly, clearly exasperated. "She's right, Dar. You're part of this family. This is for the three of us to share together."

The other man looked truly touched as he stood silent for a moment, clearly caught off guard. Adora tugged him closer so that he stood between her legs as she sat on the edge of the bed. With slow, deliberate hands, she undressed him, easing his leather leggings off and sucking him deep when she uncovered his hard cock. Darian's head dropped back, his beautiful eyes closing as her lips closed around him.

Jared knew the ecstasy Darian felt. He didn't envy his new brother the love of their mate—instead he reveled in it. Adora was theirs to pleasure, theirs to protect, and she in turn would pleasure them and give them all the love they needed. It was a rare gift and one he would never deny again.

"Enough, wench!" Darian called out with a laugh when she would have sucked him to release. Stepping back, he dove for the other side of the bed, careful not to jostle Jared's injured shoulder, but eager now for more loveplay.

Jared caught Adora gently by the neck and turned her to face him. "Give me some of what you just gave him, little one."

Her eyes flamed brightly as he pushed her head down near his straining erection. Without hesitation she took him deep and wide, her eyes holding his as she positioned herself to take all of him—all the way to the back of her throat. Adora was truly talented that way, Jared knew, thinking again what a lucky son of a bitch he was.

"She really likes sucking cock," Darian observed from beside him, leaning negligently against the headboard as he fingered his long, stiff rod. "She's got a talent for it, I think."

Jared couldn't answer around the rumble of pleasure rising from his throat as she swallowed around the tip of him. With a groan, he brought her off his dick and urged her face up to his.

"Ride me, little love. Ride me hard and fast."

She did just that as Darian moved to the side watching her ass jiggle up and down on Jared's thick cock. When she slowed, Darian slapped her butt cheeks, making her yelp and clench around Jared. When Darian inserted his wet finger into the tight spot between her cheeks, she nearly shot off the bed.

"Do you want him in you too?" Jared asked as she writhed on him. "Do you want him up your ass while I'm in your pussy?"

"Yes!" The scream was torn from her throat as she came hard over him.

Jared nodded and jerked his chin over at Darian. The other man wasted no time positioning his quickly lubed cock at her rear entrance. He eased in, not wanting to hurt her, but they both knew by now she liked the little edge of pain this position put her in. They wanted to bring her as high as they could, to show her how much they both loved her. They were of one mind in that moment, with their willing mate writhing between them. No words needed to be spoken, they simply were connected, hearts and souls.

When Adora came again, she brought both her mates with her in a glorious fireball of ecstasy that had all three of them gasping and collapsing into a dreamless sated sleep, side by side by side in the huge bed.

CHAPTER EIGHT

The next morning the dragons woke them. Kelzy nudged the huge bed with her chin, her long tongue reaching out to playfully tease her humans awake while Sandor watched and laughed in his dragonish way, smoking up the vented dome above their sandpit.

"Go away, Kelz, can't you see I'm injured here?" Jared groused as a ticklish tongue prodded his foot.

The children are coming to visit. They have news you will be happy to learn and can't hide it any longer. Do you want them to find you lounging in bed, naked as the day you were born?

"What children?" Darian asked sleepily as Adora slid over him, pausing only to kiss him good morning on her way to the bathing chamber.

"I think she means my daughter, Belora, and her mates."

And our son, Kelvan, and his mate, Rohtina, Sandor added with just a hint of fatherly pride.

"They're all coming here?" Jared finally sat up and scratched at his chest. "What for? Is there a problem?"

Not a problem, worrywart, Kelzy laughed at her knight. *Get dressed and you'll find out shortly.*

Darian decided to stop trying to fight the inevitable. He stood and joined Adora in the bathing chamber, cleansing himself before dressing for the day, stopping a few times to tickle and fondle her because he just couldn't help himself. She was so sweet, so womanly, so much of everything he had always wanted in his life. He only wished he had found her sooner, but Fate apparently had other ideas.

He realized by joining with Adora, he had also inherited an extended family in her daughter, Belora's mates, and their dragon partners. He'd gone from being all alone in the world to having a large, loving family almost overnight. The gods must be smiling down on him, indeed. Darian didn't know what he'd done right, but it must have been something big for them to grant him such happiness.

After they were all dressed and Adora had the morning tea going, the promised guests arrived with a spring in their steps and sparkles in all of their eyes. Belora rushed over to hug her mother, her face sporting a wide grin.

"What is it, baby?" Adora asked her youngest child.

"Make that babies, plural," Gareth joked, reaching out to clasp hands with Jared, then Darian as Lars did the same.

Adora's eyes drew together in suspicious delight. "Are you?"

"Mama, I'm pregnant!"

Adora shrieked and hugged her baby girl close. "Are you sure?"

"Yes, the prince told me."

"Nico?" Jared asked quickly, a grin splitting his face as well. "Was he here again?"

"No, he told me days ago but things were too hectic, and then I didn't want my news to overshadow your wedding. I had morning sickness and the prince calmed my stomach with his healing gift. Then he told me…" Her eyes grew wide with tears of joy as Lars pulled her back against his broad frame in comfort. "He told me I was going to have twin boys. One from each of my mates. And they were both going to be black dragons."

Jared sat heavily, his knees seeming to crumble at the startling news, but Darian and Adora were both puzzled.

"Black dragons, praise the Mother!" Jared spoke softly from his chair.

"What?" Adora pounced on him for answers, her eyes bright with suspicion, her mood happy but uncertain. Darian felt the same uncertainty reflected in her beautiful eyes. He sought Jared's gaze for answers, reassured by the happy expression he found there.

"Dar, since you're part of the family now, I guess you're allowed in on the secret." Jared looked over at the dragons for confirmation and both Kelzy and Sandor's heads went up and down in oversized nods of agreement. "Well, the royal lines of Draconia are descended from Draneth the Wise."

"What's ancient history got to do with my grandbabies?" Adora wanted to know. Jared took her hand and pulled her onto his lap with a smile.

"Patience, my love." He kissed her cheek before continuing. "Draneth the Wise was the last of the wizards. He made a deal with the dragons who allowed he and his heirs to live peacefully with the dragons forever after, by becoming one of them."

"One of what?" Darian cocked his head, trying to follow.

"Draneth became part dragon. As are all his heirs. You, my dear," he squeezed Adora, "and your lovely daughter, are descended of Draneth. Your sons will have his gifts as your daughters will most likely have the gift of healing dragons."

"What were Draneth's gifts?" Darian was intrigued now.

Jared smiled broadly. "Draneth was the first black dragon. Only the males of royal blood have the ability to change form from human to dragon and back again. Only they are black of all the dragons in our world."

"My grandbabies will be dragons?" Adora's eyes shot to her daughter excitedly.

Belora came over and grasped her mother's hand. "Dragons and human, just like us, only they'll be able to change back and forth, like Prince Nico. He said he showed you, Mama, like he showed me. Isn't it great?"

"It's amazing." Adora's voice trembled, her expression stunned.

"By the gods!" Darian was shocked but it was more than just hearing about the impending arrival of grandchildren. Learning the secret of the royals of Draconia suddenly made it all clear to him what Lucan was trying to do. He looked over at his new fighting partner. "Jared, this is what Lucan is driving at."

"You mean like what we saw in that tent with Venerai? You think that was the result of him trying to emulate Draneth the Wise?"

Darian nodded grimly. "In his twisted mind he probably figures he can be just as great as Draneth, can conquer the entire world, if only he has the power of the skiths on his side."

"That's insane!" Gareth stepped forward, taking Belora protectively in his arms. Lars stood beside them, a united front.

Darian nodded at the younger warriors. "Lucan is insane. Last year he brought in a witch from the north and closeted himself with her for over a month. We all thought he was just screwing her brains out but when she emerged, she was no worse for wear and he's notoriously hard on his bed partners. Then he started canceling audiences and has since gone into semi-seclusion within the palace. Only his favorites are allowed in to see him and they ferry messages and orders back and forth. He appears in public only rarely, and only when he can wear ceremonial robes that hide most of his body, come to think of it."

"You think he's like Venerai?" Jared asked shrewdly.

"Probably worse. Venerai was normal the last time I saw him at the palace, only two months ago. What we saw had to have been done to him in the last weeks. Lucan was with the witch over eight months ago. I hate to think what he might look like now."

"Who is Venerai?" Gareth wanted to know.

Jared shook his head. "He was the leader of the enemy army. We killed him when we went behind their lines. His skin was…changed somehow. Like scales. And his eyes weren't human. They were slitted like a skith's."

"Lady Kelzy, did you destroy the head yet?" Darian turned to ask the dragon.

It is over there. She pointed with one wing to the bloody sack in a far corner.

"Keep the ladies here." Darian nodded and went over to the corner, taking Lars with him. He handed the grisly burden to the other knight with grave eyes. "We need to show this to the king. I want you to keep it safe for now. Devise a case out of treated leather for it that will keep it from harming anyone. Don't touch the blood. It's probably as venomous as skith blood. When you've got it in a case, have your dragon partner burn this sack and anything else that could be contaminated. I don't want a single trace of this left anywhere in this Lair, do you understand?"

Lars nodded solemnly as he took the gruesome burden and walked briskly out of the suite, followed by his dragon partner, Rohtina. Darian shook off his fears for the future as he made his way back to the small gathering.

"I'm sorry to ruin your announcement, Belora. Your news is amazing. I can't say I ever thought I'd have littles in the family to spoil and play with."

Belora shocked him by hugging him tightly. "They're your grandchildren, Darian. I expect you and Jared to spoil them rotten."

"Grandchildren?" Darian shook his head, pleasantly stunned. The women of his new family had a way of doing that to him, no matter what their age, he realized.

Belora laughed up at him. "And Mama's not too old to have more children of her own, you know. She had my sisters and me when she was just a child herself."

Now he was completely speechless as he looked over at his blushing bride. The thought of her growing round with his child completely floored him, but that was in the hands of the gods. He would never pressure her to have a baby if it weren't what she wished also.

"Belora, have some pity on the poor man!" Gareth chided his mate as he drew her back into his arms. Gareth looked over at him with a smile. "She's a whirlwind at times, Darian. You just have to learn how to put up with it."

All of them laughed then as Belora squirmed happily in her mate's arms, showing a bit of her feisty spirit.

They left shortly after and Adora put Jared back in bed, despite his protests. She used her healing gift to treat his shoulder once more, tiring herself a bit more than she wanted, so she lay down on the sofa outside in the main chamber. Darian joined her, stroking her hair as they shared a quiet moment.

"Did your daughter say you had other children besides her?"

Adora yawned daintily and pillowed her head on his thigh. Her eyes stared straight ahead at the huge wallow where Sandor and Kelzy rested after returning from their hunting trip.

"I had twin girls who were stolen from me when they were ten winters old. After that, Belora and I hid in the forest. I had three girls, Dar. Only one was mine to raise past her tenth birthday."

"I'm so sorry, my love." He stroked her soft hair, lulling her to calmness as she recalled the sad memories. "I want you to know that I would never pressure you to have more children."

She sat up then on the wide couch and faced him. "What if I wanted more children?"

He frowned. "Do you?"

"Honestly, I don't know." She settled into his arms, snuggling close. "As a healer I know how to prevent pregnancy, of course, but since I had no bed partners until you and Jared, I haven't been doing anything to prevent it. I could be pregnant, I suppose, but it's harder to conceive for older women." She craned her head up to look into his eyes. "Would you want a child, Darian?"

He hugged her close. "What kind of question is that? I would welcome any child of yours into my heart, Adora. I would love it and teach it, be a good father to it, regardless of whether it was my seed or Jared's that did the job." He squeezed her once in reassurance. "I love you, Adora. I love everything about you. I would love your child as well. Simply because it's a part of you."

Kelzy lifted her big head and stretched lazily over to them. *You're wrong about one thing, child.*

Adora lifted her head from Darian's chest to regard the dragon. "Oh, yeah? What's that?"

You are not too old to conceive easily. By bonding with our kind, your knights will reap the benefit of a long, extended life. You're a descendant of Draneth the Wise, as well as having mother-bonded with me when you were just a toddler. You will live three or perhaps four normal human lifetimes, as will your mates. You could have many children in that time, if you choose to do so.

"Sweet Mother of All! Mama Kelzy, I had no idea."

The dragon quaked with smoky laughter. *I thought as much.*

Sandor raised his head and moved over to face them in his gentle way. *Princess, this land once teemed with black dragons. It's been many years since even one black dragon was born and my kind was beginning to despair. Now, with Belora's news, we have new hope for your race as well as our own. Any child of yours would be a blessing to our world, Adora. I hope you'll consider having at least one set of babies for your new mates. I think it would make them both happy as well.*

"Sets of babies?" Darian's voice rose in question.

Kelzy swiveled her head to look at him. *Royal blood often inspires twin births, as does mating with two knights. The Mother has a hand in all, Darian. She often blesses knights with twin sets—one from each knight. Perhaps it's Her way of equalizing things so that one mate or the other doesn't feel left out.*

"I had twins before Belora." Again sadness nearly overwhelmed her. "Arikia and Alania, we named them."

Princess, Sandor intoned comfortingly, the search for them is already underway. *Every knight and fighting dragon in the land has been told to watch for them. We'll find them. I know we will. Have faith that the Mother will bring your children back to you.*

"You're a kind being, Sir Sandor. Thank you for trying to comfort me. I'll keep your words close to my heart."

Jared walked out to the sofa, scratching around his healing wound, careful not to get too close to the sore skin around the arrow hole. He sensed the tension in the air as he drew closer to Darian and their mate. He still couldn't believe Adora was his...well, theirs. All in all, he didn't mind sharing her love with Darian. He felt good knowing Darian would be there for her if the Mother of All should decide it was time for him to leave this world.

He had come awfully close when that arrow hit him. A few inches to the side and it would have pierced his heart. Regardless, if Darian and Sandor hadn't caught him, the fall would have killed him with certainty. He had been spared that day, and he could only guess as to the reason. Apparently the Mother still had work for him to do here.

The first order of business was to cheer up his partner and their mate.

"Why so solemn?" He sat down on the couch, pulling Adora's lithe, muscular legs across his lap.

"I was just telling Darian about my twin daughters." She wiped at the wetness that leaked from her eye with a flustered smile.

"And learning that we'll have three or four lifetimes to enjoy each other."

Jared laughed. "I guess that came as a bit of a shock to you, Dar. I forgot you wouldn't necessarily know about that aspect of partnering with a dragon." He nodded over at Sandor. "Hundreds of years to drive each other crazy. Can't wait." He chuckled dryly as his shoulder itched.

"And time to have more children," Adora said quietly, shocking his eyes back to her. "If you want them."

"Sweet Mother!"

"Now who's caught off guard?" Darian teased him. "Or didn't you think about the fact that Adora could bear our children. She could already be pregnant."

Jared felt the blood drain from his face. He'd lost his son and it had nearly killed him. He didn't think he could face such devastation again.

Darian clapped a hand on his shoulder. "There are two of us now to protect her, Jared. Two fierce dragons and two warriors, not to mention her daughter's mates and dragon partners. Nothing will happen to Adora or any children we might be blessed to have."

Jared took Darian's words to heart. Relief worked its way through his system, a huge weight lifting off his shoulders that he had not even been aware was there. Adora crawled across the couch into his arms and held him as tightly as his wound would allow.

"Nothing will happen to me, Jared. I'm afraid you're stuck with me." She chuckled and he leaned down to kiss her luscious lips.

Jared sensed Darian moving around them, making a place for them all on the wide couch. They were out in the open, in the middle of the public area of their suite, but he figured it was relatively private as long as uninvited guests didn't come barging in unannounced.

He pulled back from her mouth, helping Darian undress her. Adora's leggings were already gone as Jared pulled off her top. She had her hands in his leggings and before he knew it, his cock was hard in her mouth.

"Suck me, baby." Jared's eyes closed as his head tilted back to rest on the padded back of the couch. "Oh, yes."

Adora went down on him with relish as Darian feasted on her dripping pussy. Jared opened his eyes wide enough to watch Darian's tongue delve between her legs and Jared reached out with one hand to squeeze her swinging breast. She whimpered around his cock as he pinched her nipple. Her eyes shot up to his with a devilish sparkle as she sucked harder, using her tongue in a way that threatened to unman him right then and there.

She was shoved forward a bit as Darian rose over her bent bottom, sheathing his hard cock inside her with a deep groan of pleasure. The pistoning motions in and out of her sweet pussy moved her mouth on Jared's most sensitive flesh making him even hotter.

Darian sped up as they neared completion, driving all of them forward. With a grin for his fighting partner, he slapped Adora's ass playfully. Both of them enjoyed it when she yelped and clenched on them, so he did it again with Jared's nodding encouragement. They were close to the edge now and with a final whack to her taut ass, she climaxed hard around them both, Jared coming hard in her hungry mouth while Darian spurted deep inside her womb.

All three were speechless for long moments, but finally Darian drew himself out of her tight depths as she licked Jared's cock completely clean. Adora rested her head in Jared's lap as Darian lowered her hips to the couch, taking only a moment to seat himself under her lean, gorgeously naked body.

Both men closed their eyes as they caught their breath, leaning their heads on the back of the padded couch.

"I've been thinking," Darian said after a long while.

"You can still think after that? You're a better man than I." Jared chuckled as he stroked Adora's silky hair while she dozed lightly in his lap.

"Lucan keeps a woman chained to his bed but she isn't his fuck toy." He kept his voice low so as not to wake the sated woman in their laps. "It's rumored she's a healer."

Jared's eyes popped open and he looked over at his fighting partner. "A healer?"

"I've seen the girl, Jared. Just once. She was skinny and dirty, but she had the most luminous green eyes I'd ever seen...until I met Adora." He looked pointedly at the woman sleeping softly over them both.

"Sweet Mother! Do you think—?"

Darian nodded grimly. "That poor creature could be one of our lady's lost twins."

BIANCA D'ARC

A life-long martial arts enthusiast, Bianca enjoys a number of hobbies and interests that keep her busy and entertained such as playing the guitar, shopping, painting, shopping, skiing, shopping, road trips, and did we say… um… shopping? A bargain hunter through and through, Bianca loves the thrill of the hunt for that excellent price on quality items, though she's hardly a fashionista. She likes nothing better than curling up by the fire with a good book, or better yet, by the computer, *writing* a good book.

Bianca loves to hear from readers and can be reached through her Yahoo group or through the various links on her website.

http://biancadarc.com
http://groups.yahoo.com/group/BiancaDArc/join

Coming soon from Bianca…

The Ice Dragon: Dragon Knights Book 3—Coming August '06
Lords of the Were—Coming October '06
Forever Valentine, Caught by Cupid Anthology—Coming January '07
Price of Spies: Dragon Knights Book 4—Coming February '07

Samhain Publishing, Ltd.

It's all about the story...

Action/Adventure
Fantasy
Historical
Horror
Mainstream
Mystery/Suspense
Non-Fiction
Paranormal
Red Hots!
Romance
Science Fiction
Western
Young Adult

http://www.samhainpublishing.com

CPSIA information can be obtained at www.ICGtesting.com
Printed in the USA
LVOW061614110712

289682LV00004B/112/A